RETURN TO KAITLIN

Helen Yeomans

GUARDS PUBLISHING
2015

Published by Guards Publishing, an imprint of Yeomans Associates Ltd.
www.helenyeomans.com

Library and Archives Canada Cataloguing in Publication

Yeomans, Helen, 1949-, author
Return to Kaitlin / Helen Yeomans.

Issued in print and electronic formats.
ISBN 978-0-9693219-7-2 (pbk.).--ISBN 978-0-9693219-8-9 (pdf)

I. Title.

PS8647.E65R48 2015 jC813'.6 C2015-902173-1
C2015-902174-X

"Cargoes" by John Masefield (p.134) was first published in 1903.
"Alberta Gold," (p. 94), was written by Matt Andersen in 2013.
The phrase "paved paradise" in Chapters 9 and 10 is taken from the song "Big Yellow Taxi," by Joni Mitchell © 1970 Siquomb Publishing Company

Cover design ivanzanchetta.com

Printed in the United States of America

For Matthew

Contents

Chapter

One

The Nissan Pathfinder wove along the wet road. Tyler Hogan squinted at the center lines. Which one was real? A slight rise, a shallow bend in the road and he missed the flashing red light in his rear-view mirror. Ahead, a car backed out of a driveway.

"Oh fuck."

He steered to the left and the curb came out to meet him.

"Oh shit."

He corrected. Back to the middle. Which line was it? Overcorrected. The Pathfinder was a heat seeker, heading straight for the car.

"Oh no."

His hands flew up off the wheel and covered his eyes. Thus he failed to appreciate the other driver's speedy reaction as the car shot back in toward its garage. Missing its taillights by a hair, the Pathfinder crossed the driveway and buried its nose in a tree. The tree was a hundred years old, a large cedar with deep roots, a scarred veteran of encounters with tanked-up students.

Uncovering his eyes a bare second before the collision, Ty managed to brace himself with the wheel, and suffered no more than a sharp bump on the head. He frowned at the tree trunk and turned his head. No car.

Car. The revolving red light of the police cruiser pulled in next to the Nissan. Ty sighed and turned off the ignition. His day was about to get worse and an hour ago he hadn't thought that was possible. He cracked the door and climbed out.

"You idiot! You stupid moron—look at you! You can't even focus!"

The voice was female. A girl about his own age. Piss on her. Piss on all girls. "Sorry."

"You shouldn't even be on the road."

The cop joined them. Ty had seen him before, though not up close and personal. His name was Fanning. The girl turned to him. "He shouldn't even be on the road."

Fanning looked at Ty. "License and registration."

Ty stared at the ground, considering this request. He half-turned toward the Pathfinder, then thought better of it. Lunging forward past the girl, he took off up the street.

Her voice followed him: "Are cute guys always stupid?"

* * *

"The wheels on the bus go round and round, all through the town."

Ty crooned as he sat on the wet lawn of an unknown house, head on his knees, waiting for death or retribution, whichever came first.

"The wheels on the bus go round and round. . . ."

Dad used to sing to him when he was little. Before he left. He lived in Minneapolis now with his second wife. A continent away from Vancouver Island.

Ty wondered why he had run away. His life was effectively over as of that moment. He heard the scrunch of tires on gravel and raised his head. This moment.

The cop walked over and stopped near him. "On your feet."

Ty lifted his head. "Sorry I ran away."

"Get up."

"Girlfriend dumped me."

"Uh huh."

"Wouldn't normally be like this."

"You're wasting time." Fanning reached down, grasped him by the arm and hauled. "Come on."

Ty half-turned and threw up. Fanning waited patiently. Bent over, Ty wiped his mouth with the back of his hand. He stared at the mess. "Carrots?" He resisted the steady pull on his arm. "When did I eat carrots?" He looked back as he was led toward the cruiser. "I should clean that up. . . ."

"There's a lot you have to clean up."

They sat in the cruiser and Fanning, having taken Ty's license, searched his database and filled out forms and tickets. Ty put his head back and wondered if hearts actually did break when someone you loved left you. His was hurting but it didn't seem to be broken. "She wants to go to Thailand," he said. "I can't just up and go to Thailand. I'm in school. Engineering."

Fanning started the car and drove back to the Nissan. Leaving Ty in the cruiser he examined the area around the vehicle with a flashlight, checking for broken glass or impediments on the driveway of the adjacent house. Its lights were out and the garage door was closed. Finishing up, he checked that the Nissan's doors were all locked, then returned to the cruiser. A streetlight cast sufficient light for him to see the figure in the back seat.

He finished writing the ticket then turned.

Ty peered blearily at him. "What's going to happen?"

"I'll tell you what's not going to happen. You're never going to drive drunk again." He held out the ticket, a business card and the Nissan's keys, and Ty took them. "Tomorrow afternoon you present yourself and your vehicle at that address. That means you'll find someone to drive you there." He held up Ty's license. "I'll keep this for now."

He started the car. "You've got no priors and no endorsements. That's the only thing saving you from losing your license."

* * *

The assistant at the F-J table held out Ty's essay.

"Good work, Mr. Hogan." Walking along behind the row of tables, the professor of Critical Thought nodded as he passed. First-year engineering students like Tyler had to take general courses before branching into more specialized disciplines. He'd nailed an A on this paper, exploring mankind's decision to develop nuclear energy using uranium rather than thorium, a cleaner and more abundant element.

He turned to look at the P-T table, where Jacey Thorsen waited to pick up her paper.

"Forget about her," Barty said.

"I'm not—"

"Yeah. You are."

Ty and Barty had been friends since Grade 8, despite their dissimilar looks and likes. Someone once called them Mutt and Jeff and they'd looked this up online. A tall guy and a short guy. That was them. They spent most of their free time together. Barty's parents were lawyers and the family was well-off. He planned to become a poet and even as a freshman had already had a piece accepted in the campus paper.

The A-E line speeded up and Barty reached the table. He took his paper and his face darkened. Unsurprised, Ty turned away and watched Jacey, in the midst of a crowd of friends.

Barty's voice rose in protest. "It was intended to be witty and light and entertaining. I thought I did a good job."

"You did, Mr. Cage. But the assignment was to discuss one of humanity's mistakes. Trading Luongo simply doesn't qualify."

Barty regarded hockey as a pointless diversion. This put him at odds with the rest of his family, if not the rest of the world. The paper had been a welcome outlet for his views.

Ty watched as Jacey and her crowd climbed the steps to the higher reaches of the lecture hall. Barty joined him, and they returned to their seats. The professor rapped on a blackboard. "Midterm in three weeks, ladies and gentlemen. This is your final reminder."

* * *

They stood in the weak autumn sun peering through the open doorway of the Nissan. A breathalyzer, a device about the size of a mobile phone, was mounted on the dash, with a tube connected to a point under and behind the ignition.

Barty was dismayed. "Can't you disconnect it?"

"If I even try, it's game over." Ty was still smarting from a furious dressing down administered by his mother.

"So it won't even start if you're over .05?"

Ty nodded.

"That's only one beer, for chrissake!"

They stood there silently mourning the loss of freedom represented by the gizmo on the dash.

"So you blow into it and it unlocks the wheel?"

"Yeah."

"That's insulting," said Barty.

"Cost me nearly eight hundred to be insulted."

* * *

The Pathfinder ran along a narrow logging road through dense forests of evergreen. Sunlight flashed across the dash at regular intervals. Ty drove, Barty next to him, with two other friends, two dogs and four backpacks behind. They clacked over the wooden bridge crossing the Indian River. Slow and wide further downstream, up here the river was a torrent rushing through a narrow gorge a hundred feet below. The road widened into a lay-by where people could park. They saw two vehicles as they drove by, one a new electric-blue Dodge Ram. Next to Ty, Barty shifted slightly in his seat.

"Dunno the one," said Alex from the back, "but that's Jacey in the Ram—" he stopped at Barty's glare, "—oops."

"Over it," said Ty casually. "No big." He glanced through the rearview mirror, then they rounded a bend and the bridge disappeared from sight.

The road climbed gradually but steadily, following the hill's contours. They passed another lay-by.

Alex looked back. "Aren't we stopping?"

"Another mile up and the trail comes out in the open. It's great."

They rounded another bend.

"What the—?" Ty slammed on the brakes in front of an iron barrier.

The dogs leaped out, followed by the four boys.

"Who put this up?"

"It wasn't here in September," said Jason, the fourth member of the group. "I was up here then."

"There was a drug bust," said Alex. "Bet that's why they did it."

"You could have said," Barty shook his head. Alex wasn't the sharpest tool in the box.

The barrier was a sturdy gate made of three-inch hollow bars welded to an iron frame, the whole attached by hinges on the right to an iron post sunk in concrete. Built to deter the public, it was attached on the left by a padlock to another iron post. There was no room to drive around it.

Ty would have liked to return to the bridge but didn't dare suggest it. Instead, he turned the Nissan and they headed back to the other trail entrance, parked on the roadside, collected their packs and set off to hike the five miles through the woods to a clearing. They gathered wood and lit a fire in an old stone fireplace while the dogs ranged far, coming back only when called, following the scents of deer and bear and raccoon.

Hot dogs, sandwiches, chips, cake and apples under a late-fall sun. They sat on logs around the fire, and talked of school and sports and gossiped about fellow freshmen.

* * *

When Barty was fifteen he drank a can and a half of beer and came tipsy to dinner. That led to the lecture, delivered by his dad. When you're sixteen you can drink beer or wine in moderation. When you're nineteen you can do as you please, except that you must never, ever drink and drive. He asked if Barty understood, and Barty nodded. He finished by saying he expected him to drink responsibly.

Ty had received a similar lecture a year earlier, because his dad was a drinker and Annie Hogan had made sure the subject never became an elephant in the room. She had always answered all Ty's questions, and those of his older sister, Emma, and like Barty's dad she had delivered the lecture.

The result with both boys was identical. They listened, digested and absorbed the words—all except the last one. "We're expected to drink," said Barty to Ty the first time they shared a beer. "I know," said Ty. They set out to meet expectations.

The evening of the hike, they sat in the basement den at Ty's place, drinking beer. Barty was texting his girlfriend, Cathy. Ty looked at videos online. It was during the third beer that he said, "I got an idea. You nominate me to drink a beer."

Barty looked over at him. "You mean like a nek nomination?"

"Yeah. I mean, look at this idiot." He held out his phone and they watched a video of a student chugging a can of beer, a student wearing swim trunks and standing on a snowboard launch. He finished the beer, pushed off, dropped ten feet, swerved wildly and fell over into a snow bank.

"Asshole."

"Yeah, but I got a better one. You nominate me."

Barty opened his Facebook page. "I nominate Ty Hogan," he typed as he spoke.

"Wait a minute." Tyler flopped on his side, laughing. "To bungee jump off the Indian River Bridge and chug a beer at the bottom."

Barty focused. "Awesome." He resumed typing. "To bungee jump off the Indian River Bridge and chug a beer at the bottom." He stopped. "When?"

That called for thought. Ty fetched two more cans and a shopping bag for the empties. They settled on Friday afternoon and fixed a time. Barty added the details and was about to post the entry when Ty had second thoughts.

"We shouldn't say where or what, in case someone tells my mother. Just the day and time. We'll upload a video. Say that."

Barty amended the entry and posted it and they discussed the details with their fourth beers. They heard Annie Hogan drive in, and realized the time. They finished their beer and cleared away the cans, and Ty walked Barty out.

"So, see you Monday," said Ty. He was going to Jason's tomorrow to borrow his do-it-yourself bungee jumping kit.

Barty nodded and walked off along the driveway, almost invisible until he reached the road and its streetlights. He disappeared down the road and Ty returned inside, considering ways to make sure Jacey found out about next Friday. Swear Jason to secrecy, he decided, then tell Alex on Thursday. Alex never could keep a secret long. And Friday night was the Ferguson party. Everyone was going to that.

* * *

On Friday afternoon a small crowd of students gathered at the bridge. Barty's Facebook entry had attracted a good deal of interest, but to all the queries on the page he had simply replied "wait and see." Now he and Alex were busy attaching the bungee apparatus to stanchions in the bridge railing. Although wooden, the bridge was built to support loaded logging trucks, so they were not concerned about its ability to support a freefalling Ty.

The man himself sat cross-legged on the bridge surface next to Jason. They were figuring out the correct length of the bungee cord. This required a complex series of calculations having to do with the height and weight of the jumper, the tensile strength and elasticity of the cord and the overall drop. The objective was to give the jumper the maximum length for his freefall without his subsequently having to be scraped off the ground. The final step in the calculations entailed solving a quadratic equation for *k*, and the previous evening, Jason and Ty had arrived at different results three separate times until they realized that Ty was dividing milligrams instead of Newtons. "Look on the bright side," Barty had said after this error came to light, "at least you're coming up with the same answer each time." On the fourth try their results agreed.

Today, they were working through the calculations again, and again they arrived at different answers. Finally, Jason leaned over and Ty talked him through his calculations.

"Where's your 1.85?" 1.85 was Ty's height in meters.

Ty stared at the paper, while Jason stared at Ty.

Barty half-turned and glanced at him. "We don't have to do this, Ty."

Ty could hear his heartbeat in his ears, and he had suspected earlier that his brain wasn't up to speed. Now it was confirmed.

He laughed. "What an idiot." He scribbled out his calculations and began again. Eventually he came up with the same result as Jason.

"Fantastic," he said.

He sat and watched Barty and Alex assembling the apparatus. "Did you jump here, Jay?"

Thin and clever, with a ring in one ear, Jason shook his head. He hadn't in fact jumped at all. "My dad said it's too risky. But I worked it out using Jenna's teddy bear and we tested it off the sundeck."

Ty thought about that. "Would a teddy bear be heavy enough?"

Jason nodded, appreciating the question. "Right. So we opened it up and added some rocks, then weighed it and recalculated."

"Jenna's so lucky to have you for a brother," said Barty.

"It was her idea," said Jason defensively. "She's crazy about bungee jumping." He looked at Ty. "Anyway, when we tested it, the tip of his fur just grazed the concrete. It was so cool."

"No kidding," said Ty, impressed.

"We don't want Ty to reach the water," said Barty. He was beginning to have second thoughts about the whole operation.

"We know," said Ty. "I'll be stopping a meter above it."

Satisfied with their calculations, they climbed to their feet. Ty wore jeans, t-shirt and a cross-body shoulder pack holding a can of beer. He climbed into the safety harness, rearranging the shoulder pack around it. Barty wrapped his ankles in a towel and attached the foot harness.

"Now remember, you guys," Ty looked at the others. "I don't want to be pulled up until after I chug the beer, okay?"

Barty and Alex nodded.

"Remember to launch forward, not down," said Jason, looking down at the river far below. "Otherwise you'll corkscrew all over the place." He added, "You sure you want to do this?"

"Sure," said Ty, thinking of Jacey. He shuffled to the railing and glanced over the small crowd. Several students waved, and he grinned and raised a hand. Couldn't see her anywhere.

Barty wanted the bungee line measured once more, to confirm the tie-off point. So he and Jason measured again, found the length, and secured the cord to the base of a stanchion. Then Alex and Jason swung Ty's legs over the railing while two students held on to the rope of his safety harness. Barty reached through the railing and clipped the carabiner on the end of the cord to the foot harness.

Ty raised his voice. "Okay, who's filming this?"

Several phones were waved in the air.

"Perfect. See you in a minute."

He grinned at Barty. Looked down. The water seemed miles away. He looked out at the dull November sky. Dark trees. Rushing river. *Here goes.* He flexed his knees. *Keep your eyes open, Hogan!* He sprang forward, arms wide.

Breathless.

Boundless freedom oh God how wonderful—

It was gone. Fleeting disappointment.

Cliffs.

Water—*Jeez!*

Cliff—*Jeez!*

Now the other side. Not as close. He laughed upside down, swinging back and forth between cliff and trees. The water rushed by, busy, purposeful . . . about a meter below his head. *Cool! Nice one, Jason.*

He raised his head and waved up at the bridge. *Right. Beer.* He reached into the shoulder pack, brought out the beer, opened it and used his abs to lift himself into a right-angle with his legs. *Hope they're filming this.* He chugged the beer, waved the can and shoved it in his pack, then waved again, and slowly, steadily, began to rise toward the bridge as the others pulled him up.

* * *

Ty reached for another piece of pizza, hoping it would soak up some of the beer and vodka. He wanted to stay sober at least until Jacey arrived. Hers was the first face he'd sought when he arrived. Everyone else had been there, everyone but Jacey. The party had been in high gear for a couple of hours now and showed no signs of slowing down.

"Nice one, Ty," said a passing schoolmate. "It's had nearly three thousand views, did you see?"

Ty grinned and ate some pizza. Barty had selected the best of the phone videos and uploaded it to his Facebook page and YouTube. He sat on the floor next to Cathy Atiqtalik, his girlfriend. Cathy was Inuit, a stocky girl with broad cheekbones and black eyes. She and Barty had been friends for years, ever since she'd come to board at the home next door to the Cages. Her parents wanted their clever daughter to have every opportunity, and Cathy was studying law. Barty and Cathy had formally taken their relationship to a new level last year, and it was soon after that that Ty had found Jacey. The girls had precisely nothing in common.

Cathy didn't drink, which made her the perfect designated driver. Barty raised his beer can. "More."

Ty got to his feet and made his way to the dining room, to the coolers filled with ice (now mostly ice water) and beer. He pulled out four cans plus a Five Alive for Cathy. He turned, beer stowed in the crook of his arm and came face to face with Jacey. His heart turned over and he felt dizzy.

Jacey Thorsen was a beauty, ash blonde hair, dark eyebrows and eyelashes, perfect skin and high cheekbones. She glanced at Ty as her eyes searched the room. "Hi, Tyler."

"Hi, Jacey. Gosh, how're you doing?"

"I saw your bungee video. What was the point of that, Tyler?"

There was no sympathy in her voice, and scant interest. It was just a filler question, but Tyler didn't register that. Jacey wanted to know what he was up to.

"I thought it might be fun," he said. And dashing and brave. But she had turned, returning to the living room and he followed and watched as she spotted someone.

"See you around," she said and he stood there flatfooted until someone elbowed him aside. Jacey had been looking for one of her girlfriends and he watched as the two girls worked their way toward the entrance hall. Two fellows stood there, one with his back to the room. He half-turned as Jacey reached him and with a pang Tyler saw his arm go round her and his hand cup her shoulder. The four of them moved toward the front door and moments later they'd opened it and left.

Chapter

Two

Ty was in the weight room at the gym when Barty came in, waving a copy of the campus newspaper. "It's in," he said, "on page three. 'Earth's Cerebellum'," he announced, "by Bartholomew Cage. It's online, too."

"Five, six," Ty counted, raising and lowering the barbell. Barty could see some serious weights on the ends and he nodded over at a guy hovering to help out and dropped the paper, moving to stand behind the bench. Ty lay on the bench, his feet flat on the floor, raising and lowering the barbell at chest level.

"Nine, ten." He raised the barbell for the last time, and Barty took hold of it as well, his hands between Ty's. They guided it to the vertical rack, lowering it to the rests. Ty grinned up at Barty, who moved around to face his friend.

"How much?"

"Two fifty."

They high-fived. "Dude." Barty was seriously amazed. "That's . . . that's nearly two me's."

"I know." Ty sat up. "Let's see the paper."

Barty held it out, open to page three and Ty admired it. They high-fived again. "First of many, dude."

Barty shrugged. "Yeah, maybe. Yeah."

"For sure."

The poem celebrated the Northern Lights, which Barty had seen last year on a trip with Cathy to visit her relatives in Tuktoyaktuk, on the edge of the Beaufort Sea. He had been offered a job on the student paper, a job he was considering taking if the hours could be made to coincide with Ty's job at the hardware store.

They discussed the problem while Ty showered and changed and then Barty recalled the midterm they'd both written earlier that day. "Say, you left awful early." He felt nervous even mentioning it because there was no way Tyler could have completed the questions so quickly.

"Pretty easy, wasn't it." Ty was toweling his hair, his face hidden.

"Are you shitting me?"

"Leave it be, Bart."

This was even worse. Barty was certain Tyler was falling behind in his work and now he feared that Ty was so far back he'd never catch up. Two men entered the locker room at that point, so he dropped the subject.

Out in the parking lot, he said, "Come over tonight?"

"Got to work," said Ty, and added, "saving up for Peru." The trip was one they'd promised themselves next summer.

Barty nodded and turned to go. "Say, Ty," he added, turning back.

"Yo."

Barty hesitated, and Ty came closer.

"Don't get mad at me."

"Nah. I'll just lift you with one hand and toss you over that truck."

"Yeah, right." Barty scuffed his shoe then looked his friend in the eye. "You know you're worth ten of her, right?"

* * *

Ty was at the desk in his bedroom, trying to concentrate on a chemistry problem, when his mother tapped at the door.

"Hi, mum."

The door opened and Annie Hogan came in. She was a tall woman who had fought to raise two children on a bookkeeper's income. She sat on the side of the bed looking stern.

"What?"

"Constable Fanning wants to see you at the station tomorrow afternoon."

"Jeez! Now what?" He realized too late what it must be.

"Possibly something to do with your having bungee jumped off the Indian River Bridge?"

He stared at her. "How did he find out?"

"The logging company wants to barricade that road completely. A lot of people are upset about that, people who enjoy going to the bridge or the trails." Ty looked away, and she went on, "How could you, Tyler? I know you're having a rough time right now, but how could you be so thoughtless? Did you even stop to think what Emma or I would do if you ended up a quadriplegic? Or dead?"

"Oh come on, mum—"

"No, dear, you come on." Her voice remained level but he could tell how much it cost her. "Fanning wants the video taken off your Facebook page and a public apology in its place, and I strongly suggest you do that before you go to see him." Ty stared at the chemistry text book and she studied her son. He'd lost weight and there was an unhappiness in his eyes. "I made him promise to smack you around. I indicated if he wanted to lock you up for a couple of weeks I wouldn't complain." Ty looked up and grinned and she added, "This is serious, Tyler. I didn't spend nineteen years raising you just to have you break your neck before you're even out of your teens. You've got to smarten up."

He stared at the floor, then muttered, "I don't even know where to begin."

She stood up. "You might try drinking less and studying more." She came closer and put a hand on his shoulder. "I know you're hurting, honey. I'm so very, very sorry, but it'll pass, I promise." She bent and he felt a swift hug.

He shook his head slightly and turned his face away. "It's just, I wasn't expecting it, mum. Caught me by surprise." He felt her hand on his forehead, the fingers cool and soothing, and turned to bury his face in her waist. She bent over him, embracing him. He stifled a sob.

* * *

"I'm getting mixed reviews, Mr. Hogan." The Dean's laptop screen was reflected in his glasses. He glanced across the desk at Ty. "Your professor of Critical Thought speaks highly of you. You seem to be competent in Calculus." He looked down again, and tapped a key. "Those appear to be the high points. The comments from your other teachers are less positive."

Positive. The other teachers weren't less positive, they were negative. Ty knew he must find something to say, something to suggest he cared. He drew a blank.

The Dean had a bald head and a muscular body. Dressed in shirt and tie, his cuffs were flipped back, revealing a tiny Rubik's cube tattooed above his wrist. He leaned back, removed his glasses, massaged the bridge of his nose. "What seems to be the trouble?"

Ty cleared his throat. He leaned forward, resting on his forearms, hands laced between his knees. "I guess I'm just adjusting to being in university."

Glasses back on, more tapping of keys. The Dean raised his head. "You had no trouble adjusting in September." He gazed at Ty over the tops of his glasses. "The competition for engineering jobs is intense. You know that."

Ty nodded.

"You appear to have the intellectual equipment. Are you having second thoughts about the field?"

"No—I don't know. I broke up with my girlfriend. I guess—I guess I've just been having trouble focusing." He straightened up, to signify determination. "I'll get it together next semester, for sure."

The Dean gazed at him, then consulted his screen. "You wrote a paper on thorium. Tell me about it."

Ty adjusted his thinking. The paper seemed like a lifetime ago. "We were supposed to write about a historical mistake. I thought it was a mistake to build uranium-powered nuclear plants. Thorium's cheaper, it's more common and less dirty. I figured they chose uranium because it can be weaponized. Thorium can't." He shrugged. "That's all."

"Alternative fuels interest you?"

"Not really—well, yeah, I guess."

"You expressed an interest in learning about power generation through ocean currents."

How long ago it seemed, that Physics class! Ty gazed into the middle distance, trying to remember who that was, that person who had asked those questions.

"Mr. Hogan, we're going to relieve you of the burden of learning for a while."

"What?"

"Go away and discover what interests you. If you still want to pursue an education next September, come and see me." The Dean tapped a brief note and closed the laptop. "We'll evaluate the situation then."

He stood up and leaned across the desk with a smile, extending his hand. "Thank you for coming in, and good luck."

* * *

"Look on the bright side." Barty swigged largely and went on, "You'll make a shitload of money working full-time. We'll have a great time in Peru. Then you can come back next September and—well, and get going again." Barty had been blown away to discover that Ty had been kicked out. "Everything? You failed everything? How could you fail English? How does anyone do that?" He still hadn't fully adjusted.

Ty said nothing. He pictured himself working full-time at the hardware store with Dave, the Downs Syndrome kid. His classmates would throw pitying looks his way and ask how he was doing and get the hell out of there as soon as they decently could. Barely more than minimum wage. Hardly enough for Peru, never mind that he had to pay his own fees now. His mother had said little when he broke the news. But the small college fund she had built up over the years was not, she said, earmarked for re-taking failed courses. He'd be a year behind everyone.

He scanned his messages while Barty fetched more beer. They were mostly condolences: "I can't believe what I just heard, Ty. Tell me it isn't true!" And now one from Emma, too: "Oh Tyguy, I'm so so sorry. Thinking of you and see you in a few days, love love love Emma."

He sighed and put the phone away and settled down to some serious drinking. They were on their fourth or fifth beers when Jason arrived, full of important news. He managed to wait until Barty returned with more beer, then uncapped a bottle, took a swig and leaned forward. He sat on one of the two sofas that formed a right-angle in the Cages' basement. Ty lay on the other and Barty sat cross-legged on the floor.

"Ever think of going up north, Ty?"

"It's cold up north."

"Freeze-your-balls-off cold," added Barty. "Very very cold, Jason." Barty was a known authority on the north because of Cathy.

"Yeah, that's why the pay's so good."

"Pay?"

"Listen, you can make seven or eight thousand a month, Ty! You can rake it in up there. Come back in six months, you got it made. School fees paid, buy a new car, see the world," he included Barty in his gaze. "I been talking to this guy. They're always looking for people, Ty. You're strong, you'd be just what they want."

Ty had not heard anything beyond "seven or eight thousand a month." He looked at Jason. "Hm."

"You can get a hot oiler job. It's great!" He recalled something. "Only you need clothes. Like—thermal underwear. And socks. That kind of thing."

Ty gazed through Jason. The appeal of the open road. The call of the wild. His heart responded. "Socks? I got hiking socks." He remembered something and sat up. "Wait. I got thermal socks last Christmas!"

"Listen, you need to talk to this guy. He's just come back from Fort St John. He just bought a—" he pulled himself up short.

Barty saw it coming and tried to stop him. "Forget it, Jason."

But it was too late. "Forget it? Why?" Ty swung his feet to the floor. "What did he just buy?"

"See, that's the thing. He just bought a brand new Dodge Ram."

Tyler stared at him. "A blue Dodge Ram?" He enunciated carefully. Jason nodded. "You're killing me, Jason."

"You have to forget all that, Ty." Jason spoke sharply. "This is important. This is your life. And—and he's not such a bad guy."

Barty spoke into the silence. "We actually owe him a lot." He ignored Ty's glare.

"I'll give you his address if you want, Ty. You go and see him. He knows about you."

"What do you mean? What did you tell him?"

"Jeez, Ty, relax. I just told him you were looking for work and you'd be perfect for the job. You go and see him," Jason repeated. "His name's Stefan Anderson."

* * *

The Ram was parked in the driveway as Ty drew nearer. He had pedaled past the house three times in the last day, hoping to catch the truck's owner outside. He had no intention of showing up in his battered Pathfinder, so he had wheeled the mountain bike out of the garage, wiped off some of the dust and cycled over.

He gazed at the blue truck as he pedaled by. Its gleaming surface seemed to exude a magnetic warmth in the winter daylight. As he drew past the driveway entrance he saw a pair of boots protruding from under the driver's side of the truck, so he braked and wheeled around and into the driveway, stopping near the boots.

"Hi," he said without enthusiasm.

The boots' owner slid out from under the truck and stared up at him.

"I'm Tyler Hogan. Heard you were working up in Fort St John."

The other stood up. "Stefan Anderson." He held out a hand and after a momentary hesitation, Ty grasped it and they shook. Stefan was perhaps an inch or so shorter, the dark-haired guy he'd seen with Jacey at the party. Ty pushed the thought away.

"Nice," he said, looking at the Ram.

He was invited to inspect the engine, so he laid his bike on the lawn and walked over. Stefan had popped the hood and the engine lay there, filling every inch of the available space, pristine.

"Vee six?"

"Eight. Five point seven litre. Three ninety-five horsepower. She'll tow ten thousand pounds."

Ty took off the radiator cap for something to do, as Stefan went on.

"Eight-speed transmission. Twenty-eight to the gallon." He glanced at Tyler. "Forty on the highway."

"Get out!" Ty was impressed. He replaced the cap and Stefan closed the hood. They climbed inside the cab where Ty smelled the new-car smell for the first time in his life. He was shown the gauges, the satellite and CB radios, the CD player and Bluetooth. Eventually, they worked their way to the rear and explored the toolbox. A set of wrenches. Hammers, saws, assorted power tools. "I'm going to hire out," said the proud owner. "Have truck will travel. That kind of thing."

He glanced at Ty, who nodded. He was beginning to like Stefan. "What kind of thing would you do?"

"Anything. Hauling. Construction, anything. I figure there's got to be a need for a guy with a good truck." He shrugged. "We'll see. I can afford to try it for six months or a year. If it doesn't pan out I'll head back up north." He eyed Ty. "That why you're here?"

"Yeah. I heard it's good money."

"Can be. Depends what you do. It's expensive living up north. I mean, shit, you can make sixteen an hour just at Tim Horton's."

"Are you serious?" Fast-food jobs in Ty's experience were minimum wage.

"Yeah, but it all goes in room and board, see." He shut the toolbox. "My boss told me to look out for guys. He's short a couple of hot oiler crews. You interested?"

Ty shrugged. "What do I do?"

"Basically, you sit in a truck for ten days at a time, monitoring a pipe feeding heated oil into a well. Then you come on back to town for three or four days and get cleaned up. Then you go back out again to that rig or another one."

Ty considered. "Doesn't sound difficult. You on your own?"

Stefan shook his head. "You work with another guy. He'd be the senior man on the crew." He appraised Tyler. "You have to be able to get along with people."

"I'm okay with that."

Stefan had asked around and knew it. "Pay's twenty-five an hour for eight hours."

A thousand a week, thought Ty, that's not so bad—

"Plus time and a half for sixteen hours."

"Holy shit!"

"I know."

"Are you kidding me?"

"That's why they're picky about who they hire."

He went on to explain that Ty would be interviewed on Skype, would have to send a resume and agree to a police background check. He'd have to get his first aid and H2S certificates. "If you get approved, you'd likely be starting early in the new year."

* * *

Emma was not happy about the job, and expressed her disappointment that Ty would be working for Big Oil. He ignored her, his mind full of earnings that promised to assuage his bruised ego. She was reluctant to let go and referred to it again at dinner. Emma was an accountant with a firm in Victoria. Her boyfriend worked for a government ministry and their ambition was a place of their own where they would be energy self-sufficient.

Finally, Ty put down his fork and spoke distinctly. "I don't have a choice, Em. I need work."

"That's such a cop-out."

He stared in astonishment.

"It's a cop-out, Ty. I'm sure there are other jobs around. You haven't even looked, have you?"

"You're right," said Ty, "I haven't looked around. Why would I? I get megabucks in this job. There's nothing like it down here."

After a silence, Emma said, "At least we're not adding to the problem." She glanced at her mother. "We're going off the grid next year. Chauncey's parents are coming through with the loan."

"That's a cop-out," said Ty.

"Why is it a cop-out?"

"Because it's too expensive for most people. And because there isn't enough land for everyone to do it. Too many people on the planet, Em. And you know it."

He was still not used to arguing with his sister, who had always been the thought-leader because of her four-year advantage, but when she didn't respond he took a breath, and went on: "We have to move forward, Em. We have to find ways to live better. Maybe we need to find new energy sources, maybe I'll be the one to find them. Or maybe it'll be adapting existing sources, to make them more efficient."

Annie said, "Did I ever tell you about granny and her reforestation project?"

"God's trees," said Emma, and sipped her wine.

Ty had not heard the story.

"When granny was in college," said Annie, "she spent one summer planting trees. There was a group of protestors picketing the road up to the site. Granny saw this little old lady carrying a placard. 'Why are you protesting?' she asked her. 'We're planting seedlings to take the place of the trees that were logged.' 'Yes,' said the little old lady, 'but they're not God's trees.'"

Ty stared at her. "What's that supposed to mean?"

"It means, my dear, that some people aren't going to be satisfied, no matter what you do." She looked at each of them in turn. "Try not to be among them."

Ty finished his beer and crushed the can with a flourish.

Emma shook off her mood and smiled. "At least you're back to your normal bumptious self."

"Tell you what would make a big difference to the world." He tipped his chair back.

"Don't tip your chair back, Tyler."

He sat forward with a thump. "Sorry, mum. More engineers and artists."

Emma laughed. "Naturally."

"And fewer bean counters and bureaucrats."

Emma opened her mouth but Annie beat her to it.

"Clear the dishes, dear, and bring dessert. If you can stand to eat pie baked by a bean counter."

"Oops," said Ty cheerfully.

* * *

"Hi dad!" Ty stood in the middle of the living room, ankle-deep in discarded wrapping paper. He was wearing thermal underwear, long wool socks and a wool shirt that was so thick it was actually heavy on his shoulders. His face felt hot. "I'm great," he said, responding to a question from his dad.

Sitting on the sofa, Annie gave an ear to Ty's call and the rest of her attention to Emma, who was demonstrating a yoga move in her new Lululemons.

"When did you send it?" Ty looked at Emma and raised his eyes to the ceiling. She shook her head. Their father's presents had not arrived, the same way they didn't arrive every Christmas. They generally turned up before the new year.

Gerry Hogan lived with his second wife in Minneapolis. He always phoned on Christmas morning and he was always a little tight, although as Emma and Ty reminded themselves, he was two hours ahead of the west coast, so it wasn't as though he got out of bed and started pouring.

Hogan had left one day when Ty was five. He would send money for his children's birthdays, if he remembered, and he always called at Christmas. Annie had never disparaged him, but his children weren't fools. Dad was a nice guy but totally unreliable.

Now Ty, getting even hotter, was telling his dad about the new job. He rang off eventually and took off the wool shirt. He went upstairs to rid himself of the other clothes, and Emma followed him.

"Did he sound okay to you?"

"Yeah," Ty stripped off the socks and underwear and clad only in his boxers pulled on a pair of jeans. "I mean, he was pretty tight but that's normal." He looked at his sister as he buttoned his shirt. "He was all 'You have to come visit when you get back'."

"Oh sure," Emma paused. "I spoke to Marla for a minute. She sounded okay but a bit uptight. I wonder if he's still got a job."

"He said he was off on a big sales trip tomorrow."

"Talk's cheap, Ty." She watched him hunting out a shoe from under the bed. "I just don't want you spending all your money supporting him."

He straightened, shoe in hand, and stared at her in surprise. "That's not going to happen."

"I hope not."

Annie's voice floated up from the kitchen and they returned downstairs, Ty to help his mother stuff the turkey, and Emma to start cleaning up the living room.

CHAPTER

Three

"TRYING TO THINK, *thinking to try, can I wait? no way, it's like I'm lookin' to fly,*" rapped Ty as the highway spooled under the Pathfinder's tires. He kept an eye on the speedometer as he drove. His mother had made him swear a fearsome oath on his sister's life. He'd protested but Emma had been unfazed. "I don't want to hear about you being maimed and killed on the highway," she'd said. "At least not until you have thousands of dollars in the bank. Made your will?"

She had dodged Ty's swipe with a laugh and at his mother's insistence he had taken the oath not to exceed the speed limit and he was keeping his promise. "*. . . Breakin' all the barriers, yeah, Movin' out, takin' on the country.*" Another car passed him and he frowned momentarily then forgot it. Emma's life was not to be taken in vain.

Barty had thrown an uproarious going-away party and someone had poured Ty into a cab at two in the morning. At seven he threw his duffel in the back of the Nissan, admired the new snow tires once more, then sat down with his mother for a substantial breakfast. Afterward, she'd given him a hug, a kiss and a bagged lunch and he'd caught the ferry. He got through Vancouver's outskirts without incident and reached Hope at lunchtime. There he had pulled in, eaten his sandwiches and updated his Facebook page.

Up the TransCanada he drove, along the Fraser River, through the tunnels of Hell's Gate. Past the clay cliffs at Spences Bridge and the dry grass touched with green at Cache Creek. Everywhere was new to him, everything an adventure. Now in the late afternoon he was in cattle country, rolling hills of grassland dusted with snow, the hillsides dotted with lodgepole pines like stark black sentinels.

The snow was old: the road was dry. He felt as though he could go on driving all night. He had never felt happier in his life. The misery and shame of the past few months was behind him. Right now there was nothing else he ought to be doing, nothing except what he was doing, and it felt good. His future lay in his hands. He was on his way to a real job with other men in a tough environment where he would be richly compensated. He could hardly wait.

A sign approached in the dusk and flashed by: Williams Lake 20.

He came to a decision. It had been a long day and he was getting sleepy. Better to stop, have dinner and an early night. He came into town in darkness, with bright neon signs like welcoming beacons: McDonald's, Tim Horton's, Wendy's. These were familiar, known entities. He checked into a motel and set out on foot to explore the town, stretching his legs and getting his bearings, wearing a light jacket instead of his parka because it was a mild evening.

Williams Lake stood at the head of a lake in a shallow valley. The main street ran along the eastern side, and earlier, Ty had seen the western fork of the highway running by the lakehead before climbing the valley slope on its way to the coast. He explored the main street and walked uphill until he reached a residential area before turning back. Eventually, he began to think about food, and dinnertime found him in a pub eating ribs and baked potato, washed down with a pint of beer. He followed the ribs with another beer and leaned back to look around.

Two separate hockey games were displayed on the large-screen televisions mounted high on opposite walls. No sound came from the screens but the pictures told the tale. The lighting was dim, the room warm and the hum of conversation punctuated by cheers or groans from the action on the screens. Headgear ranged from stetsons to toques to none. On the far side of the room was a small dais where a country singer was channeling Luke Bryan. Ty sat at the bar and took it all in, enjoying himself and feeling at home.

The waitress came over. "Finished with that, tiger?" Ty nodded and she took the plate. He still had half a mug of beer left. "What else can I get for you?" Her eyes promised anything his heart desired. *Jeez. . . .*

"I'm okay for now."

"You just let me know."

She leaned over and wiped the bar in front of him, then turned away and he watched as she put the pie plate and fork in a container under the opposite counter. She had a neat waist and a scooped neck on a tight tee-shirt, and he liked the look of her. Only she was older—much older, he thought. At least thirty. She turned back and caught his gaze and her eyes flickered.

Ty had not had sex since the break-up with Jacey, in mid-September, and he had never had sex with a stranger, much less a stranger who was also an older woman. He gazed at the Canucks game without seeing it, listening as the singer pined for a girl in torn blue jeans. . . .

His phone vibrated. Barty: *'Sup?*

That reminded him: he updated his Facebook page, then texted Barty, while the Red Wings scored on the Habs and the singer could be heard over the groans. "She's kinda nice looking," he finished, "and I think she wants me. Should I meet up with her?" Some moments later, he saw Barty's answer: "Go with the flho."

Jeez, he thought. He was about to reply, "She's not a ho," when Barty added: "Don't forget the Big C."

That brought him up short. He had a condom in his wallet but it had been there for at least a year. Probably past its best-before date. But girls always had condoms, didn't they? That shouldn't be a problem. He was working through the ramifications when the waitress returned with his bill. She smiled and her hand brushed his as she laid it on the bar. "Got a shift change. I'll be going off soon."

Ty met her eyes. They were so knowing he felt as though she had read his texts, and he was suffused with awkwardness. "Thanks," he said uncomfortably and looked away. After she'd returned to the other end of the bar he turned the bill over. *Jeez* he thought for the third time. Nearly fifty bucks for dinner, on top of the motel and tomorrow's breakfast. He had fifteen hundred in the bank but that had to last until his first paycheck. Still thinking about the waitress, he finished his beer, put down the cash for the bill plus a tip, and left.

He thought about the waitress as he walked, the country song playing over and over in his head. He wandered, because it was too early to return to the motel. He walked up a rising street, by small businesses and through residential areas. He walked past neat houses with windows lit, some with curtains drawn, and others not. He saw a family sitting round a table; he saw a man and woman facing each other in a living room; he saw TV screens lit. He imagined families inside, in the warmth, while he was out here alone in the cold and dark.

Being alone was okay for a while—he was after all on something of an adventure—but he'd be glad to be among people soon, doing a job and making friends. He came to an intersection and debated which way to turn. Cars were passing regularly to his left, about three blocks away, so he headed in that direction, back down the hill, and came to a wide street at the bottom: Railway Avenue. He turned again to the left, heading back in the direction of the motel. Stores and warehouses began to appear, left and right.

He was half a block past a warehouse when he heard a bark. He cocked his head and kept walking. It came again, a bark with a note of distress. He drew abreast of an alley, dark except for a light bulb encased in wire mesh over a utility door at the far end. He could discern a small light-colored dog. It barked again and backed up and he saw a youth advancing on it. He kicked, and the dog, unreacting, yelped when the boot met its side. Its ribs showed through its short coat, and behind it the contents of a garbage can were strewn on the ground.

"Hey!" Ty jogged toward them. The alley had another entrance, he saw, at right-angles, and the youth and dog were in the right-angle. The dog yelped from another kick and sprang to one side. "What do you think you're doing?"

"Look, man. It's blind." The youth had a stick in his hand.

"So it's okay to pick on a blind dog?"

"Fuck off! Who asked you?"

"No, you fuck off." Ty was furious and when the dog's tormentor turned, stick raised to strike him, he stepped forward, wrenched it out of the youth's hand and threw it away, then swung at him. More by luck than design, his fist landed on the other's shoulder, half-spinning him around. He took in Ty's size, hesitated then ran off along the other arm of the alley. Ty bent down and spoke gently to the dog, extending his hand for it to sniff.

"Not going to hurt you, pup." The dog stood motionless, shivering, waiting for another attack. It did not seem to see Ty's hand but its nose twitched. He drew closer and ran a hand along its back and it whimpered. It was a small crossbreed of some kind, short-haired, and he carefully picked it up, scratching behind its ears, and walked over to examine it under the weak light bulb. He moved one hand back and forth in front of its eyes, but they remained fixed, staring ahead. Its heart thumped wildly but it appeared to be uninjured. When he spoke to it, the ears twitched.

He heard a noise from the direction of the bully's disappearance and turned, still holding the dog. He could make out a figure, a man, big, with camouflage pants and a dark beard.

"Hey," began the man.

"Everything okay?" Another voice, this one from Ty's end of the alley. Up in the entrance, a car idled and a man looked over the top of it at Ty. There was light at that end and Ty, feeling he'd had enough surprises for one day, nodded at the bearded man and carried the dog along to the street.

The man had a pleasant, slightly pudgy face.

Ty addressed him. "Do you live here?"

"Sure. Why?"

Ty explained about the dog. "I think I should take him to the pound or the SPCA or something."

"No problem. The SPCA's on my way home. Hop in."

Ty looked across the roof of the car. The guy was medium height with broad shoulders and big hands, one of which he was extending. "Brad Clarke," he said.

Ty shook it and took the passenger seat with the dog. "Good you came along," he said.

"I was finishing up some paperwork," said Clarke. "Just back from a sales trip. Cattle feed and supply." The car turned up a lane and came to the main street. He glanced over at Ty. "You new in town?"

Ty explained that he was on his way to the oil fields and they chatted about that as Clarke drove block by block along the main street then along the lakehead. He had a pleasant manner and Ty held the dog and scratched its ears as Clarke spoke of other young men who had come through town, all seeking their fortunes up north. "Guess this is a good stopping point," he said, and Ty agreed.

Eventually the car pulled up in front of the SPCA building, now dark.

"Doesn't look promising," said Clarke and Ty agreed but decided to see if there was a bell or a phone number. He got out holding the dog and walked over to the entrance. No bell, no sign except for one stating office hours. He put his ear against the glass door and heard a distant bark, answered by another. The dog was motionless.

"Well, puppy, it's not looking good." The ears twitched. Ty looked down at it consideringly. "Maybe I should just take you with me."

He returned to the car.

Clarke had been busy with his smartphone. "There's an animal shelter back over the other side, up on the hill. Let's try that." He waved off Ty's objection. "No problem, it's not that far. Have you there in a few minutes."

They pulled away from the kerb and Clarke asked what Ty was going to do with his oilfield earnings. He explained about the abrupt hiatus in his education and that the earnings were to enable him to travel with his buddy and return to university. Why wasn't the buddy here with him, Clarke wanted to know, and Ty laughed and explained that Barty was a poet and no way would anyone persuade him to work in the oil fields, and in any case, Barty hadn't been kicked out of school—

He felt something large and warm on his thigh. On his—

"What the fuck?" He shifted against the door, the dog whimpered, he looked over at Clarke.

"Sorry! Hey—I'm sorry. Just wanted to pat the dog."

"Dog, my ass! Let me out."

"Listen, you've got it all wrong—"

Ty explained forcefully that he had not got it wrong and scrambled out when the car stopped. "Thanks, he said tersely. "We'll manage from here." He slammed the door.

Clarke leaned over and the passenger window opened. "I hate to leave you out here, Ty."

Ty started back the way they had come. "We're fine." He picked up the pace. After a minute, he heard the car drive off.

He looked around. He was not far from the pub, and he oriented himself and started along a street that angled up the hill overlooking the valley. "Okay, pup," he said, and opened his jacket, shoving the dog inside and making it easier to support. "Looks like it's going to be you and me." He had considered simply putting it down by the road, but the idea did not sit well with him. Grateful that it was neither raining nor especially cold, he lengthened his stride and ate up the blocks.

Forty minutes later they came on to the same street he'd walked earlier, though much further up. He'd seen no sign of an animal shelter, and he turned in what he hoped would be the direction of the motel. A few blocks later he heard highway traffic and came to a parking lot with a lit-up one-story building and a familiar sign: Greyhound. "How about we go inside and sit down for a minute?"

They crossed the parking lot and Ty glimpsed a spark of light in the shadows under the eaves at the far end of the building. A figure stood there, smoking a cigarette. Ty recognized the black beard and the camouflage pants. A bulky man, wearing a shirt and a padded vest. He watched Ty and the dog, which Ty had brought out of his jacket and which was parsing the light breeze coming toward them. Its ears cocked forward and it whined. Ty looked from dog to man, now approaching them.

"Is this your dog?" The dog was whining almost continually. "Hey, I'm so sorry, man." He held it out. The man halted. The dog barked sharply, eagerly.

"It's not my dog." White teeth showed through the beard. "But I guess it's kinda lonesome."

He reached for the dog and it licked his hands ecstatically, wriggling with excitement. Ty watched.

"It's not your dog? Sure looks like it's yours."

The man bent his head and said something to the dog and it licked his neck, snuffled through the beard and licked his cheeks. "Whoa, Rover, take it easy."

Ty felt somehow inadequate in the realm of canine appeal.

"My bus'll be here soon. Let's wait inside."

They sat down near a large duffel bag, Rover straining closer to the man, whose name was Eric Helgeland. He shrugged when Ty asked him his secret. "I seem to have something they like. Lot of strays in Afghanistan. It was painful, you couldn't help them all." He crouched down and opened the duffel bag. After some rummaging he produced a thick beef sandwich, half of which he put on the floor, the dog next to it.

"You meet up with that waitress after?"

Ty's jaw dropped. Eric rummaged some more and came up with a travel water bowl and a bottle of water.

"I was down the other end; guess she was too busy with you or I might have stood a chance."

Ty said, after a pause, "She was older. . . ."

"S'right. Old enough to be your mother and then some." He saw the look on Ty's face. "How old did you think she was?"

"Maybe thirty," said Ty weakly.

Eric laughed. "Mid forties, I guess."

The dog demolished the beef sandwich and drank its fill. It had no trouble knowing where Eric was, and when it had finished it crouched, ready to jump up but hampered by its lack of sight. He reached down and lifted it onto his lap. "Let's save that for another time, Rover."

"You going to keep him?"

"Yeah, I guess." The dog's teeth were yellow but not broken. "Looks like he's about ten or so. Probably has a few years in him." He glanced at Ty. "So the guy was no help, huh?"

Ty snorted. "The guy was gay." He shook his head.

"Oh. You've had quite an evening." Eric fell serious. "Wish I'd got ahold of that kid in the alley."

"Yeah, well I decked him pretty good," said Ty, in whom the memory of that fight had grown somewhat in the past hour.

Eric snorted. “You didn’t deck him, kid. You hit his shoulder and he ran off like the coward he is.” He went on to describe in detail the suitable punishment for one who would torment an animal; his description involved a Grohmann number three knife and slow evisceration. Ty sat and listened in fascination, wondering if he should have joined the army instead of going to the oil fields.

“Am I scaring you, kid?”

Ty shook his head.

Eric looked at him. “How come?”

“The dog loves you.” He hesitated, then added, “Listen, you really going to keep him? He’s blind.”

“Like the guy said, nobody’s perfect.” He reached into the duffel and pulled out a jacket, substituting it for his vest, which he dropped on the bag.

Ty was curious. “Where are you headed?”

“Dunno. Been going all over. Criss-crossing the country. There’s a lot of it to see.” He leaned back. “And when I’m on the bus there’s nothing else I can do. Kinda relaxing.”

Ty nodded; he’d had something of the same experience. He wanted to ask another question, and after a silence, in which they could hear the bus a few blocks away, he did. “Is that enough?”

“It’ll do me for now.”

Eric stood and took Rover outside to water the weeds next to the wall. He came back and repacked his duffel bag, shoving the half-sandwich in one jacket pocket and the water bottle in the other. He studied Ty then nodded abruptly. “You got good instincts, kid. You just need experience." They shook hands. "Good luck up north."

When the bus arrived and the driver stowed his duffel underneath, he climbed aboard looking like nothing more than a bulky man with a beard. He lifted a hand to Ty from a seat in the rear and the bus pulled out, bound for Grande Prairie and points east.

Ty reached the motel an hour later and soon after, lay in bed thinking over the events of the day, in particular Clarke and the waitress. "Prime rib," he said aloud. "That's what you are, Hogan. Just a piece of prime rib that people want a piece of." He turned on his side. Dogs wanted love, just like people. He wondered what it would be like just to wander from town to town.

He fell asleep with a smile on his lips, thinking of the waitress.

CHAPTER

Four

TY ARRIVED IN Fort St John mid-afternoon, driving in behind a cement truck and looking around with interest. It was the largest town on the Alaska Highway, with a population approaching twenty thousand. Passenger vehicles seemed to be scarce: mostly the traffic consisted of SUVs and pickups and laden semis. It was a muddy town, busy and noisy. Ty liked it immediately.

Grizzly Exploration consisted of a plain white trailer on a large lot. Ty joined a short line-up of men in an entrance room with a counter and smaller offices on either side. The man ahead moved away and Ty stepped up to the counter. He recognized Stan Pulaski from their Skype interview and waited while the manager finished filling out a clipboard form in front of him. A blue hardhat sat on the counter near his left hand.

"Name?"

"Tyler Hogan."

A quick glance. "Got here all right."

"Yes, sir."

"Okay. The next five days are orientation over at the high school. You're expected to be there on time. Eight tomorrow morning." He took a paper voucher from a stack near his hand, stamped it and handed it to Ty. "Hotel and meal allowance for the Caribou Arms. You want to stay someplace else, it's your dime. Got it?"

"Yes."

"You pass orientation and the drug test, you'll be issued gear and you and your partner will head off next morning. Okay?"

"I thought we had to provide our own gear?"

"Outer gear. Flame retardant. We don't want you getting burned to a crisp, Hogan. Bad for business. Next?" He continued filling in the clipboard form.

Ty took his voucher and walked outside. When he'd arrived, he'd had eyes only for the trailer, with its "Office" sign and arrow. Now he looked around. He stood on a side street. The trailer was parked in front of a chain-link fence. He walked over and peered through the fence at a small fleet of oiler trucks. *One of those is mine*, he thought and his pulse kicked up a notch.

"Is that a hot oil truck?" A stocky fellow about Ty's age had joined him at the fence.

"Looks like it," said Ty. "Least, they look like what I found on line." He poked a finger through the mesh. "See that square cabin behind the truck cabin? That's where they heat the oil."

"Oh yeah?" The other looked at him. "Do you know what we'll be doing?"

Ty grinned. "No idea. Guess we'll find out tomorrow." He introduced himself.

"Dougie Wilson," said the other. "Doug."

"Hi, Doug. You get a voucher?"

"Yeah."

Ty used his phone to find the hotel address as they walked back to their vehicles and Doug followed him in a rental car.

An hour after checking in, Ty made his way to the bar. It was a long, low-ceilinged room almost entirely filled with men. Two couples had a table near the entrance and were playing darts, women against the men. Ty saw Doug's hand go up and joined him. A waitress appeared next to him and he ordered a beer.

"Room?"

He looked perplexed.

"Tell her your room number. You can run a tab."

All right! After Ty had given his room number, the waitress left and Doug, on his second beer, asked what had taken him so long.

"Checked out the high school," said Ty. "I'd hate to get kicked off the job for being late."

The beer came and he took a long swallow and looked around. The men seemed to be of all ages. Young guys like himself sat elbow to elbow with men in their thirties and forties. Nor were they all working for the same company.

"You guys with Lodestar?" The speaker was a crewcut man in his forties, calling over from an adjacent table.

Ty shook his head.

"Who then?"

"Huh?"

"Who you with?"

"Does he mean Grizzly," wondered Doug.

"Grizzly," called Ty, and the man raised a thumb and turned back to his companions. Ty learned later that Grizzly accounted for only twelve of the men in the bar.

He heard Doug's life story over steak and fries. Unlike Ty, he had no plans for higher education. He just liked having money. He had flown up from Vancouver after deciding, reluctantly, not to become a fisherman. "I really liked that idea. Fishing's great, but deep water makes me nervous." He had a scheme that he had adapted to fit the oil sector. "You know how fishermen, like on the east coast, they work six months, make maybe sixty thousand or more, then they go on EI for the rest of the year?" Ty nodded. He'd heard this one before from school mates. He ate and listened.

"That's my plan," said Doug. "I just want me an RV and I'll work six months, travel six months."

"Do they let you do that? Don't you have to apply for other jobs?"

"Oh yeah, but you can dummy up a list of names and numbers if they ask." He chewed thoughtfully. "Or maybe I'd go on disability. I can be flexible." He waved a french fry. "I was talking to a guy before you came. He's a rig manager, what they call the toolpusher. They're always getting injuries with the apprentices. I'd rather be a hot oiler, though. Sounds like easier work."

* * *

"Getting interesting." Ty came out of the high school classroom with Doug. It was the third day of orientation and today they were learning about the truck. Day one had been an overview of drilling, including sideways or horizontal drilling as well as vertical. On day two they'd learned about well upkeep and paraffin wax buildup, the condition hot oilers fixed. They'd been introduced to flow rates, temperature and pressure, and glimpsed the balancing act required to remove the wax without causing a worse buildup.

Ty had enjoyed all of it. He'd discovered that hot oiler trucks could handle many of the tasks required of frack heater trucks, and sometimes handled smaller frack jobs. Natural-gas production was a growth industry and he hoped to be able to get into that area once he'd proved his worth as a hot oiler.

Doug didn't care. He had feelers out all over the place, and every chance he got he talked to rig managers and roughnecks, water truckers and long haulers. "You never know," he said and reminded Ty of the environmental protest that had shut down a number of wells west of town, putting hundreds out of work.

Classes were eight until five, with two short breaks and an hour for lunch. Ty had found a gym where he went after class to work out for an hour or two. Evenings were spent drinking at the hotel bar.

They'd met the other Grizzly hot oilers, each of them one-half of a two-man team. But unlike Ty and Doug, most of them came from other jobs in the oil patch, a couple from office jobs, some from haulage, others from jobs requiring hard physical labor. Their partners, the men with experience, would come in on the last day to meet their apprentices and go off to get acquainted with their trucks. Next week they would take off for their designated camps, at which point, as Ty and Doug liked to toast each other over a beer, the Big Bucks Begin.

Ty used his lunch hour to explore and on the first day had driven around town. The streets were horrible, full of frost heaves and potholes, a marked contrast to the pristine highways. "Too much heavy equipment," said a man filling an SUV next to Ty at the gas station. "Then you got your winter wear and tear. You from the coast?" Ty nodded. "Ninety percent of the population live along the border, did you know that?"

"Yeah, I did."

The man replaced his pump and waited for his receipt to print, "You're in the land of the ten percent now. Things are different here." He lifted a hand and walked off to the gas station office.

Ty finished filling the Pathfinder and decided to drive north along the Alaska Highway. He'd turned off toward the small town of Cecil Lake, and it was there, near the roadside that he'd seen the moose. Pulling in to the side of the snowy road he'd walked back to where it lay, a massive beast with a huge spread of antlers and a bloody hole behind its shoulder.

He squatted, regarding it with admiration, wishing he could have seen it alive. Its one visible eye was glazed and white and he could only move a leg with difficulty: the moose had been dead a while and was beginning to freeze. He stood up, listening in the silence, but no one came and no cars passed. Eventually he noticed the time and left for school. But he was troubled by the memory of that great beast, forsaken by the roadside, and drove back out the following day. The carcass was still there, but the head, that magnificent head with its spread of horn, was gone, roughly sawn off. The gaping neck wound had dimmed to a brownish-grey. To Ty, the butchered carcass was unseemly and he did not linger.

Today he'd stayed in town and joined Doug at the hotel for lunch.

The blow fell in the afternoon. They were back in the classroom waiting for their instructor, a former frack operator. Conversation died down as he appeared and surveyed the class. "Hands up, Grizzly employees? For you guys, this course is over." His voice rose over the protests. "Check back with your employer immediately."

"What the fuck happened?" It was one of the long-distance haulers.

"Far as I can understand it, Grizzly's contracts with Global have been canceled. So you guys are shit outta luck." Global was the oil company for which Grizzly provided exploration services.

They pressed him for information. He looked wry. "You'll find out that things change daily in the oil patch. But this is a new one on me." He scratched the back of his head. "It seems Grizzly's VP of Marketing has been doing a little drilling of his own with the wife of Global's CEO." Muffled snorts of laughter came from some of the other attendees, while the Grizzly employees looked on, unamused.

Doug headed for the door and left, and the others began to follow. Ty was furious. “What the fuck kind of way is that to run a business? I came seven hundred miles for this job, to lose it because some asshole can’t keep his pants zipped?” He heard murmurs of agreement. He was sincerely shocked. Adults weren’t supposed to behave like this. The adult world was supposed to be run on better lines than a frat party.

Later, when he had time to think calmly, he realized what a dumb assumption that was. Kids had fresh proof every day of the idiocies of the adult world. He knew that, yet he’d been raised in a house where actions had consequences, where by and large order and reason reigned. This was, he now realized, poor preparation for life in the real world. He made a mental note to tell his mother.

He shook off the instructor’s rough sympathy and made his way out of the room and back to the Grizzly office. The other trainees, except for Doug, were milling around outside, their breath rising in the cold air. Pulaski arrived soon after. “Your vouchers are cut off as of now,” he said. “Lunch was covered, but that’s all. I suggest you get over to the hotel and check out, unless you want to be charged for tonight.”

Doug returned half an hour later, when Ty had cleared his room and was standing with others at the hotel reception counter, waiting to check out.

“Hey, man!” His grin was wide. “I got me a job!”

They regarded him with respect. He went on, “I’m an apprentice on a rig. Shipping out this afternoon. Fifteen on, six off, big bucks. Like, big!” He gestured widely and Ty good naturedly high-fived him.

"Say, Ty, wait for me, okay? I'm just going to pack up then I'll buy you a beer."

Another shock awaited Ty when he saw his bill. He'd been mentally totting up his finances and had counted the past three days as free of charge, until the clerk presented his bar bill, with more than a hundred dollars worth of beer and—what was *that* at ten bucks a pop? Fifty bucks of it, whatever it was, all last night. He queried the clerk who perused his computer screen. "Ah—rum and coke. Five of them." He smiled vaguely in Ty's direction. "Doubles."

Ty winced and recalled the headache he'd woken up with this morning. A facsimile of it reappeared as he proffered his credit card. After he'd settled the bill he carried his duffel over to a cluster of armchairs and sat down. He was filled with admiration for Doug. Scuzzy schemes aside, he had taken nothing for granted. As a result, he'd landed on his feet while Ty had been a trusting fool and ended up being caught flat-footed. He made another mental note: always have a backup plan.

A newspaper stand caught his eye and he bought a local newspaper. *Take a quick look through the want ads,* he thought, *then go online*. When Doug arrived he was working through the oil and gas jobs in the slim classifieds section of the paper.

"Listen, Ty, I asked if they wanted two guys. He just got back to me," Doug closed his phone as Ty looked up hopefully. "Hired someone else. But I'm texting you his name and number and some other leads."

Over beer, Doug's long-term plan made a return appearance. He was describing the camp. "You work twelve-hour shifts and there's a lot of lifting and stuff. I figure I should be able to come outta there with a solid disability in four months."

Ty laughed shortly. "You be careful," he said, and stood up. "Listen, man, take care. I gotta go find a job and someplace to sleep." He lifted his duffel. "Have a good one."

* * *

By mid-afternoon Ty was beginning to panic. He'd checked every online job board, without success. He'd left his name and number with everyone who would take it, and signed up for job alerts from the main career sites. Now he sat in the idling Pathfinder in a Safeway parking lot, working his way through the classifieds while the phone charged. His eye ran unwillingly down the Hospitality listings, where several entries offered waiting, maid and cleaning jobs. His face felt hot. He'd worked in the fast-food business at fifteen. He was damned if he'd do that again.

Below the hotel listings was a box ad for a "Hydrovac swamper, $23/hour." What the hell did a hydrovac swamper do? Clean toilets? He hesitated but the money exerted a powerful pull and he reluctantly circled the ad then kept on looking. He glanced at his watch and turned the page to look at rooms to let. The prices, oh God, the prices. And food would be extra. What could you live on, per day, he wondered. Say ten for breakfast, twenty each for lunch and dinner. That's—*Jesus! Fifteen hundred a month just for food?* He'd been paying his mother two hundred and fifty and complaining about it.

Okay, calm down. With a furnished suite he could cook for himself. He walked over to the Safeway armed with a rudimentary grocery list—eggs, bacon, milk, bread, steak—and did some quick pricing, substituted hamburger for steak and added a few vegetables, and discovered he could probably feed himself for seven or eight hundred. He returned to the car and checked furnished suites. Anything from one to two thousand. So either way, he needed up to three thousand just to survive.

He looked through the oil and gas jobs again, wishing he had a Class 1 driver's license. The service companies were crying out for drivers for water, sand, cement, chemical trucks. He thought hard. Those jobs all had the same drawback: no overtime. For that you wanted a frack or hot oiler job, or to join a camp like Doug was doing. He cursed Grizzly again and bent his head, checking his phone for messages. Nothing.

He'd marked three jobs in the paper. All were hotel jobs, two at $17 an hour. The third was the toilet job, the hydrovac swamper. He studied the box ad and picked up his phone, thinking as he dialed the number that it seemed familiar.

"Grizzly. Pulaski."

Ty recovered. "Hiya, Mr. Pulaski. I'm calling about this hydrovac swamper job you got in the paper."

The manager invited him to come on in, so he left the Safeway parking lot and drove back to the Grizzly office.

His boots clumped across the trailer floor, the silence a reproof for the now-canceled hot oiler contract.

"So you want to be a swamper, huh?"

"I want a paying job," said Ty. "I'm not going to tell you I drove seven hundred miles to become a swamper, because I don't even know what that is." The day's events dictated a small degree of pushback, and the manager seemed to recognize that, smiling faintly.

"We use hydrovac trucks to find buried utility lines, clean up small spills, that kind of thing."

Ty's spirits soared. "Not toilets?"

Pulaski eyed him then turned and pointed out the rear window. "There's one of the hydrovacs. You've got your tanks and your eight-inch vacuum hose, see?"

Beyond the fleet of hot oiler trucks stood a larger vehicle. He could see the two tanks and the wide hose looped along one side of the larger tank. Pulaski went on: "Ever use a pressure washer?"

"Yeah."

"You're using high-pressure hot water to cut through the ground until you expose the utility pipe or wiring. Then you mark the location and move on to the next one." He eyed him enquiringly and Ty nodded. It was so much better than he'd expected.

"It's standard office hours, eight to five, no overtime. Got that?"

Ty nodded again as the manager came round the counter. He opened the door of a tall cupboard against one wall on the office end of the trailer. Shelves of gear: hard hats and coveralls, blue with the Grizzly logo on them. "Find one that fits," he said, pointing to the hard hats. The coveralls were in sized stacks. He picked out a large. "Get yourself some earplugs, we don't supply those." He glanced at Ty's boots. "Those look fine, Baffin?"

"Yeah." It was a popular make of steel-toed boot that Stefan Anderson had advised him to buy.

"Take a pair of goggles," he reached over to a lower shelf and handed a pair to Ty, "and you might want to get a pair of those rubber-dipped gloves and some glove liners."

"I got glove liners," said Ty, "but I'll look into the rubber gloves."

"Working with water all day long." Pulaski returned behind the counter. "Wind can be worse than the cold. Got a balaclava?"

"No. Should I?"

"Depends on the wind chill. You might want to take one out with you, or a liner." He meant, a hardhat liner. "Make sure you get a mouth hole on the balaclava, or the air'll come out the eye holes and fog your goggles."

"Okay!" This was real progress at last. Wearing the hard hat, Ty picked up the goggles and coveralls. He glanced out at the truck and had a thought. "Am I going to be driving the truck? Because—"

"No. You're the swamper. You take your orders from Cyrus."

"Cyrus?"

"Cyrus Connolly. He's the driver."

"Okey dokey."

"You should know, Cyrus is a little—eccentric."

Ty had aged since lunchtime and the Jeopardy buzzer sounded loud in his ear. He put the gear on the counter. "Eccentric?"

"No need to look like that. I wouldn't send you out with him except I think you can handle the situation."

"Situation?"

"Cyrus has anger issues. He tends to take them out on his truck. I put up with it because the truck's old and so is Cyrus. He's forgotten more about the oil patch than you or I will ever know. He doesn't like people. He's not wild about college kids, but you can play that down, right?"

Ty gazed out the window, thinking over what he'd heard. Finally, "So I'm supposed to go off to the bush with this crazy guy and wait for him to pick up an ax and try to off me?"

Pulaski looked shocked. "Cyrus wouldn't do that. What he will do is drive around all day long to each site on his list and expect you to do all the work. That's about as bad as it gets."

Chapter

Five

Ty worked the wand over a shallow depression in the frozen ground. A jet of hot water cut through the soil with the force of twenty-five hundred pounds per square inch behind it. *Like cutting butter*, he thought. Dirt and stones spat at his coveralled legs as he stirred the earth in a rectangle approximately two feet square. There. That should be enough to get going.

He switched off the wand, left it next to the hole and jogged to the truck. He could see Cyrus reflected in the large rearview mirror, staring ahead at the distant trees, smoke spiraling up from his cigarette.

The hydrovac was parked in a field. Ty unhooked the eight-inch suction hose from its place on the side of the sediment tank, unspooled it and dragged it over to the hole. He returned to the truck and threw the switch on the pump and was glad of his earplugs.

Back at the hole he sucked out the loose mud and rested the hose in the depression. It lay there, sucking air, the hole too shallow to hold it, while he picked up the wand and resumed digging. Cyrus had informed him that he should be able to dig a hole five feet deep in twenty minutes. Still new to the truck and the equipment, he wasn't yet close to that time.

He worked the wand, so intent on his excavation that he failed to hear Cyrus's approach. Suddenly the suction hose dropped into the hole.

"It works better when you stick it in the hole, fucktard."

Ty kept playing the wand. "It wouldn't stay in there!" he yelled back but the other ignored him.

Cyrus Connolly had a three-day stubble, long grey hair tied in a ponytail and pale blue eyes. He was missing some key teeth: a couple of molars, two or three incisors. His vocabulary appeared to be restricted to words of one or two syllables and his favorite word was "fucktard." Sentences addressed to Ty contained either this word or "swamper boy," sometimes both.

Now he held one foot on the suction hose until the hole was nearly a foot deep. When it stayed in place he turned away. "Get the lead out, swamper boy, we're running way behind." He headed back to the truck.

The deeper he got, the more ginger Ty became, knowing the power washer could cut through a cable. When he exposed the electrical pipe he found it lying next to a large rock, too large for the hose. He used the wand to loosen the soil until the hose could clamp on to the whole rock, then he pulled rock and hose up to the surface, ran back to the truck, turned off the suction, then back to the excavation, where he lifted the rock and threw it to one side. Back to the truck to turn on the suction again, explaining the reason for the delay to Cyrus, who swore ripely. Then back to digging until the pipe was fully exposed, five feet down. He finished suctioning out the mud, planted a small orange flag next to the hole and returned to the truck to switch off the pump.

He opened the driver's door. "How far to the next one?" They were spending the whole day in this field, he knew that much.

"Other side," said Cyrus and slammed the door.

Ty powered the windup switch for the water pressure hose and wound it onto its drum next to the water tank. Then he retrieved his goggles and water bottle and lifted the end of the suction hose, preparing to drag it back to the truck. Suddenly the truck moved off and he dropped the hose, swore under his breath and watched as the truck lurched over the field, hose trailing behind. If it snagged on anything . . . but it did not and eventually the truck halted on the far side of the field. Ty trudged toward it, looking forward to his pay check. "Flunk school, see the world," he muttered.

Cyrus had already started the excavation when he arrived. "Jesus, swamper boy, pick it up! We ain't got all day. Get the hose in here, pronto."

After lunch they excavated a long trench down one side of the field, exposing utility lines every five or ten feet. At the end of the day they dumped the contents of the mud tank along the fence near some trees, and Ty looked out over the empty space and tried to picture the drilling rig that would be set up here next week.

"Why's it called daylighting?"

They were driving back to the Grizzly yard. This morning, when Cyrus had come out of the trailer carrying rolls of maps, Pulaski and another man had followed him out and Pulaski had made the introductions. "You'll be daylighting all day today," he'd said to Ty, who had wanted to ask what that meant. But Cyrus was already halfway to the truck, moving in a crablike but rapid fashion, so he loped after him. His question had been ignored this morning, so now he asked it again.

"You wouldn't want to do it at night, would you, college kid?"

Ty stared at the old man. "Listen, Cyrus. You're the guy who's supposed to know everything, so why don't you back off with the insults and just tell me."

One arm draped over the steering wheel, Cyrus sniffed, hawked, lowered his side window and spat adroitly. "Fuck. Fuckin' prima donna fucktard."

Ty gave up.

* * *

Mr. Choi was reading the newspaper when Ty, showered and changed and hungry as a horse, came upstairs. He lowered the paper. "Good evening, Ty."

"Hiya, Mr. Choi. Paul," he added as the Korean began to correct him. Of medium height, in his late forties, Paul Choi spoke slow, precise English. "I am practising," he said, indicating the paper.

"Oh yeah?" Good food smells filled the air and Ty sat down reluctantly, choosing a footstool opposite Paul's armchair. The Korean wanted to know if he had found everything satisfactory. He had asked this question earlier, at breakfast. Ty made the same answer.

"It's all fantastic," he said sincerely, and his host looked pleased.

The previous afternoon, Ty had made three quick phone calls outside the clothing outfitter's where he'd bought ear plugs and a balaclava. The first place was full. Of the other two, one seemed small and none too clean. The third was a large house with two basement bedrooms and a bathroom. Ty liked the look of it immediately: the room was clean as a pin, with a TV, laptop and small fridge. A large rubber tray sat on the floor inside the basement door. Ty had seen similar trays at the hotel and school: they were for muddy boots.

The Korean owners seemed okay, especially the husband. Mrs. Choi said little and Ty later learned her English was limited. She had a long face, a heavy nose and a bad-tempered expression. Mr. Choi tended to overcompensate for this by smiling a good deal. They asked if he liked the room and he answered enthusiastically. The other bedroom was rented, its occupant away in the bush. The Chois wanted a week's rent in advance and Ty handed over his credit card and brought in his duffel. When they only had one paying guest, the family's custom was to keep him company at meals.

The dinner gong sounded and the two men entered the dining room. "Pork chops," said Paul, then added carefully, "scalloped potatoes. You like Korean food?" There were two vegetable dishes on the table.

"Not sure I've ever tried it," said Ty. "But I like most things." He sat down.

"Kimchi, and that is Hobak jun. Fried zucchini."

On his left, Mrs. Choi impatiently indicated the pork chops. *You help yourself!* He took two and passed the plate to Paul, helped himself to potatoes and the two vegetable dishes, all under the watchful eye of ten-year-old Lydia. She sat opposite him, not far from the large brass dinner gong suspended on a mahogany frame.

Ty smiled across at her. "How're you doing?"

"Okay," she said, unsmiling. She spoke English with just a hint of an accent.

Ty began to dig in, then stopped abruptly as they all bowed their heads and clasped their hands. Paul spoke: "For what we are about to receive, may the Lord make us truly thankful."

Ty took up his knife and fork again, then Mrs. Choi did some more wrist exercising, this time in the direction of the condiments in the middle of the table: ketchup, hot sauce and mustard.

"Can I pass—" said Ty but she flapped at him: *You! Get on with it.* Ty helped himself and remembering the prices in the grocery store—was it only yesterday?—he was more than usually frugal with the ketchup. He returned the bottle to the table center and found Mrs. Choi regarding him with suspicion. Now what?

She spoke. "More?"

Ty shook his head. "This is great, thanks." He loaded a fork and took a mouthful of dinner while the adult Chois exchanged words in Korean and Lydia ate sedately.

Paul spoke. "My wife asks, did you take enough catsup?"

"Oh sure," said Ty. "My mother always says I put so much on I can't taste the food, so I thought I'd ease up a bit." Paul relayed this and Mrs. Choi frowned.

"This is delicious," said Ty and glanced across the table at the girl. "You don't eat catsup?"

"No." She chewed slowly. She had her father's regular features. "I eat ketchup."

And her mother's disposition. Ty continued eating while a short spate of conversation between the parents finished with a gentle rebuke by Paul of his daughter.

"What did you call this? Hubuk—?"

"Hobak jun. You like it?"

"It's delicious, so's this other one. Cabbage and zucchini. Who'd have known?" He beamed around the table, doing his bit to keep the mood light.

He was not expected to linger after dinner, so he returned to his room and lay on the bed watching TV for a while. Then he turned on the laptop, updated his Facebook page and surfed job sites. *Always have a backup plan.* He wondered if Doug was settling in to camp life. He found an oil and gas forum and lurked for a while, reading the comments of guys talking about jobs and companies that were hiring. Having a Class 1 license seemed to be a good thing but that would have to wait until the alcohol lock came off his vehicle.

He found the websites of companies mentioned in the forum and studied their application forms. He met the eligibility requirements: over eighteen, physically fit, able to attend an unpaid orientation course—he made a rude noise at that—and on one website, scrolled down to find a list of questions. *Do the following apply to you?* He considered them.

Do you mind working in remote locations? Why would I mind, thought Ty. That's how I make the big bucks. Of course I don't mind.

Can you lift eighty to a hundred pounds at a time, many times a day? He pondered. If you could bench-press two-fifty, a hundred should be no problem. As for lifting all day long, that was a matter of using your thigh and back muscles properly, and your core. Ty had no qualms about the prospect. Next question.

Do you mind getting dirty? What kind of question was that?

Are you able to get along with different kinds of people? Of course.

This sounded like his kind of job. He scrolled back up to the top. The page was titled, "Are you cut out to be a roughneck?" It was a long form, with boxes you could check for each question plus a few fill-in-the-blanks. He filled it out and heard light footsteps on the stairs as he worked through it. The kid? A knock at his door.

"Yo!" He continued checking boxes.

The door opened and Lydia regarded him unsmilingly. Lying on the bed, laptop on his stomach and drawn up knees, Ty gave her a broad smile. "Hi there!"

"My mother wants to know if you want hoddeok for breakfast. They're Korean pancakes."

"Sounds great. Anything your mother cooks is just fine with me. Say—can you tell me your address?"

"Why?"

He explained about the applications and swiveled the laptop so she could see the screen. She turned and disappeared, leaving the door ajar and he heard her run upstairs. He shook his head. Useless brat.

He considered the form, thinking it was pointless to put his home address, then he heard footsteps flying downstairs and she returned. "Seven zero eight Woodside Drive," she said and added the postal code when he asked it.

"Perfect!" He hit send and looked for the next company.

"I'm going to be a chemical engineer," said Lydia.

"Oh yeah?" Ty regarded her. "For one of the oil companies?"

She nodded. "I'm going to find a way to make gasoline change into pure water."

"Why water?"

"No carbon dioxide. So it won't be bad for the planet."

"I getcha." He flipped to a search page. "Here, look at this."

"What?" She climbed on the bed while Ty searched and brought up a page.

"What is it?"

The page showed a tidal generator. "It's a turbine that uses ocean currents to generate electricity." He watched her as she studied the picture. "It makes power from the tides and stores it."

She raised her eyes to his face. "Is that what you want to do?"

"Dunno." He pulled the pillow up behind his head. "I want to get into engineering, just not sure exactly what, yet."

"When will you be sure?"

He looked at her.

She climbed back off the bed. "There's no time to lose, you know." The black eyes were reproving.

* * *

After a week on the job, Ty could expose a pipe eight feet down within half an hour. He was also more adept at working the boom of the suction hose. Best of all, he had discovered a remote in the glove compartment.

"What's this for?"

Cyrus glanced over as he drove. "Remote, what's it look like?" He added a predictable epithet under his breath.

"Yeah, I can see it's a remote. What's it for?"

"Use it if you want. Just try not to break anything."

Ty made an educated guess. "If this is for working the boom controls, you could have told me before. Bellyaching about how slow I was didn't do you much good, did it?"

"I was waiting for you to figure it out for yourself, fucktard."

Ty bit back a comment and they drove the rest of the way in silence.

They were digging a slot trench in a new development. It was dull, repetitive work that consisted of laying yards and yards of trench ready for utilities and power cables. As soon as they arrived, Ty experimented with the remote and discovered he need no longer run back and forth between the truck and the boom: now he had on/off switches he could toggle, and a means of making simple changes to the boom direction and angle.

Another day they began digging holes for light standards, each two feet in diameter and seven feet down. The weather turned bitter, minus forty Centigrade, and he had some trouble with his hands. He stopped in town after work and bought another pair of glove liners and some rubber gloves, and that seemed to help. Other than that, he found that multiple layers would keep his body warm as long as he kept moving.

Cyrus continued to sit in the truck for most of each day, staring morosely out the window, but Ty was just as glad to be on his own.

That changed on the morning of the rock. He'd been working steadily, extending a slot trench with the suction nozzle buried in the trench sucking up sludge as fast as his water wand created it. The noise of the suction motor penetrated his earplugs and when it rose to a high whine he reacted immediately. *Rock in the hose!* He dropped the wand, turning his head to look at the boom, pulling off a glove and fumbling for the remote in his pocket. Cyrus shot out of the truck.

"Shut it down, shut it down!" He reached for the controls just as Ty stabbed at the on/off for the suction motor, and the whine died away. Cyrus launched into a profane tirade that Ty ignored as he stared up at the suction hose. How far up had the rock gone before it stuck? He took hold of the free end and felt the pliable pipe, but it was empty for as high as he could reach.

They had to unhook the hose from the boom, uncouple it from the motor and lie it flat on the ground. From behind his seat in the truck, Cyrus withdrew a sledge hammer, and feeling along the hose found the blockage. He stood up, braced his legs and swung the hammer once, a strong, well-placed blow. It was the most competent action Ty had seen from him. He shook the hose and pieces of rock fell out.

"That's your on-the-job training," Cyrus glared at him and turned away, returning the sledge hammer to the truck. Ty grinned: he had complained to Pulaski that the hydrovac operator's job description included training the swamper and he hadn't been getting any.

Eventually the hose was rehung, connected and tested, and they resumed trenching.

It was nearly lunchtime when he looked up to see a pickup drive in on the dirt road. An Indian woman sat behind the wheel, with two small children next to her. She parked on the other side of the road, opposite the hydrovac, and climbed out. She wore long boots below a long skirt and a parka that had seen better days. Her gaze came Ty's way but her eyes were indifferent. The kids stared back at him unmoving, two small heads side by side behind the driver's window of the pickup. Cyrus opened his door. The woman spoke but her words were inaudible over the noise of the motor. Money passed from Cyrus to her and she returned to the truck and drove off. At lunch, Ty spoke up.

"Was that your wife?"

"Daughter."

"Cute kids," said Ty, for something to say. Cyrus shot him a glance but said nothing.

Ty mostly ate his lunch in the truck with Cyrus, who would take out a thermos of coffee and a dingy backpack from which he produced coarse sandwiches of thick dark bread and yellow cheese. If they were working in town Ty liked to explore, walking block after block, looking in shop windows, talking to people when the chance arose. He found it strange still to be without friends and became aware of how much he had taken their company for granted. He saw a poster for a rock concert and bought a ticket, and met a few people his own age, male and female. He enjoyed the evening but nothing came of it.

After the shock of his hotel bar tab, Ty realized he'd have to do his drinking at home. The fridge in his bedroom easily held a case of beer and after dinner he'd lean back on his bed, updating his Facebook page then checking his job sites, filling out applications, lurking on forums and pursuing leads. Sometimes he texted Barty, and found him drinking beer while writing or researching a paper and it was as though little had changed, and they'd text back and forth during the evening. Other times he watched *Jeopardy* or *Wheel of Fortune* or a movie, or played computer games.

On Friday he picked up his paycheque. "You're doing okay," said Pulaski.

Ty nodded. He hesitated then said, "I'm still looking for something with higher pay."

"I understand, kid. We're keeping you in mind."

He was able to reduce his credit card bill with his first paycheque, but the goal of paying for his schooling remained as distant as when he'd first arrived.

Chapter

Six

"We like Fort St John," said Paul. "Except for the cold."

Ty nodded but said nothing, and resisted looking at his watch. On Fridays he went to the pub. He caught a ride with the Chois, because on Fridays they went to the social at the Presbyterian church. Paul was a warden or something, Ty wasn't sure, and they were both active in the life of the church. Now Ty and Paul sat in the front room waiting for Mrs. Choi and Gemma, the babysitter.

Mrs. Choi would not hear of Lydia being left on her own on Friday nights. For one thing, she was too young. For another, she was prone to nightmares and when she woke wailing in fear, she needed a familiar face. Gemma had been a fixture for three years and Lydia was comfortable with her.

Gemma was nearly sixteen and had a crush on Ty, which he tried to ignore. He did not think Mrs. Choi would take kindly to his dating her babysitter, and since Gemma wasn't really his type he found it easy to comply.

Both females were late. He looked at Paul. "Why did you move here?"

When they first came to Canada, Paul explained in his careful English, they had gone to Richmond, a suburb of Vancouver, staying with a relative of Mrs. Choi's while they studied the real estate market and the investment opportunities. Eventually they had bought a motel in Hope, a hundred miles east of Vancouver. They had not been happy there. "Mountains all around. Close," said Paul. "It was too dark."

They had sold the motel and bought another one in Cache Creek, further north along the highway. They lived there for two years but left finally because the opportunities were limited both for themselves and for Lydia. This time they had taken great care to find a town with prospects.

"Here we have good school, good church, nice people," he finished.

Mrs. Choi arrived at that moment and overheard Paul's remark. As she put on her coat and wrapped a woollen scarf around her throat she said, just as the doorbell rang, "No much golf."

It was hardly the sort of remark Ty had come to expect from Mrs. Choi, whose conversation chiefly consisted of flapping her hand at him. He rose to get the door while Paul nodded in agreement.

"It is true, Ty. Not enough golf. But nowhere is perfect."

Gemma stood on the doorstep.

"Hi, Ty." She stepped inside, her eyes feasting on him. She was a well-built girl with brilliant green eyes and yoga clothes under her winter coat.

"Hiya, Gemma," said Ty prosaically.

Lydia came through. "Hello," she said solemnly.

Gemma greeted the whole Choi family and then—at last, thought Ty—they were off, down the basement stairs to the garage.

They dropped him outside the Caribou Arms and he waved goodbye and went inside. He would catch a taxi home.

* * *

Friday nights were an integral part of the backup plan. As he observed to himself, it would be a pretty poor plan that didn't include at least one pub night, and Friday night was for schmoozing the oil industry. Any crews in town generally began or ended the night at the Caribou Arms, so Ty made it his home base. He took a quick look around the room as he entered, saw only couples, bought a pint and joined the darts players. The noise level rose as the night warmed up, and eventually a group of men came in, a group that included the rig manager who had hired Doug. They sat down around two tables pulled together, attracting waitresses like moths to candles. Ty gave them ten minutes to settle, then bought another beer and joined them, pulling over a chair near the rig manager.

"Hi, Pete," he said. The rig manager glanced at him, nodded in recognition and continued talking to his neighbor. Ty waited patiently, listening to the table talk, determined to be one of these guys one day soon. A break came, Pete laughed and took a long drink of beer. Ty leaned forward.

"How's Doug doing?"

"Doug?" He looked at Ty. "Oh—Wilson."

The man on Ty's left overheard and laughed. "Dougie!"

"He shipped out," said Pete. "Couldn't handle the work."

"Said his back hurt," added the other man, "give me a break."

The waitress was back with another round and one of the men took a couple of twenties from the table and put them on her tray. Ty went over to the bar to replenish his own drink. He returned to the table as Pete stood up and turned. He appraised Ty from head to toe, taking in his size and broad shoulders. "Just going to make a call, kid."

Ty took that as an invitation and sat down again. The talk had shifted.

"Ace are good people. Ace Drilling. I'll work for them anytime."

"Stick with the bigger companies, that's my rule."

"—stuck it out for six weeks. Never again—"

"Who?"

"—decent meal allowance. But the beds—Jesus!"

"Dacon Mackey. There was a guy there—"

Ty made mental notes of the companies, for checking on the computer.

Pete returned and sat back down. "Here's the thing, kid. Rig work is hard. Your friend didn't seem to get that." He took a drink and before Ty could speak he went on: "Seemed to think we owed him something." He studied Ty. "Sometimes you work hurt. We teach you how to work safe, but some guys just won't listen. And it's easy to strain a muscle. You just ice it and keep going. It's that simple."

Ty nodded. “I don’t have a problem with that. I work out, keep myself in good shape.”

“You look pretty well set up. That Doug—I thought he was wiry but I was wrong. He just wasn’t strong enough for the work. That simple.” He drank some more beer and went on: “Said he’d hurt his back so we had him checked out. Doctor cleared him for light duties so we had him in the office filing papers. He only lasted a couple days. Said he was bored.” Pete reflected, then added, “Of course, he was only getting office wages, on a forty-hour week.”

Ty laughed abruptly. Pete seemed to divine his thoughts, saying, “We often get people going on modified duty. If we processed all the strains and muscle pulls as injuries, our insurance would go through the roof.” He leaned back. “Don’t need anyone right now but I’ll keep you in mind. Got a job?”

“Yeah. Swamper on a hydrovac.”

The rigger on his left turned and looked him up and down.

“All I could get,” said Ty defensively. He didn’t like the way the man eyed him. Talk had died at the table and he heard “What’s he do?”

“Swamper.”

“Shit—who’d work on a vac truck? Super skeezes.”

“Cyrus.”

Nods and general laughter.

Pete asked, “You working for Cyrus Connolly?”

Ty nodded and heard more laughter. Someone launched into an anecdote; he heard “fucktard” from someone else.

Pete eyed him. “How you getting on?”

Ty could have told a story or two about Cyrus and the way he abused the truck. He'd texted several to Barty. But Barty was far removed from the oil and gas industry.

"I've learned a lot about daylighting," he said with a touch of defiance, and swigged his beer.

The rig manager nodded and promised to keep him in mind. "You're top of my list for a leasehand."

Ty left them soon after, not wanting to overstay his welcome. The room had filled up and he stayed at the bar for a while, listening to the talk from a couple of frack men drinking vodka tonics. Later he looked up a job description for a leasehand. It sounded more menial than what he was doing now. He found it odd that a complex piece of equipment like a hydrovac truck should command so little respect from other parts of the industry.

* * *

"Got a change of pace for you," said Pulaski.

Ty waited for the curve ball.

"You're going to be working about two hours north of here. Site's being dismantled and they want us to clean the mud tanks. It's about forty hours' work."

"So—all week?"

"Noooo," Pulaski was in high good humor. "They're in a hurry. Maybe two days' work." When Ty said nothing he added, "Overtime, kid. You work nonstop and get paid big for it."

"All right!"

Before he could compute the pay, Pulaski went on, "Assuming two days, you'll get sixteen hours at regular, then time and a half, and double time after midnight." He came out from behind the counter and walked over to the closet. "Oh—and an extra one-fifty just because we're great guys."

"What?"

"Okay, because we're required by law to pay you that. Cyrus, too."

"Why," asked Ty warily.

"You'll be working with invert. It's a type of mud sometimes used in drilling, a mixture of diesel and base oil and other chemicals. It can smell bad and it may cause a rash. If you want to decline the job, now's the time."

Ty thought it over for at least two seconds. "I'm okay with it."

"Fine. Take an extra set of coveralls and a couple of face masks. Go home and change if you want. Wear clothes you don't mind throwing away because it can be hard to get rid of the smell."

"Jeez," Ty stared at him. He was wearing jeans and a thick shirt. "I'm okay," he said at last.

"There's a service crew out there dismantling the site. You'll eat your meals with them."

* * *

Cyrus pulled the truck up beside the mud tank. According to the job specifications, it was fifty-four feet or nearly seventeen meters long. The truck cab was roughly ten feet high, and when Ty looked over, the top of the tank was above him. As he would soon discover, it was divided into several compartments, all of them filled with mud.

"Let's get on it, swamper boy." Cyrus pulled the truck ahead and they began. The truck was revved to 1400 rpm to run the suction and power hoses, and it would stay that way until the job was finished. Ty dragged the suction hose up the side of the tank and dropped the end into the viscous contents, holding it in place. Cyrus worked the controls on the mud tank, turning the blender blades, helping to thin the mud. With the approach of night the temperature dropped, making an already difficult substance even harder to work with.

It was twenty hours before the tank was empty and for the last two of them, Ty had had to work inside the tank, squeegeeing mud off the walls and blending blades. He'd slipped several times and was comprehensively filthy by the time they'd emptied the tank—except that the tank wasn't really empty: it was coated top to bottom in mud, like Ty himself.

Cleaning it was the next stage, but after their last two-hour trip to town, emptying the last load of invert at the soil remediation plant, they called in at the service crew's trailer for breakfast.

"Better take off your coveralls," said Cyrus, and added, "I don't want them refusing me breakfast is all."

Ty exchanged his filthy coveralls for fresh ones. When he entered the trailer he found Cyrus eating at the far end of the long room, while the service crew sat near the buffet table. There were five guys and four of them were eating and watching the fifth, who was sorting through a pile of objects in front of him. He looked up.

"Help yourself to breakfast, kid," he said, then held out a watch to his mates. "Lookit. Still running. Told you it would be."

Ty listened to their chatter while he helped himself liberally to bacon and eggs, hash browns and toast. They were sifting through items they'd brought up from the casing at the bottom of the well, four thousand meters deep.

He took his loaded plate and a cup of coffee to the end of the same table as the crew. "Okay if I sit here?"

"Yeah, sure," said the leader. He slid the watch down the table. "Take a look at that. Sat in water for a month with a cracked face and it's still running."

Ty chewed and glanced at the watch. "Rolex? Expensive."

"The owner freaked," said one of the other crew members.

"You wouldn't believe the stuff gets dropped down the bore. Rings, watches." He lifted a wrench. "Screwdrivers, you name it."

The food was hitting the spot. Ty wasn't interested in much else. He finished the bacon and eggs, gulped some coffee and spread jam on a piece of toast.

"Let's get to it, swamper boy." Cyrus had dumped his tray near the buffet and was heading for the door. Ty stuffed the toast in his mouth, added jam to a second piece and followed Cyrus out.

Now the fun began. Ty climbed down into the tank and began to pressure wash the walls of each compartment, top to bottom. The invert clung like glue and he spent hour after monotonous hour directing a concentrated blast around the walls until his muscles began to ache from the strain of keeping the wand steady. His ear plugs saved him from the reverberations of the washer on the steel walls and the noise of the revved hydrovac engine. His goggles protected his eyes and the smell was not as bad as he'd expected. But the prolonged assault on his senses left him dazed and disoriented. When the engine died and the hoses both stopped working, he stood blinking.

"Take a break, kid."

He looked up to see the top of Cyrus's head disappearing as he climbed back down to the ground. The words wafted up from the other side of the tank: "Or not, ya fucktard."

It took them eighteen hours to clean the tank, its compartments, piping and blending blades. Ty arrived home at noon, two days after he'd left, and found Mrs. Choi waiting for him in the basement entrance. Not only his boots were to be deposited on the rubber boot tray. When he stepped off the doormat, she flapped a hand at him.

"Pants."

"Huh?"

"My wife wants to wash your pants and shirt, Ty," said Paul Choi, coming down the stairs.

Ty was going to argue, but thought better of it. He took off his outer clothes and dropped them, as indicated, on the boot tray. He stood on the mat in his underwear and socks, swaying slightly, as Paul stooped, picked up the tray and followed his wife to the laundry room at the far end of the basement. Ty's eyelids dropped, lifted, dropped again and lifted when he felt a hand on his arm. Paul steered him to his room and after he fell on the bed, removed his socks and covered him with the comforter.

He never knew what Mrs. Choi did to his clothes but they came back smelling clean and fresh. His boots stank, however, and he used some of his earnings to buy new ones.

* * *

Ty came up to breakfast and, drawn by a familiar smell, poked his head through the kitchen door. No one was permitted inside the kitchen except by invitation, but his eyes lighted on the griddle where Mrs. Choi stood with the pancake flipper and Lydia hovered, waiting to carry in plates and platters.

"Hoddeok day!" he said, and hopped from foot to foot in the doorway. Mrs. Choi turned the Korean pancakes in the pan and Ty went off to the dining room chanting "Hoddeok, hoddeok, hoddeok day."

Hoddeok are pancakes stuffed with brown sugar, cinnamon and walnuts, and during breakfast Ty gave unmistakeable signs of being in ecstasy. When he waggled his eyebrows while chewing, Lydia put a hand over her mouth and emitted a tiny snicker. Mrs. Choi rapped sharply on the table and scowled at him. Thereafter he continued to eat but in such misery and unhappiness that Lydia had to look down at her lap.

"You like hoddeok very much, Ty," observed Paul.

"I love 'em. IHOP has nothing like this," said Ty and turned to Mrs. Choi. "Will you teach me how to make them?"

He spoke slowly and continued to eat while she processed the sentence.

She waved a hand at him dismissively, *Don't talk such nonsense.*

"I'm serious," said Ty, but got no further reaction beyond a barely discernible movement of horizontal muscles in the long face, a movement that might be construed as a faint smile.

* * *

Gemma canceled for Friday night. She was flying to the coast to visit relatives and when Mrs. Choi learned and told her husband they decided to stay home that evening. It was a pity because there was to be a Bingo fundraiser at the church social and Paul was supposed to assist the caller. But they phoned and canceled, so Ty arranged for a taxi. Friday pub night was too important to the backup plan to miss.

On Wednesday night, Lydia startled her parents by announcing that she would be okay with Ty staying home. She had decided she liked him. He always talked to her at dinner, always asked how her day had gone. If she'd done poorly on a test he commiserated; and he congratulated her if she'd done well. Lydia hated the boarders and she hated her parents for taking them in. But she had become used to Ty and when she learned Gemma wasn't coming she told her parents she would be okay with him as a substitute babysitter.

The Chois, however, had no intention of imposing on Ty. They explained to their daughter the importance of backup plans, pub nights and job searches.

Then everything changed: Ty got a job offer.

He had been conducting his nightly routine on the laptop: update Facebook, check job sites, fill out applications, lurk on the forums. He'd already checked his web mail but he went back one last time and found a fresh message from Meridian Exploration, one of the companies he'd applied to. His application was being considered, and the company would like to interview him by phone tomorrow. He emailed back, arranging to be available at lunch time, and provided his cell number. Then he mounted the stairs two at a time to inform the Chois.

"It may not come through, but if it does I'll be leaving on Sunday. Orientation's on Wednesday afternoon for three days."

"Where is the job, Ty?"

"That's the bad part. It's in Saskatchewan. So I'm giving myself plenty of time to get there and look around." It was more than a thousand miles away. "After orientation we fly into camp, then it's a 14/7 rotation. Big bucks." He punched the air. "Yes!"

At lunchtime the following day, Ty watched as Cyrus took his backpack and thermos and walked from the truck to the construction hut. They were back at work on the housing development and had been given the use of the hut in advance of the crews that would move in next week once the hydrovac had finished its work. His phone rang five minutes later.

The interview went well, forty minutes of questions about his past jobs, his schooling, present position, his physical condition. He explained that he worked out at a local gym on weekends, could bench-press two-fifty and knew how to lift without hurting himself. A final set of questions dealt with his financial status. "You'll be required to carry yourself for two weeks without pay, you understand?" Ty assured the interviewer that he had the wherewithal. "Check the clothing list on the website and get whatever you don't have. Absolutely no polyester on the site, do you understand?" The interviewer concluded, "I'm giving you a green light, Hogan. Assuming you pass orientation, and a man of your education should have no problem with that, you'll be good to go in ten days' time."

Ty disconnected once the interviewer had rung off, threw open the truck door, leaped out and yelled wildly into the freezing air.

"Tomorrow's my last day," he told Cyrus after lunch. The older man made no comment and they continued potholing, the truck moving twenty yards forward, idling for twenty-five minutes while Ty excavated another hole, then forward another twenty yards.

"That's a helluva a way off," commented Pulaski that evening. "Too bad," he added wryly. "Sorry you're going."

"If it doesn't pan out I'll be back. Let you know." Ty wasn't burning any bridges.

He told Paul the news before dinner, after he'd showered and was waiting with him in the front room. Paul lowered his paper. "We will be sorry to lose you, Ty."

"Wish I could take Mrs. Choi's cooking with me." He added, "I never knew any Koreans before. It's been good."

Paul smiled. "Your job searching worked."

"Yeah." Ty thought back over the past few weeks. "You know, you just have to keep at it and sooner or later you get a break."

Paul studied him. "Will you still go to the pub tomorrow night?"

Ty considered. "I might, just for fun." It would be good to let people know he was now a respectable rig hand. Then something in Paul's manner caught his attention. "Why?"

The Korean closed his paper and folded it, then sat with it on his knee, hands clasped on it. He contemplated his hands with a slight frown.

"What's the problem?"

Paul's gaze moved from his hands to the wall and finally to Ty. He came to a decision. "We wondered if you would babysit for us. We would pay you, of course."

"No problem," said Ty. "I can go to the pub on Saturday night."

On Friday, they finished potholing half an hour early and drove back to the yard. Ty spent the rest of his shift coiling down hoses and making it all shipshape for the next guy, a weedy kid who hovered, watching, and did not speak until Cyrus had headed for the office. His name was Jamie.

"I can use the money, man," he said, "but I dunno about Cyrus."

"The work's not that hard," Ty reassured him. "I heard you'll be daylighting a new camp the other side of Charlie Lake."

Jamie hung on his words. "What's daylighting?"

"When you dig down and expose the utilities to daylight. Also called potholing." He showed him the water pressure system, the boiler and wand. "Ever use a high-pressure washer?" And when Jamie nodded, he added, "That's all this is, but with hot water. And it's powerful. Digs through the soil and you use this suction hose to get rid of the mud. Fill up the water tank once a day; empty the suction tank twice a day. There's a remote in the glove compartment."

He turned to go, then added, "You might want to rethink the wellies."

Jamie had on a pair of gumboots. "How come?"

"You happen to stand anywhere near the hose with those on and you'll be going back to town bootless."

"Are you kidding me?"

"Maybe sockless, too. Get a pair of steel-toed work boots."

He left him to it.

Cyrus was walking crablike toward his pickup as Ty started up the steps. "Hey, College," he said.

Ty turned.

"Good luck."

Ty grinned, lifted a hand and called back, "Same to you!"

Cyrus looked disgusted and turned away, muttering as he continued toward the pickup, climbed in and slammed the door.

* * *

Ty put the laptop on the coffee table and started a YouTube video. "Gangnam Style" began to play. Lydia watched the video then looked at Ty, who was prancing around the living room in the manner of the video's dancers.

"That's silly."

"Sometimes it's good to be silly." Legs pumping up and down, hands together in front of him as though holding the reins, he set off down the hall. Lydia made no move. The music continued as the singer chanted the title refrain.

She walked over and peered along the hall to find Ty prancing toward her. Totally out of sync, he sang the refrain.

Lydia laughed suddenly and began to mimic him, first facing him then following him down the hall and back around the coffee table. Back, forth, sideways they went, chanting off-key and usually in the wrong place. When the video ended, they flopped onto chairs.

They played Casino Yahtzee for an hour, then it was Lydia's bedtime. "Call me if you need anything," said Ty. He'd been briefed on Lydia's nightmares and if she woke he would go through to her bedroom and sit with her until she fell back to sleep.

He updated his various pages, as always, and only when he reached for a beer did he realize that he had none. Friday night and he hadn't had even one beer. He glanced at his watch: by now he'd normally have had several. Time to fix that. It wouldn't affect his judgment.

Downstairs, he chugged a beer and took two more upstairs. Several people had left congratulations and questions on his wall and he kept busy responding until the beers were gone, then fetched two more.

He was elated at his good fortune and the reactions from his friends and family, and dozed off in the middle of composing a reply to a question. He never heard Lydia's wail of fear, nor her crying. He was still dozing, snoring gently, when she came out to the family room, half asleep, cheeks damp with tears, and shook his arm.

The Chois arrived home to find their daughter in her nightie curled up on the basement stairs, asleep, head cradled on her elbow. Ty they found in the family room with two empty beer cans, one tipped on its side amid a damp patch of carpet.

Chapter

Seven

"Welcome to Alberta." The road sign flashed by, followed by more signs expressing a hope that visitors would refrain from bringing Mountain Pine Beetle and Eurasian Milfoil into the province. Ty mulled over these requests as the miles clicked by. "Yes, we have no bananas," he bellowed suddenly, then grinned and found a radio station where a female country singer wanted to shake hands.

"Okay, baby," said Ty. "Let's do that."

He had apologized profusely to Mr. and Mrs. Choi on Saturday morning, putting his behavior down to excitement over the job. It was a busy day for the household: the frack operator returned and several applicants turned up for Ty's bedroom. He was glad to escape, and spent the morning at a garage while the Pathfinder was given a general checkup, oil and filter change, battery check, things he would normally do himself at home but which it was too cold to do here. He spent the remainder of the day at the gym and the pub.

He arrived home in time for dinner, almost sober, apologized again to the Chois and Lydia, then spent the evening doing laundry and packing his gear. He left midmorning Sunday while the family was at church, having said his goodbyes before they left. His departure was a little disappointing to him, the family being quite reserved and, he thought, undemonstrative.

He forgot this as the miles unspooled under his wheels. It was an eighteen-hour trip and he hadn't decided whether to break it in two or drive straight through. He enjoyed postponing the decision.

A red SUV passed him and he frowned and began to speed up. Still frowning, he took his foot off the accelerator. The Pathfinder returned to the posted speed limit. Women, he thought. They did not understand the sacrifices a guy made. He listened to another song, "Alberta Gold," about working in the oil patch. "Hey, that's me, whaddya know?" He stopped for lunch at a Burger King in Grande Prairie and headed onward. The day was overcast, the traffic was light and the skies got bigger and bigger, with wide open fields stretching south on his right.

Ty was not sufficiently experienced to know the dangers of driving at dusk, and late in the afternoon he missed seeing the pothole until it was upon him. He wrenched the wheel leftward, thereby avoiding the worst of the hole, but only when the car went into a long skid did he realize he was skating on black ice. *Steer into the turn,* he remembered, and did so, but the Pathfinder turned sideways and continued along the highway at right-angles, while he fought the wheel. A horn blared at him as a vehicle flew by in the outside lane going westward.

Now Ty was facing back the way he had come, and could see the lights of approaching vehicles. Still skidding, the Pathfinder reached the snowy kerb, slid over an icy lump on the road and toppled onto its side. Skating over the snow, it slid further away from the highway toward a gully. As gravity caught it, the car rolled onto its roof and disappeared.

CHAPTER

Eight

THIGHS PUSHING against the steering wheel, head touching the roof, tethered by his seat belt Ty looked out at the snow halfway up the windshield. Above it he could see past the hood of the car along a gully, with a snow bank on one side, trees on the other. He turned off the ignition. The engine ticked and the car settled in the snow. No windows broken. Amazing. The hood was unmarked. He conducted a personal inventory: arms, legs, everything in place, nothing hurting. In fact, except that he was upside down, everything seemed to be fine.

He undid his seatbelt and supported himself with a hand flat against the ceiling. He used the other hand to open the car door, meeting some resistance. The door edge was pushing several inches of snow as it opened.

He heard a voice, then another, then a call. "Hey! Hey! Can you hear me?"

He scrambled out of the car and stood up. He was at the bottom of a gully, he estimated about twelve feet deep. "I'm okay," he called, looking up.

"Anyone else down there?"

"Just me. I'm fine." He examined the car and saw the wide swathe the roof had traced in the snowy bank. "So's my car! Hang on." He ducked back inside and found his duffel bag and jacket, brought them out and clambered up the bank with them.

"You are one lucky young man." A middle-aged woman surveyed him critically, a younger man next to her. "Any breaks, sprains, torn ligaments?"

"No kidding," said Ty. "I really am fine."

"I'm a paramedic," she said. "I called it in already. They should be here soon." Her car was parked on the broad divider section running between the east and westbound lanes. "They'll be coming out from Kaitlin."

"No need for that," said Ty, wishing she hadn't meddled. "I just want some help getting the car out."

They were standing near a second car, evidently belonging to the man. "Say listen, kid, was that a pothole you hit?"

"Yeah. I didn't see it."

He grunted. "I was behind you ever since Whitecourt and when I saw you skid I figured there was something."

The woman smiled. "Going too fast, were you?"

"No." Ty and the man spoke together and the man went on, "He was right on the button all the way." He took out a business card case, extracted a card and handed it to Ty. The name on the card was Sam Green. "Here. The police give you any trouble, you tell 'em to call me. I saw it all and you weren't speeding."

A tow truck pulled in beyond them. The door sign read, "Arnie's Towing." The driver turned on his flashing roof light, got out and ambled over. "Trouble?"

"Take a look," said Ty. "Could you help me get it back up?"

"I called 911," repeated the woman but they were deep in discussion. She hesitated a moment and then added, "Well, I'll be off if there's nothing else." She waited until an eastbound car had passed, then jogged across the road.

Arnie had retrieved a large flashlight from his truck, and the three of them studied the slope of the gully. "Take her out along there," said Arnie at last. "See how it slopes up? Drag her along the gully on her roof—there's enough snow, see? Then flip her upright along there, where the gully starts." The other two saw what he had in mind: the gully ceased several hundred yards back along the road.

Arnie looked at Ty. "'Course, there's no guarantee the frame ain't bent."

Ty nodded. "I thought of that, but you know we just slid down the slope so gently I don't think it did any damage. The windows aren't even cracked."

Arnie exchanged a glance with Sam. "Kid, you got a horseshoe up your ass."

Sam laughed. "I'm going to leave you two," he said and shook hands with Ty. "In the distance, they heard a siren. "That'll be the 911 call." He walked back to his car.

Arnie looked perturbed and cupped the back of his neck. "Comin' out from Kaitlin, not Whitecourt." He hesitated. "Look, kid, the guy there has the contract on 911 hauls. I don't want to step on his toes."

"Aw look, couldn't we just get on with it? Be done before they get here."

"I don't think so." They turned to look at the car and gully, barely visible in the dusk light. "Let's see what turns up."

The fire engine was the first to arrive. Without doing a U-turn it drove across the divider section, across the two eastbound lanes, and came to a halt nose-to-nose with Arnie's tow truck. Four firefighters sprang out and two began placing safety cones along the verge. Orange, red and yellow roof lights strobed over the road, the trees and the snowy gully. The captain and fourth man joined Ty. "Anyone injured? Who's involved? Where's the woman who called it in?"

Ty dealt with the questions. The captain returned to his truck and got on the phone while the fourth firefighter scrambled down the bank to examine the Pathfinder. Arnie and Ty walked over to the engine and Ty examined it with interest. Smaller than a full fire truck it had "Rescue Truck" stenciled on its red flank and its sides were filled with compartments: a stack of three-foot lengths of two-by-four in one; another stack of square, inflatable air pads, three coiled one-inch diameter hoses in a recess above a piece of equipment that looked like giant pliers.

"How the hell did you do that?" The fourth fireman had climbed back up and was regarding him curiously.

Ty grinned. "It's easy when you know how."

"You know how?"

"Haven't got a clue," said Ty cheerfully and the fireman laughed.

"You're bloody lucky, you know that?"

"Yeah. Are these the jaws of life?"

The fireman nodded. "Not needed today, that's for sure."

Arnie walked off to find the captain.

Ty pointed toward a long flat compartment holding assorted struts, poles and planks. "What are those pieces up there for?"

"People are getting bigger. Notice?"

Ty looked at him curiously. "So?"

"So." As tall as Ty, the fireman shrugged. "Sometimes the ambulance guys have trouble lifting someone. Sometimes we do, too." He looked quizzical.

"Oh, man."

"So we sometimes make up a trestle or some other kind of stretcher, stronger than what they carry on the ambulance."

On cue, the ambulance came along the highway. They heard Arnie, arguing with the captain. "Jeez, Dave, I'm right here."

"My hands are tied, Arnie, you know that."

The ambulance described a U-turn and pulled in beyond the tow truck. More roof lights strobed over the scene. Two attendants sprang out and joined the group. One nodded at Arnie and looked at Ty. "Is this him?"

Ty fended them off. "I'm fine! I really am. Look—I didn't call this in."

"Driving too fast?" The captain glanced at his watch then along the highway.

"I was not speeding," said Ty distinctly, removing his arm from an ambulance attendant's grasp. "I hit a pothole. You shouldn't have potholes on a highway—" he stopped, abashed, then finished, "I don't think."

"'Kay," said Arnie, "if no one's coming, I'll get the car out."

"Crusher's coming," said the captain. "Get off it, Arnie."

Arnie shrugged, half-turned then looked back at Ty. "'Kay, I'm gone. Good luck, kid."

"We should get going," said the ambulance driver, taking Ty's arm.

"What do you mean? I'm not going anywhere." He watched as Arnie drove away, feeling he'd lost his last friend.

"You need to get checked out."

The captain spoke up. "Nothing you can do here. We'll get your car out—here's Crusher."

A tow truck pulled in and parked in Arnie's spot and a man emerged, a huge man. The four firefighters suddenly seemed shrunken next to the tow truck driver. Six foot five or more, he was big in every respect except his eyes, which were deep-set and small. He walked toward the group with a deliberate stride. "What we got?" His voice was mild.

The fire truck driver nodded. "Crusher." He pointed down to the car.

"Nothing's wrong with it," said Ty. Something, some stir of affection for his beat up old Pathfinder, made him feel anxious. "I mean, it works just fine."

The small eyes regarded him. "We'll soon fix that." A faint grin, and one of the firemen laughed dutifully.

The captain saw Ty's expression. "Relax. You go on into town. Get yourself checked out. We'll bring your car in."

Ty hesitated. Unconsciously, he was searching his memory bank, looking for prior experiences that might have a bearing on this situation, looking for guidance. He'd been raised by a mother who was strict but fair. His experience of adults was largely limited to teachers and parents, with one or two employers and the odd cop thrown in. He had not yet developed a reason to question authority on principal. So now, when the firemen told him to go into town he hesitated, torn, wanting to stay and help or at least to oversee. Then he turned as the ambulance driver tugged once more at his sleeve, and walked off, into the rear of the ambulance.

But he was not wholly compliant, as they discovered on the way into Kaitlin.

"See your driver's license?"

The ambulance was cruising along. Ty sat on a bench in the rear facing the ambulance attendant, who had a clipboard on his knees and one hand extended toward his passenger.

"Why?"

Eyes down, the attendant completed the form, rapidly filling in blanks and ticking boxes. He checked his watch and noted the time. "Driver's license?"

"Why?" Ty felt belligerent. "I haven't done anything wrong. I was driving within the speed limit—I got a witness—and I hit a pothole. I'm not hurt. My car's not hurt. Your crappy pothole's at fault here, not me."

"It's just paperwork," the attendant assured him, but Ty refused to produce his license even when they reached the hospital. Assorted pairs of boots stood in the rubber trays along one wall of the admitting area. His eye fell on them. Not taking off my boots, he thought mulishly. He'd been parted from his Pathfinder. He was not about to surrender his nearly new Baffins. He paced back and forth while the doctor dealt with a child that had swallowed a tack.

The admitting nurse came up against the same intransigence. He refused to cooperate.

"What have we got?" The doctor, a woman in her thirties, joined them.

"He won't give me any details," said the admitting nurse.

"Nothing!" Ty lowered his voice. "Nothing's what we got. Now where do I go to get my car?"

A vague unease when he had left the scene had grown into a more definable fear. He had been separated from his vehicle, the vehicle linking him to his new job, to his future. He was alone in a strange town in a strange province at night, and he was now wary, poised on the balls of his feet and ready for whatever might befall him.

The doctor smiled, took his arm and guided him along the wide corridor to a small examination room, while the ambulance attendant tagged along. "Flipped upside down. It's amazing he wasn't killed."

The voice of the admitting nurse—"I don't even know his name!"—followed them into the small room.

Dismissing the attendant, the doctor sat Ty on the side of an examining couch and asked him to pull up his sweater. "Nice abs," she said as she began to probe his ribs and organs. "Got a name?"

"Ty Hogan. Tyler."

Her fingers moved rapidly, from his torso to his head. "Any bumps, bruises?" He could feel them moving around his skull.

"No."

"Were you drinking?"

"No. I got an alcohol lock on the steering wheel."

"Well, Ty, that was quite a piece of driving. How on earth did you avoid a crash?"

No one had asked him that, and he was happy to relate the post-pothole details, how he'd steered into the skid, how the black ice had confounded all his efforts to straighten the car. "I got the speed down—I wasn't speeding, you understand, but I got it down just with small, real gentle taps on the brake pedal."

She was listening to his heart now. "Breathe in."

"You know," he took a breath, "that ABS is supposed to help in situations like this," he breathed out, "but I dunno."

"ABS? Breathe in."

"Anti-locking brakes." He breathed in again. "Anyhow, there was just nothing I could do," he breathed out. "We just flipped over and slipped down the slope." He grinned. "Really weird."

"I believe you." She pushed up the sweater on his left arm and wrapped a blood-pressure cuff around it. "Where are you headed, Ty?"

"Well—here is fine. I was thinking of spending the night here. This is Kaitlin, isn't it?"

"It is. Where are you from?"

"I left Fort St John this morning." He smiled at her. He'd nearly said Nanaimo, but they'd contact his mother if they could—and her next question confirmed that.

"How old are you?"

"Nineteen. I got a job lined up on a rig, starting Wednesday." Nineteen was an adult. Old enough to vote. Old enough to take care of himself.

"Thought you might have, coming from Fort St John." She stepped back. "Wish all my patients were as fit and healthy. Okay, Ty, here's the drill. They'll need an address at the desk. Somewhere to send the ambulance bill."

"Bill?" He felt stupid. You had to pay for an ambulance?

"Oh sure. Unless you have Blue Cross or some other insurance." She patted his arm and he stood up.

"But I didn't order the ambulance. I mean, I didn't phone 911. And I wouldn't have taken it." He was starting to become hostile.

"Listen, Ty, it doesn't matter whether you used the service or not. Someone saw your accident and rightly called it in. That means you have to pay. Now, you give the nurse your address and she'll send the bill there."

"No fuckin' way!" The words came out of their own accord. "I'm sorry," he apologized. "Look, thank you for your help, but if there's anything to pay, I'll pay it myself."

He followed her out of the examination room, mulling over her words as they walked back to Admitting. If he had to pay for the ambulance, how about the fire truck? He felt resentful: he hadn't wanted or needed either, so why should he pay for them? He told himself to get over it. All that mattered was getting to the job.

The doctor had updated the admitting nurse, who looked on him with a kinder eye.

"So—Tyler Hogan?"

He nodded. "Is there a motel near here?"

She brightened still further. "The Chinook's not far, close to the highway, just a few blocks from here. Tell you what," she became confidential, "Why don't I use that for your address."

That's more like it. "How do I get there?"

"I might be able to get you a ride. Hi, Joe."

An RCMP officer came up to the counter. He had a yellowish-brown moustache and hair that hung down over his collar. "Marcie. Looking for the driver of—." His eyes followed her nod toward Tyler. "You the owner of the Pathfinder?"

"Yeah."

"This is Officer Feeney, Tyler."

"License and registration, please."

Ty felt like a fool. "I left the registration in the car, sorry." He quoted the Pathfinder's license plate number and reluctantly took out his driver's license. "I haven't done anything wrong," he said as he handed it to the officer.

"Wait here," said Feeney and returned to his cruiser, parked outside the entrance.

"One of the paramedics is off in twenty minutes," said Marcie, putting down the phone. "He'll drive you to the Chinook."

Ty paced restlessly back and forth in the admitting area, stopping now and then to read the plaques on the wall. It seemed the locals were generous, with donations ranging from seventy-five thousand to nearly two hundred thousand. He wondered how the money was spent, what sort of equipment they needed to buy.

The area became active with emergencies: an old man coughing blood, supported by a younger one; a small girl, crying, with something lodged in her nose; a man with an injured leg. Their relatives were anxious, fearful or, in the case of the mother with the small girl, annoyed. The victims were stoic (the man), determined (the girl, who kept remembering to cry) and long-suffering (the old man). Wheelchairs materialized and patients were whisked away and then Ty saw, with relief, the fire captain approaching him.

"We got your car up. Here's Crusher's address." He gave Ty a business card. "You can see it tomorrow morning." He turned away.

See it? "Wait—what do you mean? Can I pick it up there? How—is it okay?" *See it* had an ominous, view-the-body connotation that unnerved him.

The captain lifted a hand and exited through the sliding door, disappearing into the darkness. Ty looked down at the card: AJ Harmon Towing and in small letters: "Next to Harmon Toyota on Railway Avenue."

What had they done to his car? He was worrying that question like a dog with a bone when Feeney returned with his license and a ticket. Ty put the license away and stared at the ticket. "What's that for?"

"Speeding."

"I was not speeding."

"Yeah, you were." Feeney still held out the ticket.

Ty held his temper. "How do you figure?"

"I spoke to the emergency personnel at the scene. From what I heard you were speeding. Here."

"They weren't even there!" Ty put his wallet away and his hands on his hips. "I was not speeding. I hit a pothole. It beats me how you could allow a pothole on a major highway, but maybe that's how you do things in Alberta." He recollected Sam's card and extracted it from his back pocket. "Here! This guy was traveling behind me all the way from Whitecourt. He saw the whole thing. Call him. Or—call the woman who phoned it in. She heard what he said. I hit a pothole. There was black ice. I was not speeding."

Feeney's expression of indifference had not changed during Ty's speech. He'd found out the facts and the matter was settled. "Nine hundred other people didn't end up in the ditch. You did." He put the ticket on the counter with a tiny slap. "You were speeding."

The blood rushed to Ty's head. "You asshole! You weren't there and you don't know!" He shoved forward, chin first, invading Feeney's space, and only the motion of the officer's arm toward his gun stopped Ty.

"You really want to spend the night in jail?"

Words trembled on Ty's lips. The man was an incompetent, a fuckwit with a quota to fill. He held Feeney's gaze and his eyes filled with contempt. *Son of a bitch . . . sorry excuse for a cop.* He took a small step backward.

"That's better. Take your ticket."

"Go to hell."

"Your choice, Mr. Hogan. Your driving record's not exactly spotless, is it?" These words were spoken in the presence of a third party and Marcie looked shocked at the breach of privacy. They watched as Feeney left the ticket on the counter, walked out through the sliding doors, got into his cruiser and drove away.

"He's a loser," said Donny, the paramedic who drove Ty to the motel. "Lazy son of a bitch. You don't want to think about him."

Ty tried not to, but after he'd checked into the Chinook and taken his duffel bag along to his room, he dumped it on the floor, slumped into an easy chair and stared glumly at the wall.

His costs were mounting. The ticket was one-seventy-two. He started to get angry again, and put it under the blotter on a small dresser, out of sight. He was going to get bills for the ambulance and maybe the fire truck, too. While waiting for his ride he had realized the fire department would have access to his car registration and home address and had urged Marcie to make sure they sent any bill to the Chinook.

He'd get another bill from the towing company. And worst case, his car would need work. He had a network of contacts at home who either provided cheap repair services or knew someone who did. Here he knew no one, so he was going to get socked.

He had an uncomfortable pre-Christmas memory, when his mother had freaked out on hearing that he needed flame-retardant clothing. He had a list: socks and underwear, shirts and pants, the works. After he had explained that he was not in danger of being immolated, that this was merely standard wear in the oil business, Annie had agreed to buy all of it as her Christmas present to him. "But that'll have to be it, Ty. I can't manage anything else." He had expressed his gratitude—the clothing was not cheap—and she had waved it aside. "That includes the BCAA membership. You'll have to buy that yourself." The car club membership would have provided traveler's insurance for himself and his vehicle, over and above the basic auto insurance he was required by law to carry, and it might have covered some of his accident costs. He tried not to think of that now. Because he'd had to choose between the membership and snow tires, and at the time the tires had seemed the obvious choice. Now he was not so sure.

He decided to have dinner and get drunk.

CHAPTER

Nine

A COUNTRY SONG, cheerful and upbeat, met Ty's ears as he opened the pub door. Three-quarters full, the cosy room seemed to beckon and his spirits lightened. He bought a beer and stood at the bar enjoying the music, looking around, until he heard his name. A hand waved from a corner table and he picked up his drink and joined Donny and another man.

"Thought you might come in," said Donny. "This is Brad. Been telling him about your accident."

"Nothing else to talk about here," said Brad.

"Glad to help out," said Ty wryly as he sat down.

Brad was a data programmer for a web hosting company. Like Donny, he was in his late twenties.

Kaitlin, Ty learned, had about ten thousand residents, a pulp mill, lumber companies and a growing oil services sector. "Long winters, hot summers." Brad was planning to move to Calgary in the summer.

"And drugs and gangs," added Donny. "They follow the money. We see the results at the hospital."

The talk became desultory as they drank their beer and listened to the music. Eventually, they came round to the accident again and Ty brought out the towing company card. "Know where this place is?" He showed it to the others.

"He does the 911 tows," said Donny. "Railway isn't far."

"Depends which end," said Brad, then added, "nothing's far in Kaitlin."

Donny offered to drive him over in the morning. "It's my day off and I got nothing much to do. I'm an early riser," he added, seeing that Ty was about to decline. "I'll get you there early."

* * *

Soon after eight the next morning they pulled into the yard of Harmon Towing. "There it is," said Ty, and added, "Oh my God."

Several cars stood in the fenced-off yard surrounding a small shed with an office sign on one wall. The Pathfinder was close to the gate and Ty got out of Donny's car to examine it. Glass littered the seats. Only one of the back passenger doors had any glass left, and it had a deep diagonal crack in it. On the driver's side both doors had deep dents and neither door would open.

Donny was content to wait, staying in the car, busy with messages and social media, so Ty left him and entered the shack. Crusher was leaning on the counter.

"What happened?"

"What do you mean?"

Ty controlled his temper. "Last time I saw my car it had no dents and all its windows. What happened?"

The big shoulders moved in a shrug. "Not easy to get a vehicle outta that gully and right way up."

"Can I drive it off the lot?"

"Pay first."

"I mean," he spoke between gritted teeth, "is it driveable?"

"Captain, he tried it. Said the steering don't work right."

Ty turned away and stared out the window. He couldn't drive it another five hundred miles in its present condition. New glass would probably run three or four hundred dollars. Worse, the car needed racking. He knew from friends who worked in garages that racking was expensive and not good for a vehicle. The car had cost him less than a thousand. Time to let it go.

He turned back to the counter and reached for his wallet. "Okay, let's settle up."

Crusher moved an elbow off the bill and pushed it across, his small eyes intent on Ty.

The blood rushed to Ty's head and his sight blurred. After a pause, he said, "You turned my car into a pile of junk and you want me to pay you a thousand and fifty-seven dollars?"

Another shrug. "Rough, ain't it?"

"How about I just sign the car over to you? There are four nearly new snows you can have."

"Don't want no snows."

Some minutes later, Ty left the shack and joined Donny, who looked up from his phone as the passenger door opened.

"How'd it go?" He saw Ty's face. "Oh shit. What?"

But Ty had just thought of something worse than the towing bill and black anger changed to a look of acute chagrin. About to climb in, he squatted in the doorway, hands covering his face, fingers digging into his scalp. "Fuck, fuck, fuck, fuck, fuck—"

"What? What's going on?"

Ty raised his head, face scarlet with embarrassment. "I just told that horse's ass where to put his credit-card machine."

"Good for you," said Donny heartily. He was liking Ty more and more.

"I forgot I got an alcohol lock on the wheel."

"Oh my." Donny was familiar with the device. "Is the car driveable?"

"No. Oh *shit*." Ty's hands covered his face again.

"Okay. We need to find a mechanic who can take it off."

"They're easy to take off, Donny," snapped Ty then saw his expression. "Sorry." Donny would know as well as he did that it had to be taken off by an accredited shop. He groaned in anguish.

Some minutes later, after he had composed himself, he returned to the shack. Crusher's small eyes regarded him.

"Figured you'd be back."

Ty disregarded this. "I need the keys. Forgot I left some stuff in the glove compartment."

He picked up the keys and added, "And I have to get that alcohol lock taken off. Know anyone who does that?"

"Body shop down the road. I can tow it over. One-twenty-five each way."

"That's real generous of you," said Ty furiously. "I'll let you know."

But although the engine sounded fine and he was able to drive forward, the car refused to reverse: the wheels simply locked. Eventually he stopped trying and, after clearing a few belongings from the rear and the glove compartment, returned to the shack.

"Get the body shop on the phone," he said curtly.

Crusher was offended. "You want to watch it." He stared at Ty, who held his look. Eventually, he dialed a number and Ty spoke to the manager. He arranged to have the device removed and learned it would be ready for pickup mid-afternoon. He then added a further two hundred and fifty dollars to his credit card and left.

"You look like you could use a drink," said Donny.

"What I need is a gym. I need somewhere I can let off steam."

So Donny dropped him at a gym in town and gave him directions to the motel. Then they parted. "Say, listen, Ty, sorry you had so much trouble here."

"Forget it, man," said Ty. "Thanks for all your help."

He watched as Donny drove off, then went inside and paid twenty dollars to work off his frustrations. Two hours later, showered and calmer, he walked back to the motel. Except that he hated this town, Kaitlin felt much like Fort St John: it was muddy and noisy and everyone seemed to drive SUVs. He walked part of the way along a river, coming eventually to a massive industrial site. When he saw long, high stacks of logs he realized this must be the pulp mill. Donny had pointed out the Greyhound depot earlier in the day. Over lunch he checked out the schedule and found there was an eastbound bus tonight and another tomorrow morning at ten. Plenty of seats available on both.

The motel manager called to him as he walked by the office, and he turned and poked his head through the door. "Couple of letters for you." Ty took the letters, two envelopes on city stationery, back to his room, closed the door and sat down in the easy chair before opening them. The ambulance bill for four hundred and eighty-nine dollars. A bill from the fire department for thirteen hundred, including two people at four hundred per hour and two more at two hundred per hour. He wondered briefly about applying for work as a fireman.

He sat there with his eyes closed and the numbers filled his mind. This was getting serious. After a while, he lay on the bed and tried to relax. Then he tried lying on the floor. When that didn't work he sat at the desk, took out a piece of motel stationery and listed all the charges: ambulance, fire, towing, ticket. He went online and took a look at his credit card account, then added his motel and meal charges and another hundred for the alcohol-lock removal, just to be on the safe side. Then he reviewed his agreement with the drilling company and worked out how much he would net after tax and when he could expect his first check. He felt better after that.

* * *

Snow was falling in tiny, fey flakes that swirled and circled and refused to fall to the ground. He made a bargain with himself as he approached the body shop: if the bill was under a hundred, he'd allow himself extra beers this evening, the number to be determined by the amount saved.

The shop looked busy: he passed mechanics working on cars in three bays. None of them was the Pathfinder and it was nowhere to be seen. He pushed open the door marked "Office" and went inside. A big man behind the counter looked up from a computer screen. "Help you?"

"I'm here to pick up the alcohol lock from my car. Nissan Pathfinder?"

The man nodded, finished up on the screen and pressed a button. A printer awoke and began to work. "Here it is," the man retrieved a plastic bag and put it on the counter. "We had a time with it."

Ty looked sharply at the man. To give himself a moment, he checked the contents of the bag. The man continued, "Had to clear out that glass before we could get to work on it, and we needed to take out the lock on the driver door."

"What are you saying?"

A bill came across the counter. Ty bent his head and looked for the total. Five hundred and twenty-nine. He raised his head. "What is it with this town? Did you see me coming? Did you think, oh great, college kid, let's take him for all he's got? What—tell me—what was your thinking?"

"Sorry—"

"Bullshit! This is bullshit! It's fifty bucks to take off one of these things. I doubled it because I get that you like to soak people around here. But five hundred? Five hundred? Jesus!"

As fast as his temper had flared, it died away. There was no way around this. He knew it. And the manager knew he knew.

"I told you there was a lot of clean up."

Calmer, Ty studied the owner. He had a familiar look. "Are you related to the towing guy?"

"He's my brother."

Ty started to laugh. "Where do I go to surrender?" He pulled out his wallet and slapped his credit card on the counter. He watched the manager begin to process the bill. He did not look unduly disturbed by Ty's outburst or even surprised.

* * *

At eight that evening, Ty sat in a bar drinking beer. He'd checked out of the motel, eaten dinner at the café, watching the hockey game, and walked over to the Greyhound depot. No one was there but he decided against leaving his duffel bag and took it with him down the block to a bar.

A decorative sign on one wall asserted, "The more you run over a dead muskrat the flatter it gets." Got that right, thought Ty morosely.

He was served by a blonde in her thirties with a sulky, discontented expression. He ordered a beer and looked around him.

The bar was busy and getting busier; several more people entered, stamping feet and removing parkas. Two men sat next to Ty, deep in conversation, arguing. Something to do with a parking lot. They were older men, in their forties.

"'Paved paradise', Ev? It was nothing but scrub land in the first place."

"And what is it now? A parking lot in the middle of nowhere."

Silence, then, “You really got it in for Fred, don’t you?”

“If you can point me to one contract, one retailer moving in there—”

“So maybe he’s just thinking ahead! Nothing wrong with that. Town’s growing like crazy, it can support more retail. Or maybe it’s for manufacturing. Ever think of that?”

“You better hope so, Harry. We can’t support the retail we’ve got.”

Harry swiveled on his stool, looking at his companion. “What the hell are you talking about? Town’s busting out all over.”

Ty missed Ev’s reply as he ordered another pint. The Harmon brothers entered and found a table.

Harry sounded angry. “Oh shit, don’t be starting on that foreign workers crap.”

Ty was aware of the temporary foreign workers program. Some people were against it on the grounds that it would hurt Canadians looking for jobs. He lost the thread of the conversation as the waitress brought his beer then walked over to the Harmons’ table. Ty watched in the mirror behind the bar. She obviously knew them, and let her hand rest once on the arm of the nearest brother. Crusher was facing Ty but had not seen him.

Ev glanced around at Ty, then returned to his conversation. “Fact is, the Wendy’s up on the highway is going to close because they can’t hire enough staff. So don’t tell me we need more retail. We need more workers, local or immigrant, that’s what we need.”

Harry finished his beer and slid off the bar stool. “Yeah, well.” He grinned, a stocky pleasant-looking individual. “I like my coffee black and my employees white." He left a tip for the barmaid. "See you round, Jodie."

"See you, Harry." She looked at Ty. "Another?"

Ty nodded. Ev gave him an appraising look then smiled and held out a hand. "Ev Brown."

"Ty Hogan." He shook hands with the other man.

"Passing through, Ty? Or do you live here?"

"Got a job on a rig in Saskatchewan."

Ty's beer came and they chatted about the oil business. "Good pay if you don't mind hard work," said Ev. He added, "Bad enough that we're a small town with a big transient population. We've also got work camp operators raiding our local businesses. It's unbelievable."

"What's a work camp?"

"Those are the service companies that run camps for the drilling crews." He sipped his drink and began to reminisce about the sins of the service companies, recounting one anecdote after another about the difficulties of retaining staff. "Here's one that'll curl your hair," he said. "This operator sat himself down for dinner in one of our restaurants. The restaurant owner told me this one. He went in the back to catch up on paperwork, came out a couple hours later to find all his employees had quit. Every single one. They can get twenty-five an hour plus transportation for working in a camp, instead of twelve in town."

"Twenty-five?" Ty was impressed.

Ev nodded. "Friend of mine, an East Indian, was a short-order cook at McDonald's. Got a job as a number two line cook for forty an hour at a camp in Saskatchewan."

"Your friend, the one you were talking to, sounded pretty racist."

Ev glanced at him. "Lot of people round here are. He's a good employer, though. Motel owner. Treats his people well and has no trouble getting more when he wants them." He studied Ty. "Staying long?"

Ty shook his head. "Catching the bus tonight." His mood had improved considerably.

"Buy you another?" Ev indicated both their glasses as Jodie returned, and waved away Ty's objection that he wouldn't have time to return the favor. "Two's my limit anyway."

Ty thanked him. He glanced at the Harmons in the mirror.

Ev said, "You should think about coming back this way. Kaitlin can use kids like you, kids ready to put in the hours, do the work. This is a young town, with prospects and plenty of money."

Ty recalled the donation plaques at the hospital but shook his head. As Jodie returned with their drinks, he said, "Do you know those two jerkweeds?"

Jodie shot him a look. Ev looked startled. He handed Jodie a bill for the two drinks. "Keep the change," he said, and she went away. He followed Ty's gaze in the mirror. "The Harmons? Did you tangle with them?"

"They soaked me two thousand dollars today."

"How?" And when Ty said nothing, "Something to do with a car?"

Ty glowered, then drank off a quarter of his pint. "Nothing. Forget it."

"I'd watch your mouth," said Ev quietly. "Jodie's involved with Zack Harmon." He hesitated, then added, "Arthur's okay. He's just . . . slow."

"He's not so slow," said Ty bitterly.

"He's not good when he gets riled. Doesn't know his own strength."

Ty looked at him. "How old do you have to be before you know your own strength?"

"That's what I'm saying. He's slow. Mentally challenged. You know?"

"Shit." Ty shook his head, but before he could finish his thought they both saw Jodie at the Harmons' table. She served fresh drinks and said something that caused the brothers to look over at the bar.

"Damn troublemaker," muttered Ev.

Crusher half rose then listened to his brother and sat down again.

"You lousy bastard." Ty was spoiling for a fight. He slid off the bar stool and turned toward the Harmons.

"Sit down, Ty. You do not want to do this."

Ty shook off his restraining hand and took a step toward Crusher, who stood up.

"Fellows, help me out." Ev took firm hold of Ty's arm. "Zack," he called over to the table. "You watch him. I mean it."

Zack Harmon got up and blocked Crusher's path. Most patrons by now had stood up, and many were heading for the exit. "Never knows when to stop," Ty heard one of them say. "Buy you another at the Schooner, come on." Two men helped Ev escort Tyler out.

"Thanks, guys," he said and one of them raised a hand. Both followed the other patrons along the street. Ev peered in the opposite direction. "Right. There's the depot. Get going and don't be so foolish. I'm sorry you had a bad experience but believe me, fighting Crusher would only make it much worse."

The cold air sobered Ty and he squinted up at the snow, still light and dry and swirling as it had been earlier. The ground was barely covered. He looked at Ev.

"Sorry about that." He raised a hand in farewell and headed for the depot. He remembered his duffel bag only when he reached the empty waiting room. He'd left it on the floor by his bar stool. He used the toilet at the depot then jogged back along the street to the bar. When he stepped inside, the Harmons were halfway to the door. Zack had been bent over at the bar and turned, straightening, holding the duffel.

"What do you think you're doing?"

Crusher growled and started toward him and Ty moved to meet him, light on his feet. He ducked a fist and hit out at Crusher's chest. He found himself grabbed, then thrown across the space of two tables, and he slid headfirst to the floor. He was hauled to his feet and he saw stars as a fist caught him in the cheek. He felt teeth loosen and the force of the blow spun him round. His forehead cracked against the edge of a table and he was dizzy as he hit the floor. Voices sounded, shrill and loud, male and female. Blood ran down his face and he was lifted bodily by an arm and a leg. He felt a sensation that took him back to the playground as a kid, the dizzying feeling of whirling round and round, then he was flying, his ribs came in contact with something hard and pain shot through his chest. He fell onto something round and padded—a bar stool?—then slid to the floor and lay behind the stool, his back to the bar.

More shouting, a new voice: "Stop this!" One eye was caked shut. Through the other he saw the toe of a boot coming at him and he raised an arm feebly to fend it off and succeeded in deflecting it from his eye to his jaw and as he slipped out of consciousness he heard a voice, strong but angry: "Get him out of here."

CHAPTER

Ten

COLD. HE CAME back to full consciousness. Pain. His head hurt. Panic. He'd lost an arm.

He tried to move. Groaned and stopped. Too much pain.

The ground trembled, light washed over him, something heavy blasted past with a gust of cold air. Darkness returned.

He could feel his left arm. He was lying on it. Even the small weight shift required to pull it out set up a frightening barrage of pain in his head. He lay unmoving. Tried to work out where his right arm might be. After a while he summoned the grit to extract his left arm. He felt a weight on his right slide and thump to the ground. Unable to see out of his right eye. Rolled onto his left side. The pain became hideous. He saw his right arm. Pulled his right hand over the gravel like a lump of meat. It had been resting on his duffel bag.

The cold was bitter. The white, dead appearance of his hand frightened him. He tried to think. Gloves. In his jacket pockets. He must get up. He must. The effort brought tears to his eyes. Using his left hand to unzip the parka, he thrust his right hand under his left armpit. A lump of ice.

The darkness lightened and his duffel became clearer. The light extended upward, headlights of an approaching car in the far lane. It sped by. He looked around. Four lanes. No gully. Apart from that, he seemed to be on the same highway he'd been traveling yesterday. Was it yesterday? The pain was crushing. He must move. Had to move. His left side was growing colder from the lump of ice in his armpit. He put his left hand up to his mouth, licked his fingers and rubbed at his eye. Better.

He pulled his duffel bag closer. Somewhere in there he had mitts with silk liners. He scrabbled at the opening with his left hand, suddenly able to see more clearly. Light washed over him and he saw blood on his fingers. He turned his head and through the blinding pain saw headlights. He forced himself to his knees, to his feet. The pain was overwhelming and he fell to the ground and blacked out.

* * *

"Don't be alarmed. Found him on the highway. I'll take him into town when we're done."

Ty heard a groan and turned his head toward the speaker's voice. He saw a barn and a pool of light and two people, a man and woman, joined by a third carrying a bag like a doctor's bag.

"He looks awful," said the woman. Young, of medium height, she had straw-colored hair, thick and curly, pulled back in a ponytail.

"He's just a kid," said the man, wiry and slightly taller. "Mattie, you go with Doc, see to the filly." He opened the truck door. "I'll clean him up." He nodded at Ty. "I'm Bill."

"Well," said Mattie, then made up her mind. "She's been in a lot of pain. . . ." She and the veterinarian walked toward the barn door.

Ty's head fell back. He felt Bill's hands under his arms, round his back. He groaned and half-fell out of the truck.

"Been in a war, haven't you?" Bill tried to loop Ty's arm around his neck but the pain was so great that Ty's knees buckled. "Hm. Wonder if you've bruised a rib." He stooped, and Ty felt an arm under his knees. He was lifted, carried into the house and deposited on a couch. "Be right back," said Bill.

Ty lay back, closed his eyes and heard steps running upstairs. Bill made several trips, returning with towels and cloths, a large first aid box, and a bowl of warm water. Ty opened his eyes when he felt water on his face.

"That's a nasty cut," said Bill. His eyes regarded Ty's. "Got a name?"

"Tyler. Tyler Hogan."

"Okay, Tyler. Broken any laws?"

Ty tried to move his head. Too much pain. "No."

"Okay, you lie still while I fix you up."

Half an hour later, Ty awoke to find his shirt had been removed and his ribs bandaged. Mattie and the veterinarian had joined Bill.

"Colic?" Bill sounded annoyed. "That's not like any colic we've ever seen."

"That's what I said. That filly is more trouble than she's worth."

Bill sighed. "Thanks for coming, Doc. Add it to our bill?"

"Of course. And what about the colt?"

They all turned to look at Ty.

"Hello," said Mattie. "You look a bit more human. My name's Mattie. Short for Matilda, but we won't dwell on that."

"I think he'll be okay in a couple of days, Doc. Can we give him a Tylenol?"

The vet said nothing for a moment. Then he squatted next to Ty, peered into his eyes and felt his skull. "What day is it?"

"I was wondering that myself. It was Monday when I got hurt."

"Still is. What's five and six."

"Eleven."

"His name's Tyler Hogan," said Bill. "Do you live around here, Tyler?"

Ty explained that he was from Fort St John and was headed for an oil rig job in Saskatchewan.

"How'd you end up lying on the highway?"

"I'm not sure." Three faces looked back at him, waiting. "I lost my car. Hit a pothole and skidded off the road. The guy who towed it, wrecked it. I got into a fight with him."

The vet's face cleared. "Would that be Crusher Harmon?"

Ty nodded gingerly and winced.

Bill had seen Crusher. "Big hulk," he said to Mattie. "Heard he nearly killed a guy once."

The vet glanced at his watch.

"He seems fine. Let him have a Tylenol." He studied Ty's face and arm. "He's going to show some bruising tomorrow, and one or two black eyes, I expect." To Ty, "Take a breath?"

Ty breathed in carefully. A wince escaped him.

The vet stood up. "Well, it's up to you. I can take him in to the hospital if you like."

Ty looked imploringly at Bill.

"Shoot, Doc, he can sleep here tonight."

"My duffel bag," Ty began. His right hand was thawing painfully but at least he no longer needed his mitts.

The others left him and a few minutes later he heard the vet's truck start up. Soon after, Bill returned with his duffel bag and dropped it on the floor near his feet. Mattie had been upstairs and returned with blankets and a quilt. She made Ty comfortable and brought him a glass of water. He took a sip, then felt around inside his mouth and removed a tooth.

"Oh my. A molar. You've got plenty more of those, luckily." She gave him a Tylenol and another sip of water, then put the glass on the floor by his head and took the tooth away.

"You've got to wonder what shape the other guy's in," Ty heard as she and Bill turned off the lights and went upstairs. "Did you see those abs?" He couldn't make out the response.

* * *

Ty woke to Bill's voice. "Knife and fork, Mason." A pause, then, "Don't they teach numbers in kindergarten?" He heard a toaster pop up and the chink of knives against plates. He heard a child's voice.

"Yes sir, yes sir, three bags full." A pause. "It's not the best use of my time, Daddy."

Mattie's voice. "Sweetheart, it's good for you to be with other children."

"Will Tyley be awake when I come home?"

"Tyler." Bill spoke again. "Probably. But he's pretty sick, son. We're leaving him to rest."

As if on cue, Ty's body began to clamor for attention. Painfully he reached for the glass of water and Tylenol bottle, and swallowed two capsules. It hurt to breathe. His head felt ready to split open and his entire side was on fire. He lay on the couch with his eyes closed, the kitchen voices drowned out. Had he been dumped from a truck? That would explain his side. The Tylenol began to take effect. Tuesday. He had to catch the ten o'clock bus.

He woke again with a start when he heard feet stamping. His watch showed after eleven and he stifled a groan. Mattie came in, her eyes full of concern.

"Morning, Tyler."

"Hi. Can you help me? I missed the bus. I've got to catch the one tonight."

She helped him to sit up, then stand, and showed him the bathroom, where he found towel and toothbrush and a disposable razor.

He came through to the kitchen forty minutes later. A hot shower had eased his bruised muscles but his face was a mess. Bill was seated at the table with a bowl of soup.

"Get some of Mattie's soup inside you, Tyler." He indicated a chair and Ty sat down. Mattie brought over a bowl of thick chicken soup and put it before him. "That dressing is loose," she said, looking at his forehead. "I'll fix it after lunch. I think maybe you should have stitches in that cut."

Ty declined. "They'd just want to keep me in hospital." The soup was incredibly good. He caught a glance exchanged between Mattie and Bill. "I haven't done anything. I . . . just don't want to—I just have to catch the bus tonight."

"This for your oil rig job, huh?" Bill took a piece of bread and mopped his plate.

"Yeah."

"You're in no condition, Tyler. I worked on a rig one summer. You couldn't do the work."

"You don't understand. I have to go. I need the money."

"That we understand," said Mattie cheerfully.

"How about this," said Bill. "You lend a hand this afternoon and I'll get you into town tonight."

"Deal!"

He learned a little about them over lunch. Bill and Mattie Williams boarded horses, and Mattie gave lessons. They had a son called Mason and sixty acres of fields and paddocks. Three days a week, Bill took his semi and trucked logs from one or more of the logging concessions in the hills around Kaitlin to the pulp mill. He would unload, then take on a load of hog fuel for the power plant, or wood chips for one of the paper mills down south.

After lunch, Ty walked stiffly over to the barn with Bill. He inhaled the pungent horse aroma inside the barn and would gladly have helped out all afternoon. But he couldn't even push a broom without pain, much less lift pails of water. Mattie sent him back to the house. “Unless you’d prefer the hospital. You’ve got cracked ribs and you might still be concussed.”

* * *

He woke to find a pair of huge blue eyes regarding him. “Hello,” he said.

A boy of five with straw-colored hair stood on Ty’s duffel bag and held on to the padded arm of the couch as his eyes moved over Ty’s face.

“It looks worse than it is,” said Ty helpfully, but the boy jumped down and ran off.

Ty dozed. He opened his eyes to see that the boy had returned. He was holding a book, not a thin child’s book but an adult book.

“My name is Mason. You’re Tyley, aren’t you?”

“I am.”

“Your face looks awful.”

“I’m glad I don’t have to look at it.” He smiled.

Mason considered this and nodded. “You’re lucky.” He switched subjects. “Would you like to hear a poem?”

Three bags full? “Sure.”

The boy pulled over a chair, positioned it at Ty’s middle, climbed up on it and crossed his ankles, hands clasped on the unopened book. His eyes on Ty’s face, he recited:

“Stately Spanish galleon coming from the Isthmus,
Dipping through the Tropics by the palm-green shores,
With a cargo of diamonds,
Emeralds, amethysts,
Topazes, and cinnamon, and gold moidores.”

His eyes watched Ty's reaction. They held full knowledge of the words. He stopped. "Isn't that good? Did you like it?"

"It's wonderful."

"Do you know what a gold moidore is?"

"Sounds like maybe a coin?" He saw the boy's nod as he shifted to his back.

"Moidore is hard to say," Mason leaned forward confidingly. "But some of the words in the first verse are even harder. That's why I skipped it."

"Do you know what these words mean?"

Mason nodded. He had looked them up in the dictionary. "I look up twenty words every day. Would you like to hear the third verse? It's the best of all." After that was done, Mason said John Masefield was his favorite poet so far, even better than Rudyard Kipling. "Have you read *The Jungle Books*, Tyley?" He was allowed to read all the books in the bottom shelf of the bookcase and had nearly finished them. They were good but he wanted to learn mathematics. "Cathy said I should be doing Khan Academy. She's the lady who helps Mrs. Ubecki with the milk and cookies. Have you heard of Khan Academy?"

Ty had heard of the online education center. Mason sighed deeply.

"We only have one computer. Mummy uses it for the farm accounts and I'm not allowed to use it because it's very old." He added fretfully, "Time's passing, Tyley, and I'm not getting any younger."

Ty snorted. "Where did you hear that?"

Mason was not discomposed. "Mummy said it about the Chaudhrys' bill. They never pay on time." He added, "Do you know a poem called 'The Ballad of East and West?'"

Ty had heard of it. He was beginning to feel at something of a disadvantage. "I have a friend who's a poet."

"Is he a good poet?"

"Well—I think he is. He's still learning, mind you. But you may hear of him one day. His name's Bartholomew Cage."

Mason liked that name and Ty searched his mind for a suitable poem of Barty's. The only thing that came to mind other than "Earth's Cerebellum" was a limerick about an NSA spy from Nantucket, but the last line was unsuitable for a five-year-old.

* * *

He messaged his contact that he'd been in an accident and was too bruised to lift anything. He'd be ready for work in a few days, he added. The reply was terse and depressing: "Forget it. Sorry."

His phone rang almost immediately, and he answered it without looking at the display. "Hello?" He'd changed his mind? Another job offer?

"Ty? Thank God, honey."

"Mum? Hi, how are you."

"I'm fine, Tyler." Delayed reaction colored her voice as she went on, "But you haven't updated your page and I was worried."

"Jeez, I'm sorry, mum." His inventive powers were not at their best. "I'm staying with these Mormons—" was it Mormons or the other guys? "—and they don't have Wi-Fi."

"What on earth?"

"The thing is, mum, the job fell through."

"Oh Ty, I'm so sorry."

"But it's okay! This is a great place—" he scowled, hating the words, "—with lots of opportunities. They got a pulp mill and you can make twenty-six an hour just for sweeping the floors." Bill had told him a lot about the mill. He thought it was a much better prospect than an oil rig.

So did Annie. "Oh honey!" Her relief came through loud and clear. "That sounds so much better than an oil rig."

"Listen, mum, this is expensive. I'll update my wall tomorrow, okay?"

* * *

Sitting on the side of the guest room bed, Bill scrutinized Ty. "How are you feeling?"

Ty's shoulders moved in a shrug. In truth, he was nowhere near his normal healthy self. His head still hurt and so did his ribs. Worst of all was the bruising down his arm and side.

"I'm going to be gone for three days. Thought I might take you with me, but Mattie says not."

Ty grinned. "Guess you're sorry you took me in, huh?"

Bill continued his scrutiny, and Ty wondered what to say. "Look, I'm getting better. I can do more to help." Was he worried about them being on their own? "I'll look out for Mattie and Mason."

Bill smiled faintly, nodded and stood up. Mattie, in long flannel nightie and dressing gown, poked her head through the door. "Everything all right?"

"Sure," said Bill. "See you soon, Ty."

They went out, closing the bedroom door. Ty heard Mattie's voice receding along the hall. "Are you being an idiot again?"

He frowned and turned on his side.

* * *

Ty woke up suddenly. He wondered if he'd shouted out. He had no recollection of having a nightmare, but Mattie had said he had called out on his second night, restless with bad dreams. He reached for his watch: it was nearly three in the morning. He was sleeping in the room next to Mason's and had been concerned about waking the boy. "Don't worry about that," she'd said. "He sleeps a solid ten hours every night and nothing ever wakes him."

Ty lay in bed thinking about the boy. He'd been the same age as Mason when his father had left. He remembered how he'd sat on the stairs in his pajamas and dressing gown, because it was November, holding his teddy bear and listening as his mother talked to the man. What was his name? Moulden, that was it. He'd asked his mother at breakfast the next day: "Is Mr. Moulden a friend of daddy's?" "Were you listening, love?" Ty had said he only heard a little bit, but he'd heard a lot more than that.

The voice had woken him and he came down, seeking his mother, and stopped on the stairs, listening. "But he can't have gone. We had a deal." Then his mother's voice, quieter. "I'm so sorry, Mr. Moulden. I don't know what to say." A silence, then she added, "Maybe he'll call you."

"You don't believe that. Do you?" Silence. "Mrs. Hogan, I don't think you understand my position. I'm on the hook for ten thousand units! Gerry said we'd have them sold even before they were produced. He said storage wouldn't be a problem. He said—." The man had stopped abruptly. Mum had said, "Would you like a cup of coffee?" Ty heard the scrape of a chair leg on the kitchen tiles. "Thank you. . . . I knew something was wrong when he didn't come by two days ago. We were going to have a conference call with an eastern buyer. Gerry was sure he'd take three or four thousand units. I was fit to be tied, Mrs. Hogan. I don't know how to deal with such people, I haven't a clue about selling, I'm a researcher. Finally, when it was past eleven, I called myself." Ty heard nothing for some seconds, then the tap of a mug against the table. "Do you know what the buyer said?"

"No." Mum had sounded tired.

"He said they do their buying in February."

There was a long silence, and Ty was getting ready to return to bed when Mr. Moulden said, "Gerry's a drinker, isn't he?" Another silence. "Do you think he'll be back soon?"

"I'm—" Ty had leaned forward, listening hard. Daddy had left two days ago and Emma had asked the same question. "I'm just not sure," she said at last.

Ty's world had been rocked by that uncertainty. Years later, his mother had said dad had tended to disappear whenever difficulty loomed.

He wondered now, lying in the guest room bed, if he'd recalled that long-ago incident because a small boy had reminded him of his own five-year-old self or because he was doing the same thing, running away from the Harmons.

* * *

"Parts of your face are green, Tyley," said Mason, peering at him. "Is that a good thing, do you think?"

"Probably." Tyler smiled at the boy and pulled out his chair for him. It had snowed in the night and the day was overcast. Mason sat down at the breakfast table and picked up his knife and fork, holding them vertically on either side of his place mat. Bill had left early and Mattie was at the stove making scrambled eggs. She glanced round.

"Knife and fork, Mason. Why do I have to keep telling you?"

He sighed and put the cutlery on the table. "Eating is my most favorite thing after reading," he announced and watched as his mother brought over a plate with scrambled eggs on toast. "And when I get a computer, that'll be my most favorite thing."

"Oh?" Tyler picked up his own knife and fork. "How do you know?"

"I just know. Yummy. Do you like scrambled eggs best, Tyley, or waffle and syrup? Or french toast?" He took small mouthfuls and chewed quickly, with total concentration. "I think eating while I'm sitting at the computer will be ideal. Ideal." He smiled at his mother. Problem solved. "Mummy? I think that will be ideal."

But Mattie was preoccupied with the snow and rattled off a list of instructions for Ty with regard to the snow blower, what to clear, how much and where. "Aim toward the house. That's where it'll go anyway, if the wind comes up."

However, the subject of the computer came up again later that morning, when she entered the living room and found Ty, chores done, sitting on the floor looking at books from Mason's bottom shelf.

"We do get normal books for him, out of the library. But he just devours them and then complains that he's got nothing to read."

"He's very bright, isn't he?"

She nodded. "Off the register. It was frightening at first." She sat on the couch. "We don't know where it comes from. I did well at school and Bill would have done well if he hadn't quit. He used to get bored."

Ty looked down at the book in his hand: *The Collected Works of Alfred Lord Tennyson.*

"Those were my grandmother's. Or maybe her father's, I'm not sure. But I don't think he'll come to much harm with them." She paused then asked, "Has he mentioned the Davidsons?"

"No. Friends of his?"

She sighed. "In a manner of speaking. There are five of them. Sorry, four—Scott was too stupid to live." She saw Ty's expression. "They're imaginary friends. He goes up to his room and lines them up on the bed and marches back and forth teaching them."

Ty laughed. He put the book back on the shelf and got to his feet. "Going to get him a computer?"

"I don't know." Mattie stood up, glancing at her watch. "I'll have to go in a minute and pick him up."

"Yeah, I'm off to the barn to water." They stopped at the hall closet while she put on her parka.

Her mind was still on the computer. "I know he should have one, but I'm afraid of what's out there."

"You mean, the molesters and perverts and stuff?"

"And there's the minor point that we can't afford it. Even if someone gave us a used one, we'd have to buy firewalls and software and so forth to keep those monsters out." She clasped her hands. "It just terrifies me." She added, after a pause, "The people at the university would give him one." She stared at Ty without seeing him. "But then they'd want to poke and prod and measure my little angel. Bill and I talked it over. We'd rather not be beholden."

* * *

Ty crouched motionless next to Mason and they peered through the slats into the hay stall. The large black barn cat lay on top of a bale peering down the far side. Along the row, they could hear a horse chomping. A bird twittered and fluttered in the eaves.

Muscles rippled under the blue-black skin, a rat's head showed around the side of the bale and the cat pounced. Teeth buried in the back of the rat's neck and it went limp. The cat dragged it round the back of the bale and Ty and Mason looked at each other. Mason's eyes were huge.

"Isn't he beautiful, Tyley?"

"He's like Bagheera, isn't he?"

Mason nodded.

They heard Mattie calling and Ty got to his feet. He grabbed Mason around the waist and galloped across the yard with him up to the back door.

* * *

The job search became more frantic and he was rewarded finally, a week after his arrival at the farm. He received a message from last week's contact: "Leasehand broke his arm. Are you still available?"

"Yes!" He shot to his feet, startling Bill, who sat opposite him at the kitchen table, mending a harness. Ty sent off an affirmative and took a deep breath. Hardly any pain now. Not much, anyway.

Mason was subdued at dinner. Later he appeared in his pajamas to say goodbye and put his arms round Ty's neck. "Goodbye, Tyley," he whispered.

"Dude. You take it easy, okay?"

He drew back and regarded the child, then leaned forward and kissed him. "Be good."

"I will." Mason's eyes were huge, and he turned and ran off.

A vehicle arrived while Ty was packing. When he came down to the kitchen with his duffel a short while after, he found a familiar face.

"It's Ev, isn't it? The parking lot man."

"Ev Brown. How are you, Ty?"

Bill looked surprised, then laughed. "Were you talking about that editorial? Paved paradise," he said to Mattie.

"Remember that editorial I told you about? The parking lot on the road to the airport."

Ty stared. "You're with a newspaper?"

Ev's reply was drowned out by Mattie, standing over the coffee machine. She launched into a creditable Joni Mitchell imitation that Ty liked a lot, especially the guitar vocals, "duh duh-da, duh duh duh-da."

"Yeah, okay, Matt," said Bill, who had heard it many times.

Ev laughed and turned toward Ty: "Everett Brown, editor, at your service." He took the mug Mattie held out for him and smiled his thanks. "You're looking a bit the worse for wear," he said to Ty.

Ty shrugged and said nothing. Ev looked at the Williamses. "I bumped into your veterinarian yesterday. He told me about picking up a kid left for dead on the highway." He paused but no one said anything. "A few days ago I heard a story at the hospital." He sipped his coffee. "About a kid who flipped his car on the highway, rolled down the bank and lived to tell about it." He eyed Ty. "That you?"

Ty nodded.

"Too much to drink?"

Ty shook his head. "Wasn't drinking. Wasn't speeding. Hit a pothole and the car did a one-eighty and flipped and slipped down into a gully."

"You didn't tell us that, Ty." Mattie looked concerned.

"I wasn't even bruised. I got out fine." All the anger of that twenty-four-hour period boiled over and he added, "And then your fine town gave me a royal screwing."

Bill watched him warily.

Ev said, "I wish you'd told me this the other night. I take it you went back to the bar?"

"I had to get my duffel."

Ev studied him. "You'd had a few beers."

Ty shrugged.

After a short silence, Ev said, "So—how did Kaitlin screw you?"

"Someone called 911, so I got a fire truck and an ambulance and an incompetent tow truck operator and all in all I paid four thousand dollars for the privilege of leaving my car in Kaitlin, Alberta."

Mattie was horrified. "Don't you have Blue Cross?"

Ty ignored her. He had opinions to express. "It's one thing to charge people when they ask for help. But I didn't. I could have got that car up by myself."

Ev looked skeptical.

"I don't mean me alone. But this tow-truck operator stopped and we were planning how to get the car up, but he wasn't allowed to help. Instead I got this troglodyte from Kaitlin who mangled the car so badly I couldn't drive it."

Ev made a note in a small pad. "What do you mean he wasn't allowed to help?"

"Oh—and don't get me started on the cop. He wasn't there, and he refused to call my witness, so I got hit with a speeding ticket as well." He mimicked the cop, "Nine hundred drivers didn't hit that pothole. You must have been speeding."

Mattie shot to her feet. "What?"

"Take it easy, Matt," said Bill. "We've heard that before," he said to Ty.

"I *hate* that cop," said Mattie. "Nine hundred people came round that corner without going in the ditch, ma'am. You had to be speeding." She explained: "Someone came round the corner so fast, on the wrong side, the only way I could avoid being hit was by going in the ditch. I hate that cop," she repeated.

"Joe Feeney," said Ev thoughtfully, and added, "I recognize the quote."

Bill's mind was back on Ty's accident. "Arnie's Towing is good. Too bad you didn't get him."

"I actually did," said Ty. "He's the one who stopped and we were discussing how he was going to proceed but they wouldn't let him."

"Who wouldn't let him?" Jotting notes, Ev looked up.

"The fire chief. My hands are tied. I heard him say that. So this subnormal gets the job and the car got so beat up it wouldn't reverse and the whole frame was shot. I had to just leave it." He thought of something else. "He charged me eleven hundred. And I had to pay him and his brother eight hundred more to get this alcohol lock off the steering wheel. It stops you driving if you've had a drink," he explained, but the Williamses seemed familiar with the mechanism.

"Arthur Harmon," said Ev. "And Zack."

"They could have dropped you at the hospital," said Bill. "You might have died out there on the highway."

"Get him out of here." Ty stared at the table, remembering. "Someone said that just before I blacked out. I heard a man say 'Get him out of here.'"

"Soft voice?" Ev rummaged in a satchel at the side of his chair. "Loud? Hard?"

Ty thought. "I don't know. A boss voice, that's what it was. Maybe the owner of the bar?"

Ev put a small microcassette recorder on the table and reversed briefly, then pressed "Play." A woman's voice recited details of a proposed bylaw. A man's voice, strong: "Thank you. Are we ready to vote?"

"That's him." Ty looked up sharply.

"Sure?"

"That's him."

"That's the mayor," said Mattie.

"Why would the mayor—?"

"That's Fred Harmon, brother to Arthur and Zack. The mayor of Kaitlin."

* * *

Bill pulled in at the Greyhound station and stopped in front of the bus. "Good luck, Ty," he said as they shook hands. "Stay in touch, okay?" Ty watched as the pickup left, then walked over to the bus.

The Williamses had been furious at the Harmons, especially the mayor.

"I always liked the bastard." Bill paced back and forth across the kitchen floor to relieve his feelings.

"Everyone likes him," said Ev. "That's why he's been in office so long. Too long, in my view."

"I won't be voting for him next time," said Mattie flatly.

"Have you ever?" He looked at her shrewdly.

"Ever?"

"Ever actually voted for him?" And when she was silent he added, "I didn't mean to trip you up. It's just that almost no one votes in civic elections. No one has time." He put the cassette away. "Fred's been mayor for eleven years. He's comfortable in the office. He has lots of friends who are comfortable, too." He added reflectively, "He's always looked out for Arthur. Zack does what he's told. He's the middle brother. But Fred is the youngest and he's always looked out for his brothers."

Bill wasn't interested. "What are we going to do?"

Ev stood up. "Don't know what you're going to do, but I'm going to look for connections."

Mattie stared at him. "What kind of connections?"

"Oh, say, between parking lots and potholes."

* * *

After he'd left, Bill and Mattie tried to persuade Ty to go to the police. He wasn't interested. He didn't say so, but he couldn't wait to leave Kaitlin. And now, as the bus pulled out, his heart lifted as they passed the hospital and the Chinook Motel, and entered the eastbound on-ramp.

Chapter Eleven

"THIS'LL BE ONE of your jobs." The motorhand motioned Ty to follow him over the frozen ground. "Load the pipe onto the catwalk and send it up to the rig, see there?"

Ty could see several lengths of pipe propped up against the rig.

"How heavy's the pipe?"

The motorhand glanced at him. "Don't have to do it by hand." He went on, "Every time we make a connection we add a length of pipe. You send another one along to replace it."

They had reached a stack of pipe lying on a trestle near the rig. The pipe was nearly five inches in diameter, thirty feet long. Each stack contained a thousand feet of pipe and there were ten stacks.

The rig floor was twenty feet above them and in the waning light Ty could see the day-shift roughnecks shooting the breeze. The pumps and motors sounded a background pulse for a structure that was driving pipe miles into the ground. Ultimately, the vertical depth of the bore would be some six thousand meters, twenty thousand feet. Paul, the motorhand, seemed to switch between imperial and metric measures without noticing.

"We've slowed down since Monday. Not making connections nearly as fast." He glanced at Ty. "You missed all the fun."

A catwalk ran alongside the trestles and up to the rig. "How do I get the pipe onto the catwalk?"

The motorhand gestured and Ty followed as he headed for a small hut next to the far end of the catwalk.

He'd arrived at the camp in the late morning, flying in with supplies from the town of Loon Water. He'd been given a room in one of the camp's long trailers, issued coveralls and a hard hat and driven out to the rig site, twenty minutes away.

The motorhand had been delegated to show him around, to give him a crash orientation course, one he'd normally have had in Loon Water. Instead, he was on the job, on site, and he'd been shown the shale shaker, where used mud was processed, the mud pumps and the huge mud tank similar to the one he'd cleaned in Fort St John. All the while, the rig worked away, the derrick rising a hundred and twenty feet into the air, the pumps and motors circulating mud to cool the bit and drive it deeper and deeper into the ground. The rig sat in the center of a large clearing, encircled by scrub pines. They were in northern Saskatchewan and it was bitterly cold.

They reached the hut and walked up two steps and through a door. Inside was a small room with a panel at waist height. Ty saw a joystick on it and a button.

"My ten-year-old can do this," said Paul, "so you should be okay." He reached for the joy stick. "It's all hydraulics, see? You ease the pipe onto the catwalk like so." He moved the joystick. A length of pipe stirred itself as though by magic, separated from its fellows and rolled from the trestle onto the catwalk. "Then you press this button," he did so, "and it moves up to the V-door." That was the name for the opening on the side of the rig railing where pipe was brought onto the rig. As he spoke, the catwalk's rollers had begun to revolve and the length of pipe was transported toward the rig and up an incline until it reached the rig floor. "Got it?"

"Sure. Joystick onto the catwalk, button up to the V-door. What happens then?"

"Use the tugger winch to pull it up into the mousehole. That's my job."

"Piece of cake." Ty surveyed the trestles, the panel in front of him and the rig.

The motorhand gave him a jaundiced look. "Tell you something," he said. "Accidents can happen just like that." He snapped his fingers. "Saw a pipe roll on a roughneck's foot once. It was supposed to be resting on a twobee." He meant, a two-by-four. "Must have been a splinter or some irregularity in the wood, pipe rolled off onto the guy's boot. Pushed his foot up through the top."

Ty hated being taken for a sucker. "Are you kidding me? A steel-toed boot?" He followed the motorhand out of the hut and toward the rig.

"S'right. The bones were sticking out the top every which way."

"Jeez." Ty tried to picture it. "What happened?"

"Oh—we got the medic to him, flew him out. I heard they put the foot back together."

"Wow, that's fantastic."

"Didn't last. Got gangrene in his toes and they had to take his foot off to save the leg." He walked under the platform and stopped, facing a large, bulbous piece of equipment. Ty stopped with him. He forgot disagreeable things like gangrene.

"This is the blowout preventer, right?" It would shut down the well if the pressure ever spiked.

"The BOP. S'right. You don't ever want to see a gusher, like in the movies, you get that?"

"Yeah, I know." Ty knew blowouts could be lethal, especially from the depths reached by modern wells.

Once the tour was over, Ty helped the daytime leasehand to shift hundred-pound bags of gel into the mud room. The work was repetitive but he didn't care. He was finally part of a rig crew, on a rig at last, and he was happier than he'd been since leaving home.

At dinnertime he drove back to camp with the rig manager or toolpush, a man of medium height with broad shoulders and an air of suppressed energy. Nothing escaped the toolpush. He was indefatigable and on the drive he supplemented the motorhand's safety lectures with words of his own. "You missed the orientation safety videos," he said. "Work safe. Work smart. It can get ugly here if you don't."

At six he was surveying a vast array of breakfast selections in the dining room. This was several large trailers opened into one, with tables around a buffet that ran out from a kitchen area. It was presided over by an East Indian chef whose assistants were kept busy replenishing the metal chafing dishes along the buffet. Ty loaded his tray.

"You the new guy?" A dark-haired stocky fellow in front of him in the line had been eyeing him while filling his own tray.

"Yeah. Ty. Nice to meet you."

"I'm Jerry. Floorhand. You can get dinner if you want. Other side."

"This is fine." He added some bacon as an afterthought.

The dinner tables were noisier, their crews more relaxed. The breakfast crews mostly ate silently, busy pushing in the carbs against the coming cold. Ty followed Jerry and put his tray down opposite a man in his late-twenties with a thin ascetic face and Ty later discovered, the eye of a photographer. "Cory," he said, nodding pleasantly. "Derrickhand."

Ty could feel his ribs as he sat down, and it must have showed in his face. A hardfaced heavyset man sitting next to Cory said, "Sympathy's in the dictionary there, Creampuff. Somewhere between shit and syphilis."

A grunt of laughter came from Ty's right. He looked across the table. "Thanks, Hotstuff."

Cory raised an eyebrow, then introduced the hardfaced man: Roy, the driller and crew boss, and on Ty's right, Mike, the motorhand, in his forties like Roy.

"Tyler," said Ty to both of them.

Roy poured syrup on his hotcakes and said nothing. Mike held out a hand and shook Ty's. "Welcome to Meridian 41." He had a seamed face and kind eyes.

The room had filled up quickly with tables of crews. The camp serviced six or seven rigs out in the bush. All the crews were men except for a woman at a nearby table with the toolpush and another man. Jerry followed his look.

"Mud engineer an' that's the doc. Got a thing going with the toolpush." Fragments of pancake sprayed the table in front of him and he continued to shovel in the mouthfuls.

"Better hustle," said Cory, drinking his coffee. "We'll be leaving in a minute."

By ten to seven they were at the rig site. Along with the others, Ty crowded into the doghouse next to the rig platform. The other crew were gathered on the far side of the room, the driller still monitoring the controls. Roy worked his way over to stand near him and the toolpush started the meeting.

"Less BS," he said, slowly, pitching his voice over the hum of conversation, which immediately ceased. He looked slowly round the room. "I want to see each of you bringing *one hundred percent* to work. Especially you juniors." He looked at the younger members, finishing with Ty. "Less bitching, more attention to work." Feet shifted across the room and Ty wondered if he was speaking to anyone in particular.

"Safety." The toolpush let the word hang in the air. "If you have a question, ask. If I see you out there doing something the wrong way, your driller is going to hear about it. And believe me, it won't be pretty." He glanced down at his clipboard. "While we're on the subject, we'll have visitors on the site tomorrow. Treat them with respect, and get them out of your area as soon as you safely can."

He half turned. "Safe shift," he said as he left and the two crews began the changeover. The motorhands passed Ty on their way out, deep in a discussion about steam, and followed by the two roughnecks, floorhand and leasehand, from the day shift. Jerry hastened after them. Cory, after a quick word with his daytime counterpart, beckoned to Ty, who followed him out. He stopped, so Ty did, too.

"I like to just listen," Cory said. "Get the rhythm." He glanced upward at the derrick outlined in lights but otherwise dark. The rig platform, by contrast, was brilliantly lit from fluorescent tube lighting in all the struts and girders. "Ever done any day trading?" He started down the steps.

Ty snorted. *As if.* "No," he said, following the derrickhand.

"'Kay . . ." Cory paused, then continued when they were both on the ground. "You don't just plunge in and start buying pork bellies, say. You watch. Check the volatility, see how the market behaves. You get a feel for the rhythm before you try to invest. Same thing here. Listen. Look. Ease yourself in. Get it?"

"Yeah, I think so."

Cory continued as they walked across the clearing to the collection of trailers that included the mud room. "From tomorrow, you'll be responsible for the crew truck. That means you pick up the replacement crew before the end of the shift. You be ready to leave when Roy climbs in at the end of our shift." He glanced at Ty, who nodded. "Someone's not there, you don't wait. Understand?"

"What if Roy's not there?"

"Except for Roy. Anyone else gets there after the driller, they're out of luck."

He continued with a rundown on doghouse protocol. "Some rigs they don't even allow roughies in the doghouse. Here, you're allowed in, but no gloves on the counter. You don't even open the doghouse door with your gloves on, got it?"

Ty nodded.

"Always put your gloves on the floor. You get covered in mud, don't even try going in the doghouse."

As they approached the trailers, he switched subjects. "You're going to hear lots about safety. Here are my rules: don't drop anything down the hole, don't get hurt, don't hurt anyone else."

Ty remembered the Rolex and wrench in Fort St John. He mentioned them to Cory, who said, "Must have been after they'd made the turn." Once the bit had started along a horizontal bore, he explained, it wouldn't be damaged by fallen hardware. "We've got a long way before we're at that point. Don't drop anything down the hole. Very expensive mistake. Management doesn't like it."

They entered the mud room. It seemed to be colder inside than out. "Jesus, that Paul," said Cory. Paul was the daytime motorhand, the one who had shown Ty around. Cory slapped his arms and paced around, and moments later, as though on cue, Mike entered. "Shit, Mike."

"I got it. Two minutes."

He left and soon after, hot air began to flow into the room.

"How do you feel about going up in the rigging?"

Ty shrugged. "Height doesn't bother me."

"That's good to hear. Jerry gets fussed. You can help me out once Roy okays it." He began to consult a printed list of instructions on a counter. "Got to put in your time first, you know?"

Ty knew. Cory was here to check samples of mud and prepare additives according to instructions left by the mud engineer. Ty was to take samples to the engineer. "If he doesn't have anything else for you, clean up the doghouse, okay? The other crews would be happy to work in a pigsty, but Roy hates a mess. After that you can clean the rig floor. Mud and dope gets tracked around. Rig Wash in the cleaning cupboard."

"What's dope?"

"Pipe dope. What goes on the joins when we make a connection. It's greasy. Helps to seal the joins."

Ty was aware that ninety percent of his job would involve either cleaning something or carrying something and he was okay with that. You had to work your way up. The toolpush said something similar after he delivered a report from the mud engineer. "Ask questions. Try to learn something new every day." Ty nodded and left, with the instruction to clean up the tool shed once he finished with the doghouse.

The doghouse was nothing more than a steel trailer at rig floor level, with windows on the rig side. Here the driller sat facing an array of gauges, joy sticks and other controls. Mud pressure, water pressure, the action of the kelly and the winches—everything was controlled from the driller's chair, a comfortable high-backed padded swivel chair from which Roy monitored the rig.

The driller's console was halfway along the trailer. At the far end was a small room with a window and a bed where crew could change or rest. Lockers ran round most of the walls, and safety harnesses hung near a sink and microwave. An overflowing garbage can held magazines, mostly porn, banana peels, candy wrappers and empty Red Bull cans. Jerry, back from taking the night crew back to camp, sat at a center table absorbed in a porn magazine. He lifted his head reluctantly when Ty spoke.

"Do I get one of these lockers?"

"The one next to me." He used a boot to indicate and Ty opened the locker, which held pants, shirt, sweater, socks, magazines.

"Was this the other guy's?"

Jerry dragged his eyes from some aspect of female anatomy. "Adam. Yeah, guess that's his stuff."

Roy's voice, harsh and grating, intruded. "Jerry, go and hose down the platform and the steps. Better spray the steps."

Jerry obediently put away his magazine, donned his outer gear and left Ty a clear field in which to work. He found a box of large plastic bags under the sink and filled one of them with the contents of the garbage can and floor, and the litter on the counter. He stopped briefly to study the tack board with an assortment of licenses hanging from it. "Can I ask a question?" He glanced at Roy, who nodded. "Do you have to apply for all these licenses every time you move to a new site, or do they stay with the rig?"

He continued cleaning up and finally Roy said, "Asking questions on safety issues is fine, Creampuff. But don't waste my time on anything else. Got it?"

"Got it." Ty was looking at a kind of seismograph further along one counter. It had a moving pen scribbling on paper, and next to it was a large book with "Driller's Log" on its cover. He'd have liked to find out more about both of them.

When the doghouse was clean, he swung the plastic bag over his shoulder. The muted sounds of the pumps and motors rose as he opened the door, then he was out on the platform and carrying his load over to the steps. He waited until Jerry had finished spraying them with de-icing liquid then climbed down with his load and deposited it in one of the dumpsters.

* * *

The crew was making a connection—adding another length of pipe to the drill string—and Ty had been told to watch. To drill thirty feet, the length of a piece of pipe, could take anywhere from ten minutes to twelve hours, depending on the depth and terrain. Meridian 41 was long past the ten-minute stage, which had happened back at the beginning, before Ty came on board. They had started with wider pipe and had poured surface casing when they reached six hundred meters, or ten percent of the total vertical depth. With the bore encased in cement, they had continued drilling with intermediate-width pipe. Now they were into the main hole using four-and-a-half-inch pipe.

Ty stood on one side and studied the layout. There was nothing soft to be seen anywhere on the rig floor, nothing with any "give" to it, unless it was the rag hanging out of Mike's back pocket, or maybe the coil of rope over on the drawworks. And the rig hands' bodies. Everything else was thick, hard steel and massive machinery. The drawworks, used to raise and lower tonnes of metal pipe in the bore, was nearly waist-high.

The square kelly pipe that fed mud into the drill string was nearly flush with the deck, meaning it was almost time to add another length. The kelly was connected to the square bushing in the turntable on the floor of the rig. Jerry and Mike were poised, waiting. Roy must have thrown a switch: the turntable and kelly ceased to revolve, the drawworks winch drew up the kelly pipe and the heavy collar attached to it. Suddenly Jerry and Mike stooped and lifted the slips, a conical wedge used to keep the drill string centered in the bore, and dropped it into the hole. The slips weighed more than seventy kilos.

Now the tongs came into play, two giant wrenches on hydraulic arms. Jerry pulled over the breakout tongs and locked them into place on the pipe. It revolved and the thread was disconnected. Jerry unlatched the tongs, moved the kelly pipe to one side and mud gushed out into a bucket held by Mike. A winch whined, a fresh length of pipe rose into the air. Jerry applied dope to the threaded male join and stabbed the pipe into the socket of the pipe below. Throw the tongs onto the two pipes—breakout tongs on bottom, make-up tongs on top—get your hands out of the way, tighten and torque the connection, unlock the tongs, push to one side, a whine as the winch takes the pipe down into the bore. A pause to reconnect the kelly and collar, pull the slips, another whine as the winch drops the collar into the turntable, the kelly bushing begins to rotate once more and we're drilling again.

The whole operation had taken little more than a minute.

With Mike watching, Ty took hold of the tongs and threw the locking arm to feel the weight of it. Then he watched as Cory worked the tugger winch on one side of the platform, lifting a pipe from the group of four resting on the edge of the platform and transferring it to a hole in the rig floor called the mousehole.

Then Roy told him to mop and clean the platform. After that he had an assortment of clean-up tasks around the lease area. They made more connections, and Ty worked the hydraulics to transfer replacement lengths from the trestle to the catwalk and V-door. He began to grow tired around four in the morning. It was his second night without sleep: he'd been awake for most of the bus ride.

Cory took him down to the mixing station at five-thirty to move and stack sacks of powdered mud, bentonite, calcium and gel. Just before shift change, the toolpush made an appearance on the rig, along with the daytime crew and they all had another safety meeting. Then it was time for changeover and Ty had already reached the ground and was heading for the crew truck when he heard a call. The others were walking over to the storage shed next to the mixing station. Cory waved at him to join them and he followed, wondering if he'd done something wrong.

He entered the shed last. They'd removed their hats so he did the same, and stood there bare-headed.

"What's this?" Roy's voice grated as he pointed to the bag of gel on the ground and motioned for it to be added to the gel stack.

Ty was positive he hadn't left a bag on the ground but tired and sleepy, he put his hard hat in Jerry's outstretched hand, stooped and lifted the sack. It was squarely over his head when it broke open and he was showered in white gel powder. Amid shouts of laughter, he turned to see Cory step back with a box cutter, a wide grin on his face.

"Hey, Creampuff!" That grating voice suddenly filled him with fear. He dropped the sack and whirled, crouching, eyes staring, fists clenched, and Jerry's uproarious mirth cut off abruptly and Mike stopped laughing. Roy confronted him, arms crossed, and his look altered from amusement to watchfulness and Ty realized his mistake and faster than thought his fists unclenched, his features relaxed, he straightened.

"Hey, Hotstuff," he said lightly, but this was not in the script and Jerry looked worriedly at Roy, who turned and left, Mike behind him, then Jerry. Only Cory seemed ready to cut him some slack.

"Caught me by surprise," said Ty apologetically and Cory slapped his shoulder and put the box cutter on the window sill.

Ty looked at the mess of gel on the floor. "I should—"

"Forget it. Don't want to miss our ride. Day crew can deal with it. They spend most of their time lying around anyway."

He followed Ty out of the shed with a speculative look, which Ty caught.

"I tangled with a rough customer," he said awkwardly.

"That where you got that scar?"

"Yeah." The gash on Ty's temple had healed, but still showed as a faint line. He gazed after Roy. "Guess I should lose the 'Hotstuff', huh?"

"Good idea." Cory began to jog. "Better hustle if we want to get there in time."

They sprinted up to the crew truck, and Ty climbed in the back between Cory and Mike. The truck moved off as soon as Roy's door slammed.

The adrenaline rush from the incident carried Ty through dinner, a heaped plate of stew and a side of fries, followed by a refill. The food was good and the fries went well with the stew gravy. He wondered if they ever served poutine.

The dining room was the same as the morning: the dinner crews were more relaxed, the breakfast crews intent on cramming in the carbs. Ty helped himself to apple pie and coffee and looked around as he made his way back to the table. A lot of guys looking like Cyrus: missing teeth, a couple missing fingers. A pronounced animal smell at one table. Snippets of conversation:

"What's the difference between a Shiite and a Sunni?"

"Ya dumb fuck. It's called PMS because Mad Cow Disease was already taken." A roar of laughter.

"I'm outta here next year—Cancun or I dunno, maybe Vegas."

Ty could feel sleep beginning to overmaster him. He managed to hold on until he'd finished eating. Then he muttered some excuse, dumped his tray and found his room.

He updated his Facebook page: "At last! Making the big bucks!" He added a smiley and uploaded a picture of the rig. Then he texted his mother: "Got here okay. Job's okay. People are horrible." He lay back, meaning to wait for her reply, and was instantly unconscious.

Chapter

Twelve

SUNDAY WAS SHIFT change and on Monday, the crew began day shift. Like the others, Ty struggled with the changeover and the shortage of sleep. But he enjoyed the work. He took a proprietary pride in the site's appearance and once he was on days he was able to patrol the property, washing down the trailers and actually able to see what he was doing. He was as fussy as Roy about tidiness, not that the driller cut him any slack because of it.

"Roy always gives new guys a rough time," said Cory. "Lot of young guys don't want to do the work." Ty recalled Dougie and learned to stay out of Roy's way as much as possible.

The contrast with the third crew, back from its week off and working night shift, was stark. Tait, the driller, ran a laid-back, relaxed crew, maintaining he got more work from his men that way, with fewer injuries. But Taterhead never minded that they left the rig a mess and seldom policed up the area before they came off shift.

Ty was now paired with Jerry to make connections. He'd discovered that working the tongs used different muscles and was a combination of weight and strength together. Jerry was wiry rather than big, but he was immensely strong and could trip pipe all day long if he had to.

They had a short trip, Ty's first, midweek. The first sign was a drop in pressure and Ty heard the shouts while hosing down the shale shaker. No one called him, so he finished his job then made his way to the rig. He found everyone but Cory there, the toolpush as well. Roy had noticed a sharp drop in pressure and they suspected a cracked connection. Mike was creating a rat's nest out of frayed manila rope. They would pump this down the bore and it would plug the leak. By timing how long it took for the pressure to rise they could gain an idea of where the crack lay.

Jerry's look was anguished. "Sure hope it isn't one of ours."

Cory returned soon after. He'd been down in the mixing shed with the engineer. They were adding to the mud formula, a mixture of mineral and plastic flakes that would help seal the leak. He took down a safety harness from the wall and clipped it on.

"Why does it matter so much?" Ty could sense that a drop in pressure was a bad thing but he wasn't sure why.

"Further down we go, higher the pressure. Like in deep water. You want to maintain the same pressure to protect the pipe. If the mud doesn't circulate properly it can't cool the bit or bring up the cuttings." He added, "Looks like we're trippin' today."

"You like that."

"Sure." He took a hardhat liner out of his locker. "All alone up there, nothing but trees for miles around. Going to be nippy, though."

It was a bright day but below zero and Ty knew it would be colder a hundred feet up, with no place to hide from the wind.

The virtue of a triple rig becomes obvious on a trip: the crew can remove pipe in threes, holding the thirty-meter lengths vertically on the derrick. For a well of several thousand meters, tripping is a lot quicker by threes than by taking out the string one ten-meter piece at a time.

Roy returned to his controls, and Cory and Ty went back out to find Mike timing the rise in pressure. In the end, they estimated the cracked connection had occurred at about the two-hundred meter level.

"That puts it on our watch," said Mike, and Jerry looked scared.

"Forget about that now," said the toolpush as he left the rig.

Wearing his safety harness, Cory was already halfway up the derrick as Ty and Jerry made ready to trip. Roy brought up the kelly, they threw in the slips, pulled over the tongs, attached them and disconnected the collar. The kelly pipe went in the rathole, out of the way.

Pipe is raised using an elevator, which looks like a tubular piece of tangled spaghetti. They attached the elevator to the traveling block, and snapped the top end of the string into the elevator. Roy raised the bore until the third join emerged, and Jerry and Ty used the tongs to disconnect the three-pipe string.

High in the air, the winch whined as it rose still further, guided at the top by Cory as he leaned over empty space, snapped the pipe out of the elevator and threw a length of rope around it. He stood on a platform called the monkeyboard, which had nine fingers on one side. Each finger could hold nine stands and he maneuvered the pipe to the first finger. He had room for ten columns of ten rows, or nine thousand feet of pipe.

Ty looked up, watching and wishing he could be in two places at once. Then the elevator came back down and he attached it to the next stand, and the procedure began again.

In the end, they took off eight stands of pipe and found the leak in the connection between two pipes on the last stand, where pieces of manila rat's nest had attached themselves. They disconnected the damaged piece and raised the short stand out of the way. Then they connected a fresh piece of pipe onto the ninth stand, still in the ground, brought the short stand back down, added dope and connected the two pieces, torqued and brought the other stands back down one by one, each guided by Cory out of its finger and along the monkeyboard to the elevator.

When they were done they replenished the mousehole, giving the thread on the end a careful scrutiny.

Roy held a post mortem. "Why did this happen, Jerry?"

They all stood round the driller's console. Jerry looked ready to burst into tears. "'Cuz I missed it." He meant, because he'd failed to see a damaged thread on a piece of pipe.

Ty spoke up. "How about if I check the threads too?" He looked around the group. "I can check the threads while the pipe's still on the trestle." He spoke to Jerry. "That way, it gets two pairs of eyes. Mine. Then yours."

Jerry looked immensely relieved. “That’s good, Ty. Isn’t that good, Roy? Two pairs of eyes, me and Ty both?”

Roy appraised each of them in turn. “Sounds like a plan. That’s your new job, there, Creampuff. Checking the pipe connections.” He swiveled around to face his console.

Meeting over.

* * *

“What the fuck is that?” Roy stared at Ty’s plate, his own roast pork forgotten.

“Butter chicken poutine,” said Ty, and took another mouthful.

“I didn’t see that,” said Cory interestedly. “Any good?”

“Outstanding. I told Garvit I missed poutine. This is what he came up with.” Roy continued to scrutinize the plate. “It’s fusion,” said Ty helpfully. “You know, the meeting of two cultures on one plate?”

“Fuck fusion,” said Roy. He tackled his own dinner once more. “I don’t mind the company bringing in ragheads. But they should learn to cook Canadian.”

Ty spooned a portion of his chicken onto Cory’s plate. “If you like it, tell him. He might roll it out.”

“Jesus, that’s what I’m sayin’.” Roy chewed moodily. “They should stick to plain Canadian, not this foreign crap.”

“Hard to know what plain Canadian is anymore,” said Ty. “Poutine?”

“Perogies,” said Cory.

Roy scowled at him. “What’s the matter with perogies?”

"Nothing. That's what I mean. Part of Canadian cooking now."

Roy grunted and transferred his attention back to Ty. "Where you from, Creampuff?"

"Nanaimo."

Roy gave Mike a knowing look and addressed Cory.

"You tell him, we just want meat and potatoes, perogies are good, stuff like that." He loaded another forkful of roast pork, roast potato and string beans. "If I say anything, he'd like as not bitch to the goddamn human rights commission." Mike nodded sympathetically.

"You want to cool it," said Cory later. He sat with Ty in a small recess in the huge rec room, next to a bookcase filled with books gathering dust. At the far end of the room, Jerry had joined a group playing video games. Roy and Mike were sitting with other older hands in the most comfortable armchairs in the room, clustered around a large-screen TV.

"Roy's got a temper," he continued.

"Yeah." Ty had been on the receiving end of the driller's temper more than once. "He gives me hell if I talk to anyone, but I like to learn. And I don't waste their time. Like you."

Cory nodded. Ty was always asking questions, either about the drilling mud or the derrick rigging, his two areas of expertise. "I told Roy I don't mind answering questions." Cory paused, then added, "He just thinks you haven't got your mind on your work."

"I know. He's always saying that. 'Keep your head in the game there, Creampuff.' Jeez. It doesn't take much focus to sort the recycling from the garbage. I can actually carry on a conversation at the same time."

Cory pulled out his phone. "You wait until you've made a hundred connections. Or tripped pipe twelve hours straight. You start daydreaming and someone gets hurt." He looked up at Ty. "I saw a guy once, an experienced floorhand, stand too close to the slips when the turntable's going around. He got whacked in the shins by the handles. In pain for days he was."

"Ow." Ty resolved to watch his feet next time the slips were in. Now that he thought about it, the handles did jut out a bit. He found Cory watching him. "I'll tell you why I talk back to him. Because he intimidates me."

"He intimidates everyone. He's demanding and bad tempered."

"And a racist." He considered, then added, "Do you think he's gay?"

"What?" Cory looked astonished.

"Well . . . you know. Creampuff and all."

"And all what?" And when Ty said nothing, he repeated, "You need to cool it, Ty." He stood up. "See ya."

Ty heard a raised voice as Cory left, and glanced over to the group of drillers. *Wheel of Fortune* was playing and an East Indian contestant had just won a trip to Hawaii. "My wife slept with a raghead," said one of the drillers, "I'd goddam shoot her." The Pakistani assistant cook at the buffet looked up then bent to his work again. Ty wondered what he was thinking and whether his wage rate was worth it.

That reminded him of his own position. In three days they'd be flying out for their week off. Because he had joined the crew late he would not be getting paid until sometime during his next two-week stretch. Where could he live cheap for a week? He hadn't had a chance to look around the small town of Loon Water. Estevan, a much bigger town, was not that far away, but he had a hunch prices would be worse there.

He took out his phone and searched for hotels. Eighty-five a night. No way. His eye fell on Jerry across the room and he wondered where the roughneck stayed and where, for that matter, the rest of the crew stayed.

He saw Garvit emerge from the kitchen and got up. The Pakistani assistant was carrying empty chafing dishes to the kitchen and accosted his boss. Approaching the buffet, Ty could tell from the back that he was agitated, but couldn't hear what he said. All he heard was the cook's response. "Stop sniveling," said Garvit, "and do your work." His eye fell on Ty and he stepped aside as the assistant continued on through the doors to the kitchen. "Yes?"

"I wanted to thank you. That butter chicken was outstanding."

The chef nodded austerely, his eyes moving over his domain.

"Say," Ty began, then decided not to rock the boat. He turned to go.

"What?" The chef was looking at him. "What?"

"I was wondering . . . is your job—are you a line cook?" He rushed on. "I know a guy called Everett Brown who has a friend—"

"A line cook?"

"Yeah. A number two line cook."

"A *number two* line cook."

"I'm guessing that's a no."

"Do I look like a line cook?"

"I wouldn't know—"

"Let me tell you something. Cooking runs in my family." The word "runs" came out rich and strong. "My grandfather was a *sous-chef* at the Savoy."

This meant nothing to Ty. The chef misunderstood his silence.

"All right, not at the Savoy. But another hotel in the West End."

Ty made his apology and turned away with an inward sigh.

The following evening he asked Cory for advice on accommodation. It was the first time he'd seen him since their conversation the night before. In the morning, Roy had sent him off to check the perimeter drainage ditches, and he had spent the day peering into culverts and removing animal body parts and dead branches from the ditches.

After dinner he updated his Facebook page, posting a picture of a portion of a dead muskrat, and texting Barty, then looked for Cory, who was nowhere to be found. Not in the cafeteria or the rec room. Not in the workout room, nor the pool room. He went along to the bedroom area and knocked on Cory's door.

"Yo! Come on in."

Ty stuck his head around the door. "Hiya." Cory motioned him in, so he closed the door behind him.

Cory's room was identical to his own, compact, most of its space given over to a good-sized bed. There was a small desk with a couple of drawers and a chair tucked into its kneehole, and a narrow closet. One wall held a mirror and a few pegs for outer clothes, and that was the extent of it. An electric shaver sat on Cory's desk, next to a cell phone charger. Cory was stretched out across the bed, his back against the wall. Ty pulled out the chair and sat down.

"Say listen, Cory, sorry if I was a jerk yesterday."

"What? You were fine. What's up?"

"Mind if I ask what you do in town? Do you stay at a hotel?"

Cory shook his head. "Mike stays at the hotel in Loon Water. Jerry drives home to his mother in Estevan. Roy and a bunch of other senior guys charter one of the company planes and fly to Grande Prairie or thereabouts."

"What do you do?"

"Well, Marilyn—my wife—she sets up house wherever we go. We've got a motor home," he explained, and continued as Ty nodded, "and she arrived today. She's in a campsite in Loon Water." He studied Ty. "You could stay in the hotel. Ask Mike. I'm sure it's fine."

Ty nodded again. "Yeah. I thought I'd try to find somewhere cheaper." He got up.

Cory understood. "I forgot—you're new. No paycheck for a while, huh? Listen, Ty, let me lend you some money. It's no big deal."

"Absolutely not. But thanks, anyway," he added.

"Sit down," said Cory and eyed him in silence. "How cheap?"

"Very cheap," said Ty firmly.

"Uh huh. Listen, why don't I get Marilyn to look around? She's always got time on her hands and the town's not that big. Shouldn't take her long to find out what's available."

"That would be so great, Cory. I just didn't get a chance when I arrived." He'd seen one building that interested him greatly. But it hadn't been for living in. "I can stay in a hotel for one night if I have to, but maybe I won't have to if your wife finds something."

Cory crossed his ankles and folded his arms. "Y'know, Ty, you look like a guy under a lot of pressure. It occur to you that once you start getting a paycheck you won't find Roy so intimidating?"

"Oh yeah?" It was a novel thought.

"Trust me." Cory hesitated then added, "Sure I can't give you a loan?"

"No way." Ty was adamant. He grinned. "Shit, I got a credit card. Sky's the limit, right?"

Cory laughed. "I guess." He got up. "Come on, I'll buy you a coke."

* * *

Ty was picking up bits of garbage and refuse around the building housing the power system—the diesel engines and electric generators. He had on his glove liners and balaclava today: the wind was bitter and each breath emerged from his mouth as a plume of fog. He finished around the power building and moved to the nearby boiler shed, finding one of

Jerry's Snickers wrappers lodged under the steam pipe. He heard Mike's voice inside the shed.

"Ty, you out there?"

"Yeah."

"Give me a hand, will you?"

Ty was glad to get out of the cold. Mike wanted him to tidy up the room—return tools to their proper places on the shelving along one wall. He fussed over his boiler, studying gauges while he talked. Given the outside temperature Ty was happy to learn all about steam, asking the occasional question just to keep the conversation going.

"It seems to be an issue, Ty, especially for guys just starting out on triples. Managing steam returns with just one boiler."

Ty understood the reference to triples. The rest was a mystery. "Oh yeah? Why's that, Mike?"

"We-ell, it's a big system. You need to know where your steam is going. I always take a walk around at the start of my shift. See what heaters are on, what valves are open. That heater in the doghouse, the one in that end room—know what I mean?—that doesn't always have to be on. I go in there and Jerry's turned it on and it's like an oven in there. That's just plain wasteful. Even at minus thirty, that heater isn't necessary." He took a rag and polished the gauges on the front of the boiler. "Haven't I asked you to let me know when you turn a heater on or off?"

"You have. I do."

"I know you do, Ty. I wish everyone else did." More polishing. "It's amazing what a difference one single heater can make in a big system. Not to say you should always be turning them all off, like some people, mentioning no names, but you do need to stay on top of it, keep a close watch on your returns."

Ty guessed he was referring to Paul, the motorhand who had given Ty his orientation tour. The mud room had been close to freezing when he went along with Cory on his first shift.

* * *

Marilyn's found you a place," said Cory that evening. "Don't know what you'll think about it but it's free."

"I can tell you right now. I'll love it, even if it has outdoor plumbing."

"Yeah." Cory looked quizzical as they went in to dinner. "About that. . . ."

CHAPTER

Thirteen

AN ASSORTMENT of motels and gas stations lined the highway on one side of the Greyhound depot. On its other side stood a wooden barn-like structure. The words "Loon Water Martial Arts" appeared in large letters above the door.

At one in the afternoon, Ty walked past the depot and up the steps into the barn. Most of the interior was occupied by a gym floor, with hoops at either end. Toilets on his right; a counter on his left opening into an office with a desk and a man behind it. Steps at the back led upward.

"Help you?" The man came over to the counter. Mid-thirties, wearing white martial arts apparel with one or two badges on the breast, and a black belt.

"Hi." Ty paused. "I'd like to learn . . ." he hesitated, looking around.

"Self defense?" The man opened the counter flap and came through, extending a hand. "Axel Gray."

"Ty Hogan." They shook hands and he followed as Axel walked into the gym.

"I was thinking maybe boxing? Do you teach that?"

"We teach most everything in the defense field. Boxing, hapkido, kung fu, ju jitsu, sun hang do, you name it." When his visitor made no response, he added, "Even krav maga."

"What's krav maga?"

"Developed by the Israeli military. It's violent and it can be brutal."

Ty shook his head. "I don't want that. I thought I did, but I'm not sure I could go out of my way to hurt someone."

Axel appraised him. "What happened to you?"

Ty balled his fists in his pockets and stared at the hardwood floor. Finally he lifted his head. "I got beat up. Bad." He crossed his arms. "I've never felt so helpless in my life."

"When did this happen?"

"Three weeks ago. I don't want it to happen again."

Axel considered. "You look in good shape. You can learn more than one technique or school of fighting if you like. It's just a question of time and money."

Money. "See, here's the thing." Ty explained his schedule on the oil rig. "I'd like to cram as much as I can into my off week, do you see?" Before Axel could respond, he went on, "But I don't have any money. I won't have for a month or so. And I don't want to take on more debt." He took a deep breath. "I wondered if you could use a hired hand, someone to clean up—you must need to do clean up here. I—" he glanced uncertainly at the older man, "I wondered if I could trade labor for—for lessons."

Axel took a step back and Ty was certain he was going to reject the idea. Then he paused, held up a finger: wait, and returned to the office.

Ty looked around. Mats were stacked against one wall, small mats and larger ones. He'd bet those had to be stacked and probably cleaned off. And the floor, too. Down the length of one side were a rank of what looked like punching dummies, padded torsos on individual circular stands. He peered through a wide doorway at the end of the far wall. In the darkness he could make out shelves with chest protectors, boxing and grappling gloves, groin guards, padded helmets, and in the rear, against the wall, staffs, wooden and bamboo swords, and nunchaku, the paired chain sticks made popular by Bruce Lee. He had a hunch plenty of tidying up was needed here after a day of lessons.

"You're on." Axel was back, joining him in the doorway. "If you can work mornings, when it's quiet, I'll fit you in for lessons in the afternoons. Deal?"

"Fantastic!"

They shook on it.

"I've got a busload of twelve-year-olds arriving in a minute. Here's your first lesson." His voice hardened. "Attention!"

Ty straightened, shoulders back, hands at his sides.

"Eyes up!"

He looked Axel in the eye. They were much the same height.

"Now, when I call you to attention, you say, Yes sir!"

"Are you kidding me?" He fielded a look. "Yessir!"

"Right. Now here's the basic sparring position. Get used to it. Fists—up. Right foot—back. Weight—balanced. Knees—bent." He studied Ty's posture. "Fine. Now whenever you move, I want to hear hi-ya!"

"Hi-ya," said Ty.

"Louder!"

"Hi-ya!"

"Attention!"

"Yes sir!" Ty threw himself upright.

"Sparring position!"

"Hi-ya!"

He had finished showing Ty how to throw a punch or a kick, when the door opened and a horde of pre-teens scrambled, pushed and shoved their way noisily into the gym.

"Do ten each with each arm and leg," said Axel to Ty. "See you tomorrow at nine," and he walked over to the door. The noise dropped to nothing. Axel bowed and the pre-teens bowed back. Ty heard them saying something to their teacher.

* * *

When the plane had touched down the night before, Cory and Ty were met by Cory's wife, Marilyn, driving a rental car. Both men were tired so she drove directly to Ty's vacation home. "It's an old line shack, Tyler," she explained. "The farmer doesn't mind you using it as long as you leave it the way you found it." She glanced round with a smile. "It's real primitive, I'm warning you."

He smiled back. "Don't worry about that." He'd taken an instant liking to Marilyn: she was cheerful and talkative, and glad to help.

"Anyway, he came back with me and brought some kerosene, which was nice of him, and topped up the lamp. So you've got a stove and the lamp and this crazy privy, my God, wait till you see it, out the back."

Ty laughed.

"Make sure you don't fall down it, buddy," Cory said sleepily from the front seat.

They dropped him at the roadside in the middle of open prairie. "See the trees over there, Tyler? It's around the other side."

He said goodbye and the car turned rapidly on the shoulder and was gone, headed back toward town, the sound slowly dying away.

He walked across a field toward the scrubby trees. Beyond, he could hear the ripple of running water from a stream Marilyn had said was nearby. The cabin was small, built of board and, at one end, stone. Glass gleamed in a window next to the door. He walked up a couple of steps and the door scraped on the floor as he opened it.

"Hello?" He peered inside cautiously. Marilyn had given him a cheap lighter and he flicked it. He glimpsed a wooden table to his right, with the kerosene lamp on it, and then the flame was extinguished by a breath of wind through the doorway. He moved to the table, felt for the lamp and flicked the lighter again. He worked out that you had to lift the chimney to light it, and did so, and suddenly the shadows retreated to the corners.

It was one room with a pot-bellied stove built into a massive stone fireplace. Ten or twelve feet away, a bunk was built into the opposite wall.

He'd stuffed his duffel bag with blankets and a pillow from camp and without further ado he made sure the bunk had nothing nesting in it, unpacked the duffel, removed his jacket, boots and pants and lay down. Pillow under his head, he pulled a blanket over himself and smiled: this would work. Then his eyes closed and he slept solidly for nearly twelve hours.

* * *

Ty walked along Main Street to the grocery store, well pleased with the deal he'd made with Axel. He wasn't sure what he was being taught, but at least he had some moves to work on for tomorrow.

"Hi-ya!" he said as he reached the grocery store. An elderly woman peered at him over her glasses and he grinned and bowed, waving her in ahead of him.

"Are you trying to pick me up, young man?"

He laughed and got her a basket along with one for himself and mentally ran down his short grocery list. The cabin offered a cast iron frying pan and a tin coffee pot. Nothing else. He bought a knife, a fork and a spoon, followed by bacon and eggs, hamburger, onion, carrots and potatoes, bread and cheese. On a display rack in the dry goods section he found an assortment of school backpacks. He selected one and added a bar of soap, coffee and chocolate chip cookies on his way to the checkout.

"There a liquor store in town?"

The checkout girl told him where to find it, and he packed his groceries in the backpack and walked two blocks over to the liquor store. The line shack was only a mile or two out of town but he decided a bottle of rum would be lighter than a case of beer, so he bought that plus a mixer bottle of coke to the checkout.

"How you doing?" The checkout girl spoke mechanically.

"Fine," he said. She was a thin girl about his own age or slightly older. She looked tired. "You?" He punched in his pin number.

"Fine," she said and handed over his receipt. "Have a good one." She smiled, watching him reload the backpack, adding the rum and coke bottles and putting the eggs on top.

"Bye now." He smiled back at her and set out to walk home.

Main Street ran from the highway to Railway Avenue, where a hotel overlooked the lake known as Loon Water. Along from the hotel were the municipal hall and museum, then a few warehouses, then open fields. Like most prairie roads, Railway was flat and wide. The fields lay stippled brown and white on either side, stretching to the horizon.

A car drew abreast and he was offered a ride, though he hadn't tried to hitch. But he was glad enough to accept and returned home to find the shack unoccupied and undisturbed, protected by stubby prairie poplars and caragana, bare-branched in February and covered in hoar frost.

He unpacked his purchases and put them on a crude shelf next to the pot-bellied stove. Then he crouched down, unlatched the door and added some sticks of firewood on top of the thick layer of ash. This morning he had scouted around for wood and had found a piece of particle board under the front steps. Now he crumbled bits of it onto the sticks, added more sticks, and managed to light the fire.

He straightened and looked up at the roof. It was a simple affair of boards slanting down either side of a ridgepole, with shingles over the boards. He could see daylight in a couple of places.

He spent the remainder of the daylight gathering wood, examining the area around the outhouse for wildlife. A skunk waddled off as he came around the rear of the wooden structure. "Oops," he said. "No offense, but why don't you stay thataway, just for this week." He squatted and watched the undergrowth but nothing moved. Eventually he stood and walked over to the stream running in what seemed to be a straight line from the Arctic Circle to North Dakota. It was clear and clean, with small pebbles near the bank.

He remembered his lesson and assumed the sparring position. "Hi-ya!" He punched ten times with his right hand, then kicked ten times with his right leg. A car honked on the road and he nearly overbalanced, then completed the exercise.

He rotated a full circle. On the horizon a pumpjack, looking like a grazing T Rex, pulled oil out of the ground. The only trees in sight were those in his little copse, and he wondered if the protection it offered explained the shack's existence. He could hear nothing but the water and an occasional vehicle. The sky seemed immense but not oppressive. The clouds were beautiful, bold and extravagantly large, and he walked back to the cabin feeling positive for the first time since Fort St John.

* * *

"Wider. Swivel your heels and toes."

Arms over his head, Ty faced Axel, his legs wide apart. He used heel-toe moves to widen his stance further. “Oh man,” he said at last, “that’s about it.”

Axel studied his posture then moved to his left side, reached down for his ankle and raised his leg. Ty protested.

“Just concentrate on your balance,” said Axel. He stopped lifting. Ty’s foot was midway up his chest. “This is how high you can kick me, right now.” He lowered the leg and Ty straightened and did a knee bend.

Axel continued, “Keep stretching. Your goal is to be able to kick to head height.

Ty said nothing but his eyes moved to the words on the large banner pinned to one wall. “My goal is to become a” were the words on the top line, while spaced across the width on the second line were the words: Black Belt—Instructor—Master. Ty had resolved to become a master. He’d been careful not to ask how long this might take.

Both men wore white martial arts garb with bare feet. Ty donned the garb after lunch, in preparation for his lesson. In the morning he cleaned. On Tuesday, Axel had pointed him to a door at the rear of the equipment room. Here he found cleaning supplies, a wide mop, vacuum and a side exit door. For three or four hours each day, depending on the schedule, he cleaned, finding accumulations of dust in corners and on shelves. Axel admitted it had been weeks since the place was cleaned. “It said online that the gym floor should be wet-mopped, want me to do that one day?” He received a stare from Axel and shrugged uncomfortably. “I’m just saying.”

"No, no," Axel recovered. "That's great! Please do it. I know it's bad for the surface to leave it dirty."

After cleaning, he put out equipment for the upcoming classes, and counted and sorted gear. He paired gloves and the chained nunchaku sticks, put helmets on the helmet shelf and sorted the hangers of clothing into sizes, from teeny-weeny to big person.

All this industry earned him his daily lesson, which he received after lunch, and for a couple of hours after that he practiced at one end of the gym while classes came and went at the other end. A class of seven-year-olds all shrieking "Hi-ya!" could hurt your ears, he discovered. He usually left at that point. Sometimes he sat and watched, especially when a class was covering moves more advanced than he'd learned.

"What are you teaching me?" He'd asked Axel on Wednesday after their lesson.

"Sun hang do. It combines striking and kicking with soft moves."

"What are soft moves?"

"Throwing. Joint manipulation."

"Holy shit."

He now knew three moves: blocking, striking and kicking, and practised these incessantly. Yesterday he'd watched a match between Axel and another man who wore a green belt. They moved in a balletic blur of blocks, strikes and kicks punctuated by the occasional throw.

"What good is all this if my opponent doesn't do martial arts?"

Axel laughed. He was waiting for his next class, sitting on a chair beneath the goal banner, Ty next to him. "Then you're in luck. You'll have him disabled in ten seconds."

Ty thought of Crusher Harmon and what he would do if Ty aimed a kick at his head. If Crusher got his hands around Ty's ankle, as Axel had—he voiced this worry.

Axel looked at him. "Are you planning on looking this guy up?"

Ty shook his head. "I hope I never see him again. But if someone like him got hold of my ankle like you did, he'd just take my leg off, like I'd pull off a chicken leg."

"That won't happen. You'll be learning how to prevent it."

Axel surveyed the gym. "So I'll be losing your services for two weeks, will I?"

"After tomorrow, yeah."

"Too bad." They heard the front doors open and a gaggle of children coming in. He stood up. "You'll be getting paid soon, won't you?" And when Ty nodded, he went on, "Sure you'll want the same arrangement?"

"Absolutely. I'm trying to save money for school."

* * *

He had settled into a comfortable routine during his off week. Up at six-thirty, light the stove, wash, prepare breakfast and lunch. Leave at eight-thirty, get to the gym by nine or sooner if he was offered a ride. After work, mid-afternoon, he would do his shopping, then walk home, potter around the shack during the daylight hours. Then dinner around six, in bed by nine. His body got the sleep it craved, in quantities that eluded rig workers on the job.

Even his morning routine was now relaxed, after the first day of experiments. He'd used a sock to wash himself in the stream, the water icy and his body fully exposed to the elements and the traffic, not that much of that went by. He tried to make do with the frying pan, and spent the next morning carrying a full pan back to the shack, and washing there in what was left. That afternoon he'd bought a metal bucket at the hardware store, along with an all-purpose knife. Filling the bucket after dinner became part of the routine, leaving it on the stove to heat. It was never warm in the morning, but neither was it icy, and he was able to strip down and wash himself with the sock and soap outside the front door every morning, using the sock's mate as a towel and draping it over the bar in the fireplace to dry. When he discovered his freshly washed body getting streaked with soot, he amended that practice.

Breakfast was bacon, eggs and bread, plus coffee. One morning he'd just put the bacon in the pan when he heard a train coming. He watched outside as it approached, running slowly along the far side of the road, the track lying a few feet below the road surface. First the engine, then the cars, on and on and on. Brown or yellow grain cars. Black tanker cars. He started to count after a while, got to seventy and remembered the bacon. The ground shivered under his feet as he returned to the shack.

He'd learned through trial and error how to make coffee and rather than waste firewood, he would make enough to last all day. The pot simmered on the back of the stove and by afternoon was closer to varnish stripper than beverage. But it was good enough for a mouthful or two after dinner.

* * *

The farmer came one afternoon when he was standing outside the shack, studying the roof and wondering if it would support his weight. He'd whittled a small branch into pieces the approximate size and shape of the cracks between the shingles and he planned to climb up and fit them each into place. When the pickup pulled in and parked next to the shack, he walked over. A wiry man got out, a man in his late-forties wearing a parka over a thick plaid shirt, workpants and boots.

"How you doin', son?" He introduced himself and held out a hand. "The lady said you'd be here this week. Came to see how you're getting on."

Ty thanked him for the use of the shack and explained his problem. The farmer stepped back far enough to see the roof.

"Those boards went up two years ago. Held my weight fine. Tell you what, son, you let me get up there."

He proceeded to maneuver the pickup until it was snug against the stone wall. Then he climbed in the back and cut off a six-foot length of wire from a reel on the bed of the truck, next to a pick axe, a shovel and assorted other tools and supplies. Leaving the length of wire with Ty he rummaged in the glove compartment and came out with a tube of glue. Then he followed Ty inside and they studied the roof.

"Coffee smells good," he said, but declined a cup. "Maybe when we're done."

He thought they could improve on the whittling and found some shingles in the truck. Ty returned inside while the farmer climbed from the truck bed to the chimney. Ty could hear the scrape of his boots on the chimney stones. "Okay," he heard, and poked the length of wire up through the first crack, withdrawing it on command. The crack disappeared for a moment then returned, and he imagined the farmer must be applying glue to a shingle. The crack disappeared again, this time for good. "Okay," he heard a moment later, and he moved to the next crack and poked the wire through.

"On your right, about a yard away," he called.

In this fashion they repaired the roof.

The farmer was pleased and sat on the only chair drinking coffee from a thermos cup, while Ty sat on the bunk. "Thought of tearing the place down, couple years ago," he said and took a sip. "Strong."

"What made you fix it up?"

"Dunno. It's so old I kinda hated to tear it down. Nothing wrong with that beam," he glanced up at the roof, "so I replaced a couple of floorboards that needed it, and fixed the roof and there you go." He rose to leave. "Glad it's some use to people."

"It's a life-saver for me," said Ty, and asked if he could use it again in a couple of weeks. Demand was low in the winter, said the proprietor, so Ty was welcome to come again.

* * *

On Thursday afternoon he bought supplies at the grocery store then walked along to the liquor store.

"You again," said the same thin-faced girl.

Ty's face took on a rueful look. "Friends." He wished immediately he hadn't said it.

She smiled. "It's just, I thought you were passing through last time." She watched him load his backpack. "Staying round here?"

"Just outside town. I'm working on one of the rigs."

"Oh sure," she said. "Two weeks on, one week off."

"You got it." He introduced himself and learned her name was Brenda Pasko and that she worked nine to five at the liquor store. "Maybe we could grab a coffee next time," he said and she agreed with a little laugh. He hoisted the backpack as another customer arrived at the checkout.

"Good meeting you, Brenda," said Ty, and left.

* * *

He stayed late at the gym on Saturday, watching some of the adult classes, and this time a man was working the till instead of Brenda. Ty bought his bottles and took a plastic carrier bag with him as well. He'd wrap the bottles in it and stow them behind the stove when he left, in the ash of the big fireplace. Nice to have something waiting for him in two weeks' time.

CHAPTER

Fourteen

AT TWO MILES down, they replaced the bit, doing some maintenance on the preceding shift. Roy and Cory replaced the brake pads on the drawworks, while Ty helped Mike and Jerry inspect the tongs. One of the dies of the breakout tongs showed uneven wear, and Mike used a hammer to remove it. Ty was sent to the parts shed to find a replacement while Jerry cleaned the slot and applied some pipe dope to the surface. The new die was tapped in, and then they checked the cathead cable and the snubline.

“They should be steam cleaned,” Mike reported to Roy. “Can’t inspect them properly otherwise.” The driller made a note in his log and Mike went off to examine the elevator.

They were on graveyard again and the bit trip was scheduled for midnight. Tripping out would take about six hours. Once the bit was replaced, the day crew would complete the cycle.

About an hour before tripping began, they reviewed jobs, sitting in the doghouse, Roy watching his console while he took Ty through his paces. Ty felt he had to make a point.

"It's the same as making a connection, pretty much. I'm good." He'd tripped pipe once, when they had a pressure leak, but it had been several weeks ago, and only involved a few stands of pipe.

"Oh?" Roy looked around at him, seated at the table with Jerry. "Where do you put the kelly while all this tripping is going on?"

The kelly was the square pipe that fit into the rotary platform and drove the bit, as well as feeding mud to it. "You move it over to the, uh, the side," said Ty and Jerry winced.

"The side? Where on *the side*, Creampuff?" Roy looked at the others.

"The mousehole," Jerry piped up.

"The rathole," said Mike.

"The pothole," said Cory, who had heard of Ty's Alberta adventure. The others hooted.

Ty remembered. "The rathole." The mousehole had a different purpose, being used to hold a new length of pipe before it was added to the string.

"So you got the kelly sitting in the rathole. Now what?"

"Now you start removing pipe."

"Oh. How? By hand? You just going to pull it out, you and Jerry?"

Jerry laughed, the sycophant.

"What do we use to haul the string, Creampuff?"

"Oh right! Elevator." He remembered last time. "We have to unhook the kelly from the, uh, the swivel bale, then attach the elevator."

Applause and thumping of boots on floor. Roy took them through their jobs: Cory up on the monkeyboard, breaking each thirty-meter stand out of the elevator and moving it to the fingers; Jerry and Ty down on the rig floor, setting the slips and working the tongs; Mike nearby to lend a hand and apply the spinning wrench that uncoupled each connection, once the tongs had loosened it.

They moved out to the floor at midnight. "Let's make it the fastest trip ever," said Ty and Jerry nodded.

"Hold it, you two."

The others were already outside, Cory in his safety harness climbing the derrick.

Roy looked silently at the two roughnecks. "You should know better, Jerry."

Jerry hung his head. Ty stared. "What?"

"I dunno why it is, but every roughneck that ever lived wants to have the fastest trip in recorded history." He looked at Jerry. "What do I want, Jerry?"

"A safe trip."

"What was that, Jerry? I can't hear you."

"A safe trip! But what about—"

"Hear that, Creampuff? Forget breaking the land speed record. Just do your job and keep your head in the game. Got that?"

Ty remembered Cory's words. "Yeah."

Five and a half hours later, after Cory had unclipped a hundred and seventeen stands of pipe from the elevators, after Jerry and Ty had thrown the slips two hundred and thirty-four times—"or four hundred and sixty-eight, Jer, if you count each in and each out separately"—when the sky had begun to lighten, Ty straightened wearily and watched the bit emerge from the depths of the earth. Its tungsten carbide teeth were worn to nubs and the toolpush, who had arrived shortly before, wasted no time, and supervised the hoisting of the new bit into place, the attaching of the heavy collar that puts weight onto the bit. The two were lowered into the hole, Jerry swabbed the collar threads with pipe dope, and the last pipe stand came down on the traveling block and was stabbed into the collar. Mike swung the spinning wrench over, locked it onto the pipe and Roy spun the connection. Then Jerry latched the lead tongs and torqued the connection and they were off again. The day crew arrived, and after a short safety meeting they took over the trip. Ty followed the others down the ladder and watched the sunrise as he walked over to the jeep for the drive back to camp, dinner and bed.

* * *

Barty was back from spring break and sent a long email recounting his adventures.

> "If you've never heard of Vanuatu, bro, don't worry, I hadn't either. It's an island in the south Pacific and I was flown there—are you listening, Ty?—and flown home, all expenses paid for a week of sun and sand, no women though. And why, you ask? Allow me to introduce you to Luke Aragio. Luke is attending our alma mater at his mother's insistence—a mother only a son could love, lemme tell ya, Ty, she's a fusser. She fusses and won't stop. Ever.

She fusses over Luke and she tried to fuss over me too and I don't know how he puts up with her, but like I said. . . . Anyway, Luke will never come close to filling the gaping hole left by your departure, let me make that clear. But he's kinda sweet. He has the face and body of a god and he wants to be in movies. This is not as crazy as it sounds because he has an uncle who's a producer with a place in Vanuatu, and he (the uncle) got this idea for a movie and needs a screenwriter. Are you ready for this, Ty, because the irony of it will knock you sideways. It's a movie about—yup, about hockey."

Lying on his bed, laptop on his stomach, Ty let out a laugh.

"So we flew down there and he started feeding us drinks and I can now see why people become alcoholics. Have you ever tasted Napoleon Brandy? Oh my oh my, Ty. It's deep and rich, and it flows into every crevice in your mouth and tongue and speaks to you: how did you ever manage without me, it says. Well I have no idea how I managed but beer tastes like dishwater after NB. Forget it. Ditto coke, crack, meth, whatever. I have found my muse LOL.

"Anyway, this guy has a place right on the beach, like a hut but bigger and better. And as soon as we're settled in, he pitches this idea. 'You remember the Jamaican bobsled team,' he says. Apparently, the Jamaicans put together a team for the winter Olympics one year. 'How about a Vanuatu hockey team!'

"Picture my reaction, Ty. Well, Marcus thinks I'm disputing his reasoning on the subject, which he proceeds to explain: since there are too few hockey teams in the Olympics, they'd likely lower the standards to encourage new teams.

"So I piped up, 'you don't need a reason, Marcus. This is a movie, right? Not a documentary. We can make anything work.' That 'we' just slipped out, Ty. Don't know where it came from."

"So then I'm his golden boy. I heard him congratulate Luke on bringing me down, from which you may deduce they're not the sharpest tools in the box. But hey—they're beautiful to look at and they, or any way, Marcus, seems to know how to make money. He's had a couple of movie successes.

"Then Luke pipes up, 'Would I be the goalie, Uncle Marcus?' Even I know the answer to that. You don't put a Greek god in one of those hellacious goalie masks, not if you're hoping to get bums into seats. Can't be done and Marcus explains this to him.

"Anyway, I batted out a treatment for him and he loved it. Vanuatu needs to boost its tourist trade (this is the story) so they vote to start an ice hockey team. Luke plays the son of an islander and an American woman, and he's kind of a beachcomber type until they discover he's a natural with a stick and puck. They build a team and import a manager from LA (Marcus is a huge fan of the Kings) who brings along his drop-dead gorgeous daughter who hates everything to do with Vanuatu because it's a tax haven and she's a daughter of the people, get it? Anyway, they eventually go to the Olympics and she discovers that Luke's the one for her and there you go. Kinda dumb, but Marcus liked it. I wouldn't mind spending some more time here. Like Stevenson or Maugham? Nice life. Things okay with you, buddy?"

While Barty had spring break, Ty had been listening to dining room scuttlebutt about spring break-up, that period of six weeks to three months when the ground began to thaw. Spring break-up could start as early as February and run through to June. Rigs are not permitted to move during the break-up, road bans are in place and crews are laid off. But he'd discovered that some rigs keep on working right through, and prayed that Meridian 41 might be one of them. He lost sleep worrying about it and finally broke down and asked Mike.

The motorhand shook his head. "We'd have to be outta here by then, Ty."

"But when is 'then'? When's spring break up?"

"Up here? Probably not till the end of April."

Ty's tension eased, but the work and the schedule were taking its toll on all of them. Roy had told Jerry to cut back on the Red Bull, so Jerry was chewing gum and Cory had taken to chewing tobacco. Ty had assumed it was gum until he ejected a squirt of tobacco juice as they approached the mud mixing hut one morning.

Cory caught his look.

"What? You don't like tobacco?"

Ty shrugged. "Just didn't know, that's all."

"Well, I can't smoke. Better than doing uppers or downers or something."

"Couldn't bring those in even if you wanted, could you?"

"You'd be surprised what some guys' families send them. Think of knives in cakes."

He laughed at the expression on Ty's face.

* * *

Ty logged into his bank account and grinned like an idiot. The fruits of more than three weeks of work, fifty-five hundred dollars after tax, sat smugly in the deposit column. Eventually, the banking program, which did not recognize gloating as an activity, booted him off the site. He logged back in and reluctantly transferred most of the money to his credit card account. He still wasn't out of the woods, but another payday could clear his debts and start him earning his tuition. He went along to dinner with a spring in his step.

That evening he received a long newsy email from Mattie Williams, the gist of which was that she had been bitten by the political bug.

> "I didn't even used to read the newspaper, Ty, never mind voting. But now I do, and I'm working for Diane Huynh, one of the city councillors. She wants to run against Fred Harmon in the next elections and as you can imagine neither Bill nor I will be voting for Fred again! Anyway, Diane's Vietnamese, and her parents were boat people, and they've all done well here. She and her husband own the Seven-Eleven near the high school, and she's been a councillor for eight years and wants to be mayor. They had a feature on her in the paper. Ev's doing them on all the councillors. I went along to a council meeting one afternoon and told her to let me know anytime she wants help circulating flyers or whatever.
>
> "Couple of bits of news for you. That cop Feeney's been transferred to Whitecourt. He still lives here and Bill said he still pals around with the Harmons, but at least he's not handing out tickets here. I don't know if Ev had anything to do with the transfer, he wouldn't say. But he gave Fred the heads up that the paper would be actively working to re-

> place him, and told him why, though he didn't mention you or us by name. Fred's really on the defensive now, and even though he's still so popular we think he may have trouble getting re-elected."
>
> "BTW, pot holes cost about fifteen dollars to fix, did you know that? Ev said the province is divided into regions, and each region has a contractor who's responsible for fixing potholes. Always something new in Kaitlin!"

Ty leaned back on the bed and gazed up at the ceiling. Adults were interesting. They didn't rush off guns blazing, like in the movies. But some of them didn't just let bad stuff slide by either. All because he'd hit a pothole and got into a fight.

He returned to the email:

> "Bill wanted me to tell you he went to see one of the VPs at the pulp mill and they'd be glad to talk to you, Ty. They're always looking for good people and they've been known to take young people on as trainees and help finance their education. Bill said you should think about that, and think about settling here! End of pitch. I've got to go now and pick up my precious angel. –Love Mattie.
>
> "BTW, the Davidsons have completely disappeared! I told you Scott was too stupid to live? It seems all the others are as well. Nowadays, it's Tyley this and Tyley that. He misses you very much, Ty, and we all hope you'll visit us soon. –M."

He ate a double helping of hoddeok at breakfast and gave Cory a forkful to try. He'd waited until late last week to raise the subject with Garvit, approaching him after dinner one day when the chef seemed good-humored, and asking if he'd cook up a batch.

"I do not as a rule go out of my way to create special dishes for silly leasehands," said Garvit. As Ty turned away, he added, "But I will consider it."

"I can show you the recipe," Ty began.

"Go. Away."

Today one of the chafing dishes was devoted to hoddeok, and Ty thought they couldn't have come at a better time. The wind was up, the temperature down and he foresaw a cold day ahead of him. Fresh supplies of mud, bentonite, calcium and gel had to be lugged into the storage shed and Tait's leasehand had made no discernible inroads. Ty spent the morning moving eighty- and hundred-pound sacks, in between errands for the mud engineer and toolpush, and trying to keep his face and hands warm.

He was cold and tired by mid-afternoon and varied the routine by patrolling the property, picking up garbage. He walked around the mud processing equipment, past the shale shaker and was standing in the lee of the desifter and desilter tanks when the mud pump engine acquired an elevated whine.

Every drilling operation has at least one mud pump, and some, like Meridian 41, had a backup as well. Ty entered through the wire fence gate and found the wind had plastered a piece of paper to the air intake. He peeled it off. It was a page out of one of Jerry's porn magazines, a full-page picture of a naked girl doing an inventive pole dance. The wind gusted and he shoved the picture into his pocket, put on his glove and headed for the doghouse. He saw Mike emerging from the boiler room but was in no mood to slow down.

He ran up the steps to the rig platform, removed a glove, fumbled with numbing hand and threw open the door. The wind followed him in.

"Shut the fucking door!" Roy, Cory and Jerry spoke together.

He slammed the door and ignored Cory, who was scrambling for playing cards on the floor. He pulled out the pinup and smacked it down on the table in front of Jerry, who had his forearms spread protectively over his magazine.

"This was spread over the air intake on the mud pump, Jerry."

"It's not my picture."

Ty ignored him. "I don't give a shit about your Snickers bar wrappers—" the door opened and he turned and lunged at a Snickers bar wrapper on the floor, heading for the open door.

"Shut the door!" roared Roy and Mike shut the door.

"It's Ryan's, not mine," said Jerry. Ryan was Tait's roughneck.

Ty, who had been working up to clout him across the head, instead gave the entire crew a look of comprehensive frustration and stalked past Roy into the little bunkroom, which, as he'd expected, was toasty warm. He shed clothes in front of the space heater and Mike, who had come in to turn it off, said pacifically, "Turn it off when you're done, Ty, okay?" Ty nodded curtly and sat on the bunk opposite the heater, extending his hands and feet.

"He can't talk to me like that," whined Jerry. "Can he?" No one answered him.

The phone on Roy's console buzzed. "Right," he said after a pause. "Cory, get on down to the mud lab. Engineer's report."

Taking reports up to the toolpush was Ty's job. "I got it, Cory," he called and began to put his clothes back on.

"Stay put. I want to talk to him anyway."

So Ty sat in front of the heater until his hands hurt with the returning circulation. Then he picked up his belongings, turned the heater off and went out to the main room. He dropped his gloves on the floor and met Jerry's glance. "Sorry."

"See, look, Ty," Jerry stood up and opened one of the locker doors. "Ryan's locker." He held up the picture and Ty could see that the rip in one corner matched the tag end of a photo that had been taped to the inside of the locker door. Jerry grinned. "You could probably make him pay if you want to give it back. He's crazy about this picture."

Roy's harsh voice intervened. "Give it to me. I'll see he gets it."

Ty opened his own locker and rummaged through the balaclavas and liners on the top shelf, looking for a pair of mitts he knew he had somewhere. Nothing like mitts for keeping fingers warm. A pair of mudcaked coveralls hung in the locker and he made a mental note to take them back to camp. They'd been hanging there for two weeks, a reminder of the time he and Jerry had made a connection and he'd forgotten to hold the bucket under the kelly when it was disconnected. Mud had streamed out and covered his legs. He hadn't dared enter the doghouse in that condition and Mike had fetched a change of coveralls from his locker.

At seven pm, after the short safety meeting, Ty followed the others out of the doghouse and was at the head of the stairs when he recalled the coveralls and turned back. His hand was on the doghouse door when he heard Roy's voice inside: "I don't give a flying fuck, Tait! My leasehand spent most of the day humping gel sacks your guy was too lazy to move." There was silence, then a murmured reply from Tait, cut short by Roy. "That's neither here nor there. But when your garbage goes flying out the door you could at least send him out to police up the property. My kid found this—" Ty heard a slap—"on the mud pump. On the air intake, for Chrissake! I'm not having it, Tait." Tait's reply was inaudible. Ty turned away but not before he heard Roy: "That's not the point. It's got to stop."

Ty was down the stairs and off the rig when he heard Roy's voice: "Tyler!" Staring straight ahead, he grinned—*what, no more Creampuff?*—then turned, expressionless, waiting for the driller.

"We're going to be getting a trainee when we come back." Their week off was due in two days. Ty matched his stride to Roy's as they walked to the jeep. "I'll expect you to give him the orientation, go through your own jobs, the works. Mike'll help you out."

"I can do it," said Ty. "But there's not enough work for two."

"You're getting a promotion, to floorhand. Jerry'll be senior roughie."

They reached the jeep. Roy opened his door, surveyed Ty and nodded abruptly. He turned to climb in and Ty jogged around to the driver's side.

Driving back to camp, he planned his orientation tour for the trainee and wondered if he would now be allowed up top. The question was answered for him as soon as the night leasehand drove the truck away. The others were already at the canteen door but Roy stood waiting for him.

"You going to be okay climbing the derrick?"

"Absolutely," said Ty.

A figure came round the corner of the canteen hugging the wall, a figure in a dark parka over a white uniform: kitchen staff. The canteen door opened and one of the drillers came out. Ty recognized him as the one who'd said he would shoot his wife if she slept with a Pakistani. The driller turned to the left and came face to face with the kitchen worker.

"Okay then," said Roy. "You'll also be helping Cory as needed."

Ty nodded. They both saw the two men. Words passed between them and the kitchen worker moved out from the wall and kept on walking. Ty saw it was the Pakistani assistant cook.

"What did you say?" The driller turned. "You prick." He lashed out with his steel-toed boot, kicking him in the backside, and the cook stumbled forward.

"What's going on?" Roy moved toward them.

The worker whirled, crouching and a knife blade flashed. A moment's stillness. Then he turned and dashed off around the corner of the trailer. Roy wrapped his arms around the driller to stop him following.

"Mother-fuckin' Paki called me an asshole."

"That'd be about right," said Roy and met the driller's hot glance.

The driller swore. "Let me go, goddammit. I'll kill that little prick!"

"No. You won't," said Roy. "Tyler!"

Ty had taken off after the cook, running into the darkness round the corner, ignoring Roy's call. He glimpsed white legs along the narrow lane between the serried rows of trailers, and saw the fleeing cook enter a trailer at the far end.

He jogged along the lane and entered the same trailer. In the common area he was confronted by faces of white and yellow, brown and black.

"I'm looking for the guy who just came in."

Polite uninterest. The faces turned away and resumed their interrupted pastimes: TV, board games, texting.

"Look. He's one of the cooks. Just tell him I saw the whole thing. If he wants a witness. The other guy kicked him first."

Silence.

"So—just tell him." He turned to go then turned back. "I don't think he needs to worry."

He left, closing the door and the outer door. He had taken only a few steps back toward the canteen when the Pakistani spoke from behind. "Why do you do that?"

Ty turned. "Why not?" He added, "He shouldn't have kicked you."

"He is a pig."

They stared at each other.

"Someone backed me up a while ago," said Ty. "I'm just doing the same for you. Name's Ty Hogan, if you need me."

He nodded, turned away and jogged back to the canteen.

CHAPTER

Fifteen

"BLOCK FROM THE same side."

"Sorry."

Axel kicked again with his left foot. "From the same side!"

Ty blocked the kick from the same side.

"Good! Now you try."

Ty's punch was blocked and blocked again. He whirled and kicked and Axel stepped back. "Excellent." He studied Ty. "You've been practising."

"Every chance I get."

They set to work on opening responses. "This is your only chance to lull your attacker. So you back up, arms up, hands open. He steps in, block, block, punch. Or kick. Then back away. Elbows in. Remember, your power comes from the straight line, arm-wrist-fist."

The classes were working toward some sort of final exam, so the gym was busy from mid-morning until evening. Ty cleaned early then spent hours moving equipment and later stowing it. Mats out all over the floor, then mats away and punching bags at regular intervals along the length of the gym. Sorting and matching sparring gloves and other equipment. He generally left with a headache from the piercing cries of the smaller kids, and wondered how Axel coped, day after day.

He met Brenda for lunch one day. He was telling her about his family over soup and a sandwich when they heard a loud, unmuffled vehicle approaching along the street. Brenda sighed.

"They've been doing that all morning."

A Humvee pulled up at the traffic light, its engine turning over loudly. Two men inside, both with open beers.

Ty was astonished. "Where are the cops?"

"Busy." She rolled her eyes. "They're always busy when crews act up."

The engine revved deafeningly, the light changed, a wild yell from the passenger side and the Humvee took off toward the hotel.

"Rig pigs."

Ty was startled at the bitterness in her voice. "That seems a little harsh."

"Sorry. Are they friends of yours?"

He shook his head. "They're just letting off steam." He'd seen the two men at meal times, just two of the many rig workers at the camp. His attitude had modified, he realized. He no longer regarded rig workers as small-town, going-nowhere losers without character or prospects. Some might be, but others were his crew mates, men he depended on and who depended on him. They weren't so bad.

"It's just . . ." she looked away, then faced him across the table. "They behave like they're the only people in the world who work hard, so they deserve the money they make. Let me tell you something. I work just as hard, and I don't make a hundred thousand a year. I've got a mother at home trying to recover from an operation, and I've got a brother who's hooked in with a gang, and I get tired of these guys. See?"

"Sure." He would have been more responsive, but she'd told him she was involved, her boyfriend away in Saskatoon. He went on telling her about Vancouver Island and his family. She seemed to like that.

The two men in the Humvee were still on her mind, however, because when Ty paused for a bite of his sandwich, she said, "Do they act like that at the hotel?"

"I wouldn't know. I don't stay at the hotel."

"You don't?"

"I've got a place out on Railway," said Ty, straight-faced.

She was puzzled. "Where on Railway?" She suddenly looked embarrassed. "Ty. You don't mean that broken-down old shack?"

"You're talking about my principal residence," said Ty with dignity.

She laughed. "I played there as a kid. It was just a smelly old—." She recovered. "That's amazing. Bet you're saving money."

"You got it." Ty's answer was heartfelt, and Brenda laughed outright. She looked like a different person when she laughed.

"You don't use that outhouse, do you?"

"Share it with a skunk."

"I've got to see this. Doesn't it leak? The shack?"

"Nope. Farmer fixed it up a couple of years ago. It's fine." He suddenly felt hospitable. "Come for dinner, why don't you?"

"Dinner? Get out. You can't cook dinner. What do you cook dinner on?"

"Come and find out."

"When?"

"Friday?"

Brenda considered this invitation and her face brightened. "You know, that'd be so nice, Ty. You can't imagine." She added, "Want me to bring something? Besides wine?"

"You just bring yourself," said Ty.

"Listen, Ty. I really am involved. This is just a friendly get-together, okay?"

"Fine by me."

* * *

The farmer called by. He brought a can of kerosene for the lantern and left it over Ty's protests. "Take a cup of coffee," he said, "call it square."

The days were getting longer. They sat indoors because of the cold, but it was still light at five o'clock. "It'll soon be spring, I guess," said Ty.

The farmer shook his head. "Not yet, son. End of April, maybe."

"Is that when you start planting?"

Another shake. "Ground's frozen, six-seven feet down. Even deeper on the road beds." He sipped his coffee. "We'll seed in late May." He grew flax, wheat and barley. "Like to plant soya," he said, "but my land's too stony. Damage the harvester."

Ty learned that the pumpjack was one of several on the farmer's land. "Guess you're an oil baron, huh?"

Another shake of the head. "Not me, son. Crown owns the mineral rights. I just get a lease payment." It amounted to several thousand a year for each pumpjack. He smiled and stood up, ready to leave. "Pays the taxes and a bit over."

* * *

Ty was putting out his starters when Brenda arrived. She handed him a bottle of wine, an opener and two glasses. "I've just got to take a look at that outhouse," she said, and disappeared, taking her flashlight with her.

Ty had borrowed a chair from the gym and extra plates and cutlery from Marilyn, after spending an hour at McDonald's nursing a Coke and using the free Wi-Fi to hunt for one-pan recipes. He had phoned Cory and hitched a ride to their motor home at a campsite down the far side of Loon Water. Marilyn had had the dishes waiting.

"What are you serving," she asked, "or is it a secret?"

Ty was glad she'd asked because he was a little anxious. "I'm having cupcakes from the bakery for dessert," he said. "Girls like cupcakes, don't they?"

"This girl does, for sure," she said. "What else?"

"I was thinking some California rolls to start with, from that deli in the grocery store, and some mixed veggies and dip."

Marilyn nodded her approval.

"That leaves my main course. I'm going to do baked potatoes because they're a no-brainer. And a frittata. Sausage, mushroom and asparagus."

She had sent him on his way with her blessing and the dishes.

Brenda came back from viewing the outhouse. "I won't be using that," she said with a laugh, and took off her coat, dropping it on the bunk. She came to the table, her eyes shining. "Oh Tyler, this was such a good idea. I haven't had an evening out for so long." He had opened the wine while she was exploring and now he poured them both a glass and sat opposite her at the table.

Brenda wanted to know all about his routine, how he kept himself and the shack clean. She would keep interrupting him with childhood memories of biking there on Saturdays with a friend, and playing house, and lighting fires of twigs in the big stone fireplace.

The starters met with her approval, especially since she'd never tried California rolls. The frittata thrilled her. She watched as Ty dished it up next to the baked potatoes and exclaimed over the taste.

"How old are you, Ty?"

"Twenty. Nearly twenty."

"Oh my God." She gazed at him. "Some girl is going to be so lucky."

"Aw shucks." He grinned, and passed her the butter.

"I'm serious, Ty." She took another mouthful. "This is so good. And I haven't had potatoes baked in the coals since whenever."

They had reached the cupcake stage when they heard a car pull off the road.

Ty cocked an eye at his guest. "You invite anyone else?"

Brenda shook her head.

"Brenda?" A male voice, outside. Drawing closer. "Bren?"

She stared at Ty, amazed. "Mick?" She stood up and raised her voice. "Mickey?"

The door opened and a man in his late twenties stood there, stocky, unshaven, with the belly of a committed beer drinker. "What're you doing, Bren?"

"Why are you here?"

"Never mind that. Why are you?"

"You said you were coming back next week."

"Good thing I changed my mind." He looked at Ty with disfavor. "Who's this?"

Ty got up. "Ty Hogan. Come on in and have a drink."

"Brenda? You come alonga me. Right now." He turned away, stepping off the porch.

"Mickey! I will not!" Brenda started for the door but stopped in the entrance. "This is the first fun night I've had in ages, Mickey. You and me, we never go out except to a booze up with your friends. We never have fun. So this is me having fun, Mickey."

Mickey had turned during this speech and was staring reproachfully at the girl. "I thought you liked going to the pub."

"Did I ever have a choice?"

"Well, you never said."

"Well, now I'm saying, Mickey."

He stared silently at her, then returned to the porch. "Here, you come alonga me, Bren." He reached for her arm and she shook him off.

"I'm staying. There's no harm in it. Tyler and me are having dinner, that's all."

"Brenda," Mickey said, warningly.

Tyler appeared next to Brenda. "She wants to stay. You're welcome to join us."

"There! See, Mick? You can—Mickey!"

For Mickey had expressed his opinion of this invitation by giving Tyler a hard, stiff-armed shove that caught him unawares and sent him staggering backward onto the bed.

"You stay outta my way. And stay away from Brenda." He turned to the girl. "Get your coat and come on, Bren."

Brenda had rushed over to check on Ty, who was completely unharmed. "Oh Tyler, I'm so sorry."

"Brenda!" From outside.

She looked at Ty. "I really really had a nice time, thanks, Ty."

"Forget it." He was thoroughly disgusted.

"Could I have my coat?"

Ty couldn't be bothered to stand. He lifted a hip and Brenda pulled out her coat.

"Bren! Let's go!"

"Thanks again," she said, and ran after Mickey, closing the door behind her. Ty lay on the bed staring morosely at the wall.

The voices faded. A car started, then another. They drove away. Silence returned.

Ty sighed.

"Just once, Hogan. Just once, it would be great if you could—" he bellowed at the wall, "—defend yourself!"

CHAPTER

Sixteen

THE TRAINEE WAS a girl. "Call me Cece," she said, shaking hands.

"Missy," said Mike, rather helplessly. Jerry looked as though he was mentally undressing her.

"Miss Titties," said Roy with emphasis.

"Okay," said Cece equably. She was in her early twenties, fresh off the farm with three brothers. "Boys got all the fun jobs," she explained to Cory and Ty. "I was supposed to help in the house, give me a break. I want to travel. Plenty of fresh air and manual labor here, just like on the farm, but here I get paid."

Roy, who had moved away, snorted in disgust.

They returned to work to find that the well had reached its target depth of four miles. Now they were drilling horizontally to tap into a long, shallow deposit. Progress had slowed to a snail's pace.

Ty showed Cece his duties. Her gloves seemed on the large side and she kept pushing her fingers into the ends of them. "Smallest they had," she said. "My size is on order. I'm fine."

"I guess there aren't many women working on rigs."

"You'd be surprised."

They walked over to the control shed adjacent to the catwalk, and he trotted out the story he'd been told, about the roughneck who had his foot crushed by a rolling pipe.

"I saw the pictures," she said. "We had a safety video in orientation. There's some pretty gruesome stuff on it." She reached for the joy stick. "So, drop the pipe onto the catwalk—" she moved the stick and they watched a length of pipe drop onto the conveyor, "and move it up to the rig." She pressed the button and the pipe moved toward the rig.

Cory found them in the powder room. Cece had no problem lifting bags of gel and mud powder. "The collars might be a problem," she admitted, "nothing else." Ty couldn't lift collars himself and was about to say so, when Cory interrupted.

"Engineer wants a bulk sample," he said. He picked up an empty cement sack. "Use this." To Ty, he said, "Roy wants you to de-ice the platform."

Ty accompanied Cory back to the rig. "What's he want a bulk sample for?" All Ty ever did was scoop a handful of mud from the clean mud tank into a baggie and take it to the engineer's hut. No one had ever complained.

Cory shrugged his shoulders but made no reply.

Ty had nearly finished de-icing when he turned toward the doghouse and saw Roy at the controls and behind him, Jerry laughing his head off, backing into Mike, who was also laughing. They staggered back together, laughing even harder. Roy grinned and said something and Cory appeared, amused, and tugged Mike's arm, and the three of them returned to the small room on the end of the doghouse.

Roy saw Ty and pointed to his left. Round the drawworks went Ty and looked over the side of the rig to see Cece struggling with a cement bag full of mud. She'd evidently had some trouble filling it because her coveralls were filthy. The sack was too heavy to carry and she was dragging it through the snow toward the mud engineer's lab. As Ty watched, she slipped and fell hard on her rear in the snow.

Howls of laughter came faintly from the doghouse. She scrambled to her feet and took hold of the sack, yanking it step by step along the ground. Ty remembered the gel in his hair. Much worse. Three days he'd had that stuff in his clothes and bed and stuck to his back. He shook his head at Cece's efforts and an unwilling laugh escaped him.

He returned to de-icing. Through the window, he saw Roy hand Mike a ten-dollar bill. So the driller had bet against her, had he?

"Last year we had a girl leasehand," said Cory later. "Roy told her to go shovel some muck. She laughed. 'No way,' she said."

Ty was staggered. "Are you kidding me?"

"'You're just saying that because I'm a girl,' she said. 'No,' said Roy. 'I'm saying it because you're the leasehand.'"

Cory paused.

"So she did it," said Ty.

"Nope. She refused. So Roy ordered her off the rig."

Cece, however, was made of stronger stuff. She seemed impervious to Roy's insults and they discovered she had a sly way of getting her own jabs in. Like the time he told her to police up the perimeter. It was a raw night with a piercing wind.

"Come on, Roy," protested Ty. "She can do that when we're on days."

"When I want your input, Tyler, I'll let you know. I expect Miss Titties to pull her weight—so to speak," he grinned and turned back to his console. "And that means cleaning up around the site. Get on out there, girlie."

The wind whistled around the rig and Cece's voice was heard, plaintively, "Without my chapstick?"

The back of Roy's neck reddened and he swiveled on his chair, but she was going out the door before he could say anything. He glared at Cory, who shrugged philosophically.

"She's yanking your chain."

Mike seemed to regard her as some sort of precocious granddaughter, and she was on good terms with him. She had no problem holding her own with Jerry either, as Ty discovered soon after she arrived. They were on graveyard, he and Jerry sitting in the doghouse waiting for the kelly to fall level with the rig platform so they could make a connection.

"Where's the DF?"

Roy's voice interrupted Ty's text messaging. He looked up, puzzled, and hazarded an educated guess. "Directional finder?"

"Jesus." Jerry shook his head. "She's down by the catwalk."

"Get her up here. That floor'll need cleaning in a minute."

The kelly was down, so they went out to add a length of pipe. "DF?" said Ty as they guided the kelly pipe over to the mousehole. "He doesn't mean—"

Jerry rolled his eyes. "Dumb fuck."

Ty was shocked. "He can't call her that!"

The winch whined, raising the newly connected piece.

"Leasehand's always the DF to Roy." Jerry added dope to the end of the pipe.

"I wasn't." Ty stabbed the new piece into the string.

Jerry looked sideways at him.

"I was?"

They torqued the connection.

"So was I when I was a leasehand. So's Miss Titties."

"Don't call her that."

The string sank into the bore.

"She is, though." Jerry smiled. "I got ahold of one the other night."

Ty was horrified. He proceeded to set Jerry straight. "You cannot treat Cece like that, Jerry! She's not one of your goddamn pinups, she's a real person, with feelings and—and standards."

Jerry was unreceptive. "Felt real good, too," he said reminiscently. "Just kinda filled my hand. Real nice." He sighed. "I was just reachin' for the other one and I'm all of a sudden on my back lookin' up at the stars." He shook his head. "Dunno how she did that."

Ty recovered. This turn was to his liking. "She say anything?"

"Yeah. 'Don't try that again, Jerry, or I might have to hurt you.'" He scuffed the floor with the toe of his boot. "Bet she could too. Those farm girls, they're grain fed and strong, man." He shook his head sadly. "Too bad. That nipple felt—"

"Shut *up!*"

After dinner, Ty managed to get Cece alone and brought up the subject of martial arts. She gave him a measured look and he added, "It's just, I heard what you did to Jerry. I'm looking for someone to practise with."

Cece was agreeable and one evening they went along to the weight room for some mock combat. "Don't be a gentleman, Ty," she said at one point, after she'd raked his nose with a palm heel, knocking him flat. "You're defending yourself against an attacker, right?" She held out a hand and pulled him upright. "So you may have to attack and you will have to learn how to put him down. It's hard because you don't want to hurt someone. But you have to be prepared to use whatever it takes, feet, elbows, whatever. Get him down before he puts you out. Now come at me again, and this time make it good."

* * *

Something was trapped in the crown block and Cory would have to climb up and investigate. Roy had felt it on the last connection, a resistance under his fingers when the kelly was lifted out of the bore.

Pipe is raised and lowered into the drill hole using a drilling cable that runs over grooves called sheaves in the crown and traveling blocks. These blocks are simply outsized pulley systems, and the sheaves are the exact size for the thick cable that weaves back and forth between them. The cable and blocks carry hundreds of tonnes of pipe weight, while the ideal bit weight is only a few tonnes. So the drawworks is adjusted to take up the extra. The crown block was located at the apex of the rig, more than a dozen feet above the monkeyboard.

Roy had phoned the toolpush, who hustled over and listened tautly in the doghouse. He'd emerged soon after, signaled to Cory and the two of them huddled on the rig floor discussing the problem. Cory waved Ty over at one point, and the toolpush scrutinized him.

"We're not going to stop drilling. Your job will be to make sure every other crew member is within your sight and well away from any controls. Got that?"

"Yes, sir."

Ty had been up to the monkeyboard twice, under Cory's instruction. All he would have to do now was to keep an eye on his crewmates on the rig platform and be ready to assist the derrickhand if necessary. He listened and watched as, using the toolpush's clipboard, Cory sketched out the topmost struts, explaining how he would proceed and what he would do. The longer Ty listened, the more anxious he became. Cory noticed, without surprise.

"What is it?"

The toolpush waited with suppressed impatience.

"You told me it was a safety rule." He looked from Cory to the toolpush. "Isn't that right? You never climb above your anchor point. Well—where's your anchor point here?" He waited but neither man spoke. "It's on the monkeyboard, isn't it?"

"Yeah." Cory put the pencil on the clipboard.

"You're going to be twelve feet above it."

"Yeah." He added, "Just means I'll freefall a bit further."

But it's a safety violation! Ty waited for some acknowledgment of this obvious point.

Cory waited for the toolpush to make up his mind.

The toolpush looked up at the top of the rig. The silence lengthened. "Get 'er done." He walked off the rig.

* * *

Cory slung a leg over the strut immediately below the apex. "Okay," he called.

Down on the platform, Roy stood next to Jerry, Mike and Cece. They were on the far side of the kelly, near the V-door, well away from the doghouse and the drawworks. If something went wrong in the bore, Roy would have to sprint back to his controls.

Standing on the monkeyboard, Ty could hear the pulsing of the pumps. He took a breath and shouted down, "Okay!" They could see for themselves, but this was the moment, officially, when Cory's limbs could be at risk. Ty glanced at the derrickhand then down at the rig floor, watching the others. Roy folded his arms. Nothing else moved.

Cory had pulled himself up and examined the crown block and his attention now seemed to be focused on the steel housing above the sheaves. He reached a hand in, attempting to dislodge something, and Ty had a vision of the drawworks starting on its own, of Cory's hand and arm disappearing into the block, of Cory screaming—. He shook his head and focused on the crew below, then the sky above.

Cory reached for a cold chisel from the tool belt on his hips, followed by a mallet. Ty glanced down quickly. No movement. He heard a single ringing *crack!* as he looked up, and thought he saw something black fly into the air. Minutes later, Cory was back with him on the monkeyboard. "Looked like a piece of bark," he said. "Petrified, like me. Frozen solid, whatever it was."

He look outward past Ty and downward, where the toolpush stood outside his trailer, watching. Cory lifted a hand and got an answering wave. The manager disappeared inside.

"So . . . safety doesn't really matter after all?" Ty was frowning. "It's just horseshit?"

"'Course it matters. But crunch time, the well gets dug. That's why we're here. Toolpush won't let anything get in the way of that."

Ty mulled this over as he climbed down the ladder. Rules applied—until they didn't. The world was not straightforward. It ought to be. But it wasn't, and he wondered how you got so you could deal with it. He talked it over with Mike in the boiler room. Mike hovered over his gauges while Ty sat on a bench cleaning rusty fittings with a wire brush. "Safety's good, Ty. The rigs used to be a lot more dangerous than they are now. But . . . the new hands are seeing videos and hearing that if it can't be done safely, we won't do it. Fact is, if we worked like that the wells wouldn't never get drilled."

* * *

Camp life suited Ty, though he wasn't aware of it. But he had no responsibilities except to do as he was told and keep his head in the game. His meals and laundry were provided. He was sleep-deprived, like everyone else; on the other hand, he did not wake up every morning with a hangover. What sleep he got was deep. A young man could go many months on this regimen. And if he was at the same time accumulating net worth at an eyebrow-raising rate he might even come to enjoy it.

His first day back in town, Axel reviewed his progress and gave him a new series of moves to learn, which kept him busy for a couple of hours. Afterward, he did his food shopping, ordered a taxi, put his groceries on the back seat and told the driver to wait. He entered the liquor store, filled a box with twelve bottles of rum and another with bottles of coke, and swaggered to the checkout.

"Oh brother," Brenda regarded him disparagingly. "What is it with you guys?"

Ty held out his credit card. "I'm just enjoying being back. Your boyfriend around?" He had dreamed that sometime in the last two weeks Brenda had broken up with Mickey and was now desperately seeking solace.

"He's picking me up at five," she said with a smile, a tinge of color in her cheeks. "We're getting married in June."

"You are?"

She nodded. "We kind of had a good talk after that dinner and we finally set the date."

She handed him his credit card and he put it away, thinking she no longer looked pale and washed out. "So . . . you're not coming to dinner again?"

She laughed. "No."

Ty picked up his boxes one under each arm. "Your loss," he said stoutly and went out to the waiting taxi.

He enjoyed the short ride out of town. The driver pulled off the road as directed near the grove and Ty paid him. He hoisted his backpack into place and watched, boxes under each arm and a bag of groceries hanging from one hand as the taxi wheeled around and headed back to town. Then he turned and walked slowly through the long grass toward the shack in the trees. Was it his imagination, or did the caragana bushes have a greenish tinge?

He heard the bark of a dog and saw the smoke almost simultaneously. He always banked the stove in the morning so someone must have lit the fire. Another bark. A dog had an awfully settled sound, as though the owner were planning to stay a while. His heart sank. He could afford to move now, but he'd come to enjoy the solitude of the shack. The dog emerged through the open door and Ty stared. It was an older dog, so it didn't bound toward him, but made its way in rather deliberate fashion and he had time to see that it was none other than his old friend Rover, the blind mutt he'd befriended in Williams Lake. He trotted up to Ty, tail wagging, and Ty crouched.

"Hey, guy," he reached for the dog. "How you doing?" Rover licked his hand avidly, sniffed at the groceries and wriggled as Ty's fingers found the sweet spots behind his ears.

"Figured it had to be you." Eric Helgeland approached, hands shoved in the pockets of his camouflage pants, beard as bushy as before. "How you doing, Ty?"

Ty got to his feet with a wide grin. “What brings you out here?” They greeted each other with slaps on the arms. “Have you stayed here before?”

“I think I know every line shack left on the prairies.” Eric helped him with the boxes and they unloaded the groceries on the wooden table. “Came here in January, didn’t we, Rover? Stayed a couple nights then moved on. Been in around Winnipeg. Came back to Moose Jaw, we’re working our way back to BC, hey guy?” A whine from Rover, lying next to the stove. “Yeah, thanks,” he said as Ty held up a bottle, “what is that, rum? You expecting company?”

Ty grinned. “Never know, do you?”

Eric laughed. “Guess not,” he agreed. He supplied a plastic mug and watched as Ty poured two drinks, then took the mug and added coke. “Years since I had a rum and coke.” He tasted it. “Anyhow, we got in this afternoon. Arrived here couple hours ago. That skunk gone?”

Ty had shooed the skunk away from the outhouse as he did on every return. “He’ll probably stay away until Sunday. That’s when I go back to camp.”

They sat in front of the fireplace. Ty stretched out his legs toward the stove and Eric raised his glass. “Rover went nuts when he smelled that bunk. I couldn’t figure who would be here, thought maybe it was his old owners. Decided to wait a bit and find out.”

“I’m sure glad you did. Listen, I got lots of food. You’ll stay, won’t you? You can have the bunk.”

“Hell no, kid. We’ll stay till tomorrow, but I’ll sleep on the floor. Slept in worst places, I can tell you.”

It was still light out. Ty buried two potatoes in the coals, then they poured fresh drinks and walked out to the stream, Rover with them. Eric was taking the southern route back to BC. "Probably hang around Williams Lake till the rodeo," he said.

They sat down on the bank, and watched Rover nose his way down to the stream, pushing his way through young foxtails, their feathery heads not yet in evidence.

"Last I heard, you were going to Fort St John," said Eric.

Ty told him about Cyrus and the hydrovac, and about getting the job with Meridian, and about the accident and how much it had cost him. "Let's get some dinner," he said and they made their way back to the shack.

"Were you hurt?"

"A little bit," said Ty. "I missed the job, but lucky for me a block of ice fell on the leasehand so I got on board the following week."

"Are you serious?" Eric shook his head. "Man, now I don't know who to be sorry for." They both laughed at that.

Once dinner was ready, they ate in silence, then Eric thought of another question. "So is that why you stayed here? Because you were broke?" And when Ty nodded, he went on, "But you're making good money now, right?"

"I'm raking it in. It's great."

He poured them both drinks and Eric heard all about tripping pipe and climbing the derrick, and preparing mud samples and moving pipe from the catwalk to the platform. Most of all he heard about Ty's mates and the crews. "They're a rough crowd, missing fingers some of them, and teeth, too.

They're sexist and racist and they often don't smell too good, either. But some of them are educated, like Cory and Cece, and all of them—all of us—have to put up with some pretty rough conditions." He poured another drink.

"Well, so why—no thanks," Eric waved the bottle away, "why go on living here?

"I'm saving money big time. Finally."

Eric shook his head. "So—you get a week off, what do you do, just sleep?"

"Yeah. And I'm learning martial arts. There's a gym in town. I work there and he gives me free lessons."

"Axel?"

"You know him?"

"Sure. We were in the same unit. Called in to see him this afternoon, but he was too busy to talk."

"He's got a lot happening. I was probably in the back counting shin pads, or I'd have seen you."

Eric harked back to the night they met. "You poking that kid in the shoulder and thinking you'd scored a knockout. Thought you were pretty good, as I recall." Ty didn't share his amusement. "What got you into martial arts?"

Ty took a long gulp of his drink and met Eric's gaze. "I had the shit kicked out of me in Kaitlin," he said evenly. "That's what."

He told Eric the story between drinks. How Crusher had wrecked his car, how Ty's comments about him had been passed on by the waitress, how they'd fought. "He totally dominated me. I was just like a rag doll, or a chew toy. I never felt so helpless in my life."

Rover whined, standing by the door, and Eric got up to let him out. "Let's grab some fresh air," he said. "Don't like to let him go far, because of coyotes."

So they stood on the porch and watched Rover fossick around the yard in the moonlight. A single car passed, the only sound other than the stream and the stirring of branches in the light wind. Ty visited the outhouse and when he returned the two men followed the dog inside.

Eric poured them both drinks. "So there you are on the barroom floor. Then what happened?"

"They dumped me by the highway." He told him about being picked up by the vet and cared for by the Williamses.

"Jesus. Didn't you go to the police? You could have frozen out there."

"I didn't know who to trust, Eric. I mean, you hear about people disappearing for years and being tied up and raped and stuff. I already knew that cop was crooked. I just wanted to get the hell out."

* * *

They talked late into the night and the following morning after breakfast they walked into town together. Eric had Rover on a leash in case he decided to drift into the road, and the little dog trotted contentedly at his heel. Ty was feeling a whole lot better with eggs and bacon and toast inside him and several cups of coffee. "You can certainly pack away the booze, kid," Eric had said over breakfast. And as they left the shack, he added, "This place is okay for a guy like me but you should be having fun with your mates."

CHAPTER

Seventeen

THE CREW ATE in silence. Everyone except for Jerry was eating hoddeok, even Roy, although he'd only taken one. It was segregated on the side of his plate of bacon and eggs and he ate it quickly, to reduce the risk of it contaminating the regular food. Ty looked over enquiringly.

"Okay, it's not bad, for Korean shit. Wouldn't want it every day but it's not bad."

Ty nudged Jerry. "Come on, Jer, just try a bite."

But Jerry crammed in another forkful of pancakes and shook his head.

Cece finished and went to get another helping, coming back with more for Cory and Ty as well.

"You guys got a broken pipe?" The speaker, smartphone in hand, was a driller from another rig.

Cece looked at him curiously as she distributed the hoddeok and sat down.

"What do you mean?" said Roy ominously.

"What I'm hearing, your toolpush is looking for a fishing expert. We've got one, on a rig out in the bush." He meant, on a rig even more remote than theirs.

He went on his way.

Cece looked along the table. "Broken pipe?"

Roy answered her as he pushed away his plate and picked up his coffee cup. "He means somewhere along the string a pipe snapped. So now we're tripping and once we clear the string we'll try to grab the snapped pipe so we can pull it up and replace it."

He finished his coffee and pushed himself back from the table, pulling out a toothpick. "Let's hope it's this side of the bend."

Cory looked at Mike. "They got fishing insurance, d'you think?"

Mike shrugged. "Hope so."

Ty looked up quickly. "What does that mean?"

Mike shrugged again. "Can take days to snag a broken pipe. Weeks even. If they don't have insurance—"

"That's enough of that, Mike." Roy looked disapproving.

"—we don't get paid."

"We'll get paid, don't you worry."

Ty sighed inwardly. No use worrying. He and Jerry exchanged looks. "Four miles to trip out," said Ty. "Assuming it's before the bend. That's—that's—" he was trying to work out how long it would take.

"Shut up and finish up," said Roy, getting to his feet.

"A shift," said Mike, and Jerry and Ty looked at each other as he added, "a shift each way. We're in for some misery."

Cory gave a short laugh. "Bet the toolpush is pleased."

The well was nearly completed and every day counted as spring break-up loomed. Delays drove up stress levels in everyone, from leasehand to toolpush.

They arrived at the rig to find the night shift hard at work tripping out. The rack had its full load of 9,000 feet of pipe and they were now coming out sideways, winching each stand over to the V-door and down to the trestles. The toolpush was already in the doghouse. "We've got an expert flying in later today, but he won't stay if he can't do his job. So work safe but work fast."

Roy quickly laid out the plan: they would work as two teams, Mike and Jerry, and Ty and Cece. Cory would operate the tugger winch, moving each stand over to the V-door. Later, when they were back on the rack, Ty would spell Cory on the derrick and Cece would do clean up. It was a neat plan and it worked, for most of the day.

They filed out of the doghouse and did stretches and knee bends while they got the rhythm. "Sure glad you're here," said one of the roughnecks briefly. He stooped to pull out the slips and stepped back as the string rose out of the ground. "Pulled a muscle in my side couple hours ago."

He would ice it when he got back to camp and hope for the best. Mike took his place as Jerry replaced the other roughneck and heaved the tongs over. Roy had already taken the chair warmed by the other driller. The three-pipe stand was unscrewed and lifted to the mousehole, where Cory took over and winched it to the V-door.

They quickly acquired a rhythm, getting the tongs on the string almost before it stopped moving, locking, loosening, spinning the connection free and sending the stand over to the mousehole, to the V-door and down to the trestles. The deck was a mess and so was the trestled pipe, dripping with mud and dope. A greasy snow was falling, large wet flakes that forced them to concentrate on their footing.

The fishing expert arrived and the medic came over to update them. The toolpush wanted to know how much longer.

Roy glanced at the weight gauge outside near the drawworks. "Another hour."

The trip out finished at midday and soon after, the toolpush arrived with the fishing expert, a small man with bottle-thick glasses and a large suitcase. Along with Roy, they clustered around the short stand, the bottom end a jagged tear.

The crew stood back, watching and listening. "Overtorqued?" "Looks like pipe fatigue." Eventually, the length of pipe was disconnected and winched over to the V-door. A forklift transported it to the machine shed and the three men followed. "Give the platform a good clean," Roy instructed, "and the pipe, too."

While the racked pipe sat in a hot-water bath that kept the ends clean and hot, Jerry and Ty hosed off all the trestled pipe, and Cece cleaned the rig platform.

* * *

The rest of the day they spent tripping in, with an impression block on the end of the pipe. The crew was disgusted, having expected to be sending down some tool that could snag the fish. To get it over with. Instead, this guaranteed they'd be tripping again tomorrow. Ty and Cece were on the tongs, while Jerry cleaned the rig floor.

The impression block was a short piece of pipe with a filled-in end. "What's it do," Ty wanted to know.

"That's lead in the end," said Mike.

"So we're sending this block thing down there just to get a picture?" Ty's voice rose on the end of the question: it was a backbreaking amount of work for a seemingly paltry result.

"They need to see how the fish is lying," Mike explained. "If it's settled, see, we need to know the angle in relation to the bore."

Cece spoke up. "Why couldn't we just send it down on a piece of rope?"

"For one, because it needs the weight of the drillstring to make an impression."

Jerry looked from Mike to Ty. "What the fuck's he mean, Ty?"

"Lead's soft," said Ty. "If this block thing lands on the fish, the ends will press into the lead." He swung the tongs over to torque a connection.

"Plus, if the broken section has settled, the mud will circulate out through the impression block and clean the top of the fish so it'll make a clean impression."

Knowing what they were doing and why did nothing for their moods. On and on they went, hour after hour of clanging and banging, punctuated by the whine of the drawworks and the tugger winch. Once the trestle pipe had gone back down the bore, Cory returned to the monkeyboard and on they went. They grabbed brief breaks when they could, glad to get away from the rig and sit in peace and quiet in the boiler room. Cece especially was finding the noise difficult.

The hours crept by. Eleven hours into the twelve-hour shift, when their minds were tired and their legs weak, Jerry gave a sharp cry and swung away from the tongs. Cece took his place and Ty joined Jerry, on his knees cradling his left hand. Blood ran over his right hand and agony distorted his features.

"Caught it in the tongs, Ty," he cried.

Ty could only think of the screwed up crew pairings. "Why the fuck d'you do that, Jer?" He glanced over at the doghouse, but Roy was already on the phone. He put an arm round Jerry's shoulders. "Gotta keep your head in the game, man," he said with rough sympathy.

The medic arrived with her bag and Ty told her what he knew, while Jerry rocked back and forth. She filled a syringe and managed to get him to hold out the injured hand.

Jerry gave a ragged sigh as the painkiller took effect. The hand trembled. "Am I gonna lose it, doc?"

It was an ugly sight, red and raw where it had split along the outer edge. Jerry held it out while the medic felt along the fingers and the outer edge. After a while, she said, "Finger's not broken, but the knuckle is and one of the metacarpals." Ty helped him to his feet as she continued, "Let's get you back to the infirmary." She rigged up a sling to hold the hand, and a few minutes later Jerry climbed carefully down the rig stairs and walked with the medic over to the trailers.

He joined them at dinner, his forearm and hand in plaster.

"They sending you home, Jer?"

"Hell, no. I wouldn't get paid then. I'm leasehand again, and Miss—and Cece is floorhand."

"That where she bit you, Jer?" One of Jerry's cronies walked by and leered at Cece. "Or did they plaster the wrong part?" He roared with laughter and returned to his own table.

* * *

The world outside was a welcome relief. That evening, Ty lay on his bed and read an email from Mattie Williams with a link to a story in the Kaitlin *Courier*. Written by Everett Brown and entitled "Pothole Paradise," the story asked if Kaitlin was getting a reputation for bad roads. A spokesman for a local law firm was quoted:

> "We hear far too much of this and frankly it's embarrassing. Drivers call us, irate over the condition of the highway and the damage they say it has caused their vehicles. We generally refer them to City Hall."
>
> When contacted for comment, Mayor Harmon advised local residents to contact the Road Works department. "Our people work very hard to keep Kaitlin's roads in top condition," he said. "We'd certainly want to look at compensation for anyone who can provide proof of damage on roads under our jurisdiction."
>
> But highway repair is a provincial rather than municipal responsibility. When asked about the issue of highway potholes, the Mayor had no comment. Nor could a spokesman for Dunstan Construction & Paving be reached for comment. Ken Marquet, scheduling manager at Dunstan, is a cousin of the Mayor's. He is currently on vacation.

Ty leaned back on the pillow and gazed up at the ceiling. So the mayor had a deal going with the paving company? They held off filling potholes, at least long enough to generate some business for the Harmons. He lifted his head to read what the law firm had said. It was immensely comforting to find he wasn't alone. Other people had hit potholes, maybe had to get work done. Only they probably had insurance so it hadn't hurt them as much.

* * *

A second day of tripping, and a third, twelve hours of bending, lifting, pushing and shoving, punctuated by the incessant clanging of the pipe and the whine of the drawworks.

The crew began to get careless. Cory dropped a stand during a trip out. Jerry yelled, Roy halted the elevator's downward path and Ty grabbed his safety harness, buckled it on and started up the ladder almost on the run.

Cory was waiting for him. The pipe leaned across the internal space of the derrick. He had his rope wrapped around it and as Ty's head came level with the monkeyboard he said, "Hook your safety onto the ladder. Then grab the elevator and snap it round the pipe." Almost before he'd finished speaking, the elevator had started up toward them. It drew level with Ty's chest and stopped. He took hold of it and snapped it around the pipe.

"Good! Now climb up here and get out of the way."

Once Ty stood on the monkeyboard, the elevator resumed its upward climb and the pipe fell to vertical once more. Then Roy lowered it, and Cory broke it out and maneuvered it over to the fingers. Ty returned to the rig floor.

Another time, Cece nearly lost a foot. They were between trips and she was pressure-washing the trestle pipe. For something to do, she washed the few remaining lengths that had yet to be attached to the string. They lay on a trestle gathering mud and debris and she hosed them down then saw a twig sticking out between two lengths of pipe. She pulled on it, and the uppermost pipe rolled over the lower, trapping her glove but luckily not her hand. She whipped it out of the glove and stepped back as the pipe continued to roll right off the trestle, narrowly missing her shin as its four hundred pounds hit the ground. She heard a yell and Ty, scrubbing pipe ends, ran to join her.

"You okay?" He found her staring at the pipe lying next to her foot. She looked up whitely.

"Fine."

Ty's glance traveled from her face to her foot. "Looking at the bones, huh?"

"Don't—say anything, okay?" She retrieved her glove and put it on. "I can't believe I could do something so stupid."

He knew the noise bothered her. "You ready to be committed yet?" He grinned at her expression. "Kidding."

"That's not such a reach," she said, and pulled out a pair of earplugs.

They finished up and walked back to the boiler room and Ty said nothing when Mike asked Cece if she was feeling okay. Then Jerry arrived to say it was time to get going and they returned to the rig floor to begin yet again.

* * *

At six pm on the third day, Roy hooked the fish. An overshot, a device designed to grip and hold the broken pipe, had been attached just before their shift began, and they had spent the day tripping in. Mike gave them the play-by-play as the overshot neared the broken pipe four miles down. Inside the doghouse, the toolpush and fishing expert looked on.

The drill string moved downward imperceptibly.

"See? They're making a note of the weight." Ty looked over to see them staring through the glass at the weight gauge. The toolpush made a note on his clipboard. "It's landed on the fish," said Mike. "Remember that lip on the lower end? That's the guide. He's using it to slide over the top and down one side. Now he'll rotate it. That opens the grapple." Mike shook his head admiringly. "He's right down in that bore with it," he said, glancing over at Roy. Through the glass, the driller could be seen motionless, hands on his controls, eyes half-closed.

They turned and watched the drillstring. Finally Ty spoke. "Ever see one of those moon landings? This is like that."

"Yeah," said Cory, "and it'll be one giant step for mankind if he hooks it."

The drill string rose slightly. The occupants of the doghouse peered intently at the weight gauge. The toolpush gave a thumbs up.

"It's hooked," said Mike. "They got a bunch of extra weight on the string."

The crew exchanged cautious looks. No one wanted to be the first to celebrate.

They were right to wait. The string rose smoothly but almost imperceptibly. The doghouse door opened and the toolpush came out followed by the expert. They stood watching tautly.

"What's the problem," Cece muttered to Ty.

"We could still drop it," said Mike as management left the platform.

“Are you serious?” Ty stared at him.

Cory spoke. “We don’t know what’s down there, or what shape the string is in, whether there’s another weak spot. Whatever.”

It was another fourteen hours, fourteen stress-filled, nerve-wracking hours of tiptoeing around, afraid to breathe, afraid of jerking the overshot loose, or jarring the string each time they put in the slips—another fourteen hours before the broken pipe emerged into the air and eager hands grabbed it. Eventually, when the string below the break had seen the light of day, the toolpush, relief in his face and voice, pronounced them ready for business again.

They tripped in for the remainder of their shift and sometime during the night, drilling recommenced.

* * *

Ty began to smile as he climbed the ladder. “I just want one last look around,” he’d told Cory. “You know, kind of saying goodbye.” The well was finished. Today was their last day, and the toolpush was about to make a speech to the troops. Ty had pestered Cory, who finally relented, checking his harness and telling him not to take forever.

He let his head fall back and looked up at the pale blue sky, feeling the sun on his shoulders. He counted absently as he always did, *thirty-three, thirty-four*. Five weeks off for the others, while the rig was dismantled and moved to its new location, north of Fort St John. Ty was pleased about that, but he couldn’t afford the time off and the toolpush had found him a job on a single in northern Alberta, a four-week job, leaving him a week's R&R before meeting the others in Fort St John. *Fifty-seven, fifty-eight.* He had ten thousand in the bank and the sun felt good. It was the first time he'd climbed the rig without full winter gear and he had on a tee shirt under his coveralls, with the sleeves rolled up. *Seventy-two, seventy-three.* Jacey's birthday was September 3. How completely he'd forgotten her! He looked back ruefully on the memory of her. Barty had said she was just a face, but Ty had refused to listen. Did you always see qualities that weren't there in people you loved? His heart contracted as he recalled those feelings, that passion. *Eighty-six*—the traveling block was next to him, stationary, its elevator empty. Relieved of half a million pounds of weight for the first time in weeks, the blocks and drawworks awaited disassembly. Mike had told him an old story about an overeager service crew that unbolted the derrick without checking for crew. The derrickhand rode the rig down and survived, but his hips were driven up into his armpits, said Mike, and he never walked again. Ty shook his head in the weak sun, putting that recollection aside. The clouds were small, puffy like cotton wool in the vast dome of the sky—except for two or three that had drifted into each other to form a larger shape like—he smiled, realizing what it reminded him of. Like Mason's galleon, sail billowing.

He looked out over the trees. Would he ever find someone real, not a face like Jacey? The air was sweet with the promise of spring and he stopped climbing for a second, then realized the monkeyboard was right above him and continued the last few steps, moving the safety line carefully to one side for Cory, hearing his instruction *(I hook it into my D-ring, first thing I do when I get up here)* and stepping onto the platform. Someone who could love wholeheartedly, someone who would want to love him and to be loved by him.

He held onto the railing and gazed southward over the forest. What would she be like, look like? Would she have a sense of humor like his sister? Would she be fanatical about some cause? Would she be a neat freak, a vegetarian, a tree hugger? He came back to the present. I'm going back to university, he vowed silently, and I'll meet someone and we'll love each other totally and she'll have my back and I'll have hers and we'll build a future together.

He smiled and turned a full circle, gazing out over the vast and peaceful land, dreaming of a sun-touched future with the girl he would love and honor and protect.

When Cory's voice came faintly to his ears, he started and looked down over the side and saw them assembled below, faces upturned. He turned toward the ladder. The monkeyboard railing extended all the way around except for the bay normally filled by the traveling block. Now the block was several feet below and as Ty approached the ladder, his foot slipped on the safety cord, lying on the platform instead of being clipped to his harness, and as he fell forward toward the gap he realized with a marrow-freezing horror he would never entirely forget that he was unattached and he grabbed for the railing and missed—

—and fell off—

—cries below—

—and the rig floor was far far below and his flailing arms hit the shoulders of the elevators, seized, grasped—

—Jesus Christ, oh Jesus Christ—

—and his fall was arrested, wrenchingly, and his cheek was pressed against the S hook and his legs flailed frantically in empty space. He stared out at the rig structure, eyes fixed, the horror of the fall still printed on his retinas, his arms wrapped around the elevator.

—hold on, Ty, bringing you down, hold on, kid—

Oh Tyley your face has green bits on it is that a good thing, do you think? No, Mason, it's not.

His vision cleared and he looked up. Sky still there, still blue. Sun still warm. He wanted to cry because the sun was warm and he could feel it. He was still alive and his body flooded with thankfulness as the traveling block began to move. Roy, in his last act as driller on this site, brought the block slowly down the rig until Ty felt the deck under his feet, and hands holding, patting, gripping him and anxious-happy faces all talking at once. His legs gave way and people helped him to a seat on the drawworks casing.

Roy stormed out of the doghouse. "Have you got shit for brains? What were you thinking?"

Ty put his face in his hands and felt Cece's arms around his knees. "Oh Ty." And Jerry bent down and peered into his face, his injured arm held awkwardly to one side. "Shit, Ty," he said, when Ty took his hands down and wiped his eyes with his sleeves, "Shit, you really had me worried there." Ty laughed along with the others. "Did I, Jer? Sorry about that. Had me a bit worried too."

The rig fell silent. Ty looked up and met the toolpush's icy gaze. A boot scraped.

"Do you think we're running an amusement park?"

He stood up. "No, sir."

"Turn around," said the medic, and began to examine Ty. He hardly noticed her.

Roy leaned against the drawworks, arms folded. The silence on the rig floor was complete.

The toolpush continued. "What were you doing up there?"

"I gave him permission," said Cory, stepping forward.

"It's all on me," Ty faced the manager as the medic turned him round. "I kept pestering him." He grimaced. "I just wanted one last look around."

He looked at Cory and then Roy. "I know how bad this looks and I'm so sorry."

"Didn't anyone teach you how to attach your safety line?" The toolpush was not appeased.

"Cory did. That's the first thing he taught me." He hung his head and added, reluctantly, "I was thinking about a girl."

A muffled snort from someone in the crowd seemed to relieve the tension.

"Good Christ, I don't believe it." The toolpush's voice rose. "Don't we tell you every day to keep your head in the game?" When Ty said nothing, he barked, "Well?"

"Yes. You do."

The toolpush became businesslike. "Okay. This is a firing offence." He looked at Roy. "It's up to you. You have to work with him. Want him fired?"

Roy stared at the rig floor. No one breathed. He straightened and addressed Ty. "You going to do that again?"

Ty shook his head mutely. The mere thought of it nauseated him.

Roy raised his voice. "Tyler's a member of my crew. He does about three times as much work as most of you assholes. So we're going to overlook his little lapse, there."

Cory grinned and so did Mike. Cece cheered and Jerry looked hugely relieved.

"Besides," Roy added, "I don't need the fuckin' paperwork."

* * *

That night, partying at the hotel, Ty got into a crap game run by a friend of a guy from one of the other crews. Mike, who had a long and unlucky history at craps tried to dissuade him from playing. If it had been earlier in the evening, when he was not quite so drunk, he might have listened. But when the subject came up he was hammered and therefore perfectly capable not only of playing but of doing well. "I fell off the rig and lived, Mike. I can do anything. Lemme show ya."

He followed Mike out to the elevator and up to one of the rooms where the game was in noisy progress. There, during the course of the next two hours, he lost five thousand dollars.

CHAPTER

Eighteen

DRINKING HIS coffee, Ty contemplated the two inches of scotch left in the bottle. Pour it out or take it with him? He pulled back the curtains. A bright, sunny spring morning. His hangover made itself felt and he turned to regard the bottle. Drink it now?

Hangovers were a part of his daily life, ever since the crap game. The month-long rig job had wound down two days ago and had consisted of twelve hours' work followed by twelve hours' booze and babes in the small town east of Grande Prairie.

The offer had come out of the blue.

"Want you to fly down to Edmonton tomorrow, Ty," said the toolpush, a tall man with wire-rimmed glasses. "One of our people wants to talk to you."

"I do something wrong?" It had been a rough month in a rough camp, but he didn't think he'd screwed up too badly. On the other hand, anyone stupid enough to fall off a rig or lose five grand in a crap game was probably capable of other idiocies.

"Not at all." That was all the toolpush said.

He learned the rest when he met with the recruitment VP. That had been yesterday. Meridian wanted to hire him fulltime and fast-track him in their engineering program. They would help to finance his education and he would spend his summers doing fieldwork. The company had drilling operations in North America, Europe and Asia, the salary was good, benefits were great and he thought he'd be a fool not to jump at the chance.

He hadn't mentioned the crap game or the fall to Barty, telling him only about the change in rigs and location. Barty was forging ahead, finishing his freshman year and trying his hand at an epic poem about the country's origins. "We're still on for Peru, right," Ty had texted. "You betcha."

Now he drank his coffee and planned his day. He had a week until he was to join the crew of Meridian 41. All he had to do was stay out of trouble until then. The best place for that was the line shack at Loon Water.

He finished the coffee, hoisted his duffel and went to the door. A quick check round the room. Leave the scotch for the hotel staff. Time for a break from booze. He was conscious of a sense of relief.

Returning the alcohol lock was the first item of business once he'd had breakfast and checked out of the hotel. He'd taken a cab to the company's local office and now he stood at the counter while the clerk recorded his details. The damn thing had been an albatross around his neck and now he was free of it.

A text arrived from Cece while he waited for a receipt. She was working on a rig west of Edmonton and he debated briefly going to see her then decided to wait until he was en route to Fort St John. He asked the clerk for directions to the nearest car rental and hoisted the duffel, now marginally lighter.

The day after the party, the four of them—Cece and Ty, Cory and Marilyn—had met for lunch at the hotel. They'd all been hung over. Cory had dropped several hundred on coke the night before and lit cigarette after cigarette between fingers that shook. Cece had a splitting headache and Ty had the worst hangover of his life.

They sat at a table on the terrace overlooking the lake and by the time they'd finished lunch, the mood had lightened.

"Hate the thought of breaking in a new driller," Cece had said. "Roy was just beginning to see things my way."

Cory and Marilyn had announced that they would soon have enough to leave the oil patch and open their own studio. They were both photographers. Marilyn had a knack for capturing people on film and had taken a picture of Ty searching for the skunk around the outhouse in the fading light. Cory's work leaned more to black and white mood pieces, mostly landscapes. But they were both talented.

"It's probably a crazy idea," said Marilyn philosophically, "when everyone takes pictures all the time. But it's what we've always wanted."

"Weddings," said Cece. "People want more than a smartphone snapshot for their weddings."

"Grads, funerals," added Ty.

"How about you, Ty?" Cece looked at him curiously. "Whole life ahead of you. What do you want to do?"

"Give him a bottle and a straw and put him in a corner," said Marilyn, "he'll be happy," and the others laughed. Ty finished his drink and ordered another. "Ty . . ." she shook her head slightly. "That's your fourth."

"Fifth," he said. "You're not my mother."

"Sorry."

"Me, too." He gave her a wry look.

Recalling that conversation now, he realized he'd never got around to telling them about his interest in alternative fuels. He walked along the street in the spring sun. Was he still interested? Would he be restricting his options if he took this job?

He'd stayed another two days in Loon Water after the others had left, spending most of his time with Axel at the gym. On Ty's last day they had a mock fight. Axel had been pleased with his progress and they had gone on to review various scenarios: being attacked from behind, by one or several aggressors, daytime or night. Ty had demonstrated his defense under each set of circumstances.

"Knowledge is power, remember," said Axel at one point. "Use every opportunity to size up your opponent. Does he look like a puncher or kicker? A wrestler? Does he come at you swinging? Has he had any training at all?" He looked at Ty. "How can you gain time to increase your knowledge?"

"Back away with my hands up."

Axel nodded. "There's another benefit, too. You want any onlookers to see that you're not the aggressor."

Ty shrugged. "Okay."

"What's the first thing the cops ask when they arrive on the scene?"

Ty had no idea.

"Who started this? Right? Now, your friend Cece, they wouldn't look twice at her because she's just a girl. But you—you're a guy and a big one. We know you're just a meek little lamb—"

"Hey!" Ty took a jab at him.

"But the cops don't know that, do they? So you back away, hands up and if anyone is watching, you make it plain that you're not looking for trouble."

"Which I'm not."

"Which you're not. And at the same time, you're watching your opponent, how he walks, how he holds his head and arms, his size, agility—"

"And I'm thinking of his opening move and what I'll do."

He was far more aware of his surroundings as a result of Axel's training. Walking along the street today he found himself sizing up approaching pedestrians, planning his defense against this man or that woman. When he caught himself doing this with a middle-aged woman, he gave himself a mental shake. He watched idly as she turned into a used car lot and walked toward the office situated in the middle.

He could see the rental-car office on the opposite corner but as he was about to cross the street, his eye was caught by the sight of a Nissan Pathfinder in the car lot. He stared at it, aware suddenly of a longing for the past, a yearning for happier times, a vague wish that he could do some things over. Then he stepped over the barrier and made his way toward the car. Same model. Same year. A sales rep materialized at his elbow.

A test drive was arranged. Haggling ensued. Before lunchtime he was the happy owner of a second Pathfinder, paid for with negligent ease on his credit card.

He swung the duffel into the back seat and climbed in. One more task and he could set off. He drove to the store he'd visited yesterday, the store across from the hotel. "I've come for that computer," he said to the clerk.

* * *

He came onto the highway heading east in the afternoon. He had last seen this stretch of country in the waning light of a midwinter afternoon. Now in late May, the somber pines were lightened by tender greens of birch and alder and maple. A road sign flashed by: Kaitlin 40. He became conscious of an elevated heart rate and relaxed his grip on the wheel. *You planning on white-knuckling it all the way there, old man?* He grinned to himself and calmed down.

The Pathfinder was behaving nicely, with only a slight tendency to pull to the right. He watched his speed and slowed slightly, gazing at the near side of the road. There! That was where he'd gone over the bank—and it was past and gone. A car went by him and he accelerated. It's history, he thought, forget it.

He'd never driven into Kaitlin but now he discovered the highway ran through town. Construction was going on near the first traffic light. He sat waiting for the gravel truck to turn, and the light to change, and thought again how like Fort St John this town was, the same busy, dusty, noisy kind of town. There was the mill, down by the river, white smoke issuing from a stack, a massive pile of logs running alongside the plant. He wondered if Bill was down there, loading hog fuel for the power plant.

He had no idea where on the highway the Harmons had dumped him, but on the assumption he had been dropped just before the first exit beyond the town—there—he reckoned the vet might have turned off at the second. It rang no bells with him, but the third exit seemed somehow familiar, and he turned off and followed a country road for a mile or so, arriving at the Williams's farm in late afternoon. He stopped at the entrance and gazed at the wooden sign: The Haven. *Who knew?* Underneath, in smaller letters, "Horse Boarding and Training." He followed the lane as trees gave way to fenced pasture and the green and brown dirt patchwork of fenced paddocks. Three long-legged colts skittered around a paddock with wooden green-and-white jumps as he came past.

Bill's semi was parked next to the barn and the pickup stood outside the house. Ty pulled in and parked next to it as the door opened and Bill appeared in jeans and a shirt with the sleeves rolled up. He said something over his shoulder and came out with a wide smile.

* * *

Ty and Mason were in the bakery section of the grocery store. Ty had his eye on a large chocolate cake. "What do you think?" he asked.

Mason, sitting piggyback, had a different idea. "Ooh Tyley, look at that one."

Ty followed the boy's pointing finger to an equally large cake with orange and green icing. "Oh yeah? That what we want?" He felt a vigorous nod and walked round the table.

"Can I carry it, Tyley? Please?"

Ty lifted the cake. "It's heavy, Mason. Better let me take it. Hang on."

They made their way through the store, looking for Bill.

Mattie had sent them into town for groceries, including a store-bought dessert. "This is worth a celebration," she'd said. Bill drove, and Ty swiveled round in his seat so he and Mason could discuss desserts.

He'd forgotten how large the child's eyes were, and how direct. There had been an awkward moment when they first met, halfway up the porch steps. He'd hugged the boy and drawn back, saying something, and Mason had pulled a face.

"Ooh, Tyley, your breath smells like Grampa's when he's had a few too many."

Mattie's jaw had dropped in horror. She looked accusingly at Bill.

"Aw, look," he said weakly. "I never said that."

"No? No? He just—pulled the words out of thin air?"

Ty had grinned and gone into the kitchen with Mason, who began to tell him all about Janice, who was Diane Huynh's granddaughter. Ty brought out a roll of breath mints. He'd taken to carrying them ever since Axel, throwing him down during one lesson, had made a comment about drinker's breath. While Mattie and Bill argued, he and Mason sat at the kitchen table sucking on mints and he heard all about Mason's first sleepover and how he and Janice had played a game on the computer, and it was evident from the boy's words that he still hadn't a computer of his own.

"Ty, I'm so sorry." Mattie was sincere, but there was also a wariness in her eyes that Ty failed to see.

"Forget it. Really. I got a job offer yesterday. Went overboard last night, I guess."

Soon after, once it had been settled that Ty would stay for dinner, she'd sent them into town for a few groceries.

They found Bill filling a bag with potatoes. The cart held nothing else. "Got talking with a school friend," he said by way of explanation, and they picked up a large milk and a dozen eggs, paid and walked out of the store.

Standing in the express line, Jodie, the waitress from the bar, girlfriend of Zack Harmon, watched Bill, then gave a start of surprise as his companion turned, laughing, and said something. She recognized him, the guy from the bar, the guy Crusher had nearly killed.

* * *

Mattie was meeting her candidate later, following a Chamber of Commerce dinner. "She wants to float some ideas on zoning but it's really more of a meet and greet. They know her husband better than her."

The contrast with his earlier stay played in the back of Ty's mind through dinner. February had been freezing and dark and he'd been hurting and deep in debt, but now Mattie had the beginnings of a summer tan and so did Mason, and the kitchen was bright with evening sun.

Bill looked at Ty ruefully. “Getting rid of Fred isn’t going to be easy. He’s kept taxes low—”

“We like that,” Mattie interrupted. “And getting people out to vote is like pulling teeth.”

Bill changed the subject. “Remember Arnie? Tow truck? He’s set up a branch in town. Now there’s no more Harmon monopoly on highway towing, he gets his share.”

“Fred denied there ever was a monopoly,” said Mattie. “And now that the potholes are getting fixed on time, the towing volume’s gone down.” Bill began to remove the plates as she went on, “No one minds if oil companies have to pay to get their vehicles towed or fixed. But we very much do mind when it’s tourists or penniless college students. It’s like preying on the weak and helpless.”

Ty laughed. “I was called a lamb not long ago, so I guess weak and helpless is about right.”

Mason looked interested. “Why were you called a lamb, Tyley?”

“Because I wasn’t ba-a-a-ad enough,” he said, and Mason laughed.

Then Bill brought the cake to the table along with a knife and plates and forks, and Mattie served it and they all agreed it was wonderful.

“I bumped into Jodie Paterson,” said Bill as he ate. “She’s talking about moving to Ontario, be with her parents.”

“Hasn’t she married?”

“Involved with a married man.”

Ty might have followed this conversation except that Mason had got himself into difficulties trying to emulate his hero by taking big mouthfuls. His mouth was now so crammed with cake that he was unable to chew, and icing was oozing out and down his cheeks. His eyes held a mute plea, and Ty resisted the urge to laugh, turned Mason's head toward him and using a teaspoon carefully excavated, removing a large portion of cake. Suddenly freed, Mason's jaws began to work overtime and he gave Ty a look of gratitude and bent his head to hide his embarrassment.

Mattie insisted he stay put when dinner was over, while she and Bill did the dishes. So he listened as Mason told him all about the Huynhs, and how Janice was descended from boat people who got attacked by pirates looking for their gold, and by sharks. Then it was time for his bath and he hugged Tyler and took himself off upstairs.

Dishes done, Bill scribbled a list of names while Mattie rummaged in her purse for lipstick. She took the list as Bill said, "Make sure she gets in front of them. They all said they'll listen to what she has to say." He pointed to a name. "He's having trouble with his new car."

"Oh come on!" Mattie was skeptical.

"I'm just saying," Bill replied. "He might be a little pissed off with Fred right now."

"Why don't you both go?" Ty leaned back at the table.

They regarded him.

"No way," said Bill.

Mattie's face had lightened momentarily, then she turned away.

"Look." Ty lowered his voice. "I brought Mason a computer. That's really why I came. You were so good to me last

February. I wanted to do something for you and this seemed like a good idea." He added, as they exchanged a glance, "If you're not quite ready, you could put it away for a while, no harm done."

"No, listen, Ty." Bill stopped, then added, "We're on board with the idea, but—"

"It's incredibly generous of you," Mattie said, reluctantly, She had difficulty meeting Ty's gaze.

"I remember how bad off I was back then. You didn't have to keep me here. You could have sent me off to the hospital."

He won his point eventually and after they had thanked him, he reverted to the meeting. "Why don't you both go? Tell me where you want this and I'll set it up. I thought the front room, where all his books are, but whatever. I bought a hard drive, so it could stay in one place where you could watch. There's a desk and printer, too."

Mattie remained silent but Bill was tempted. "You're going to stay for a while, aren't you? Couple days, anyway?"

"Bill," Mattie protested, "we can't just leave Ty to baby-sit when he's just got here." But Bill had come round to the idea and went upstairs to change. Mason had gone to bed when Ty went out to unload his car.

"Tyler."

He straightened and turned, arms full of computer boxes. Mattie was studying him.

"Are you going to be drinking this evening?"

He met her gaze then turned away, partly to put the boxes down again and partly to hide the hatred that shot through him. She had no right to ask that.

He faced her again and smiled. "Guess that's a fair question. I'm taking a break from booze, so the answer's no."

Mattie's gaze faltered. "I'm sorry, Ty. But I had to ask." She crossed her arms and came down the porch steps, staring at the hardpan. She lifted her head. "Bill and I have the occasional beer. But my dad's a drinker, as you may have guessed."

"Yeah."

Her eyes moved from the paddock to the barn. "He nearly drank this farm into the ground. We're slowly getting back on our feet. . . ." She studied Ty as though wondering if she could believe him.

"I brought nothing to drink, Mattie." He added, "I wasn't planning to stay."

Her features relaxed and she smiled and touched his arm. "Of course you'll stay. For as long as you can."

* * *

The first attack came an hour later. He had the computer set up on its small table with the adjustable swivel chair. He stepped back, admiring the set-up, and Mattie's words still rankled and he wished he had a drink.

No drink. No bottle. He cleared away the boxes, flattening them into a neat pile on the porch. No bottles in the car, none in his duffel. He knew this, yet he must look. He went out to the yard and emptied his duffel on the back seat of the car. He'd had a mickey in there at one time. Socks, shirts . . . not anymore.

He'd been deliberate this morning, when he'd left the bottle at the hotel. *I need a day off.* One day. Maybe two. It depended on the Williamses. If he wasn't invited to stay at the farm, he'd had some thought of driving on, stopping at the first motel he found. He'd been vague beyond that point.

I need a day off. His desire shot up. His tongue twitched, anticipating the bite of the scotch. Whisky had become his beverage of choice when he tired of buying mixer. He paced the yard in a circle, then took the porch steps two at a time and returned inside.

Bill and I have the occasional beer. Nothing in the fridge—nothing on the bottom shelf at the back, nothing in the freezer. Basement? He was searching, bent over, the low-ceiling basement when the phone rang. He ignored it but it rang on and on. Up the stairs. Calm down. He lifted the receiver. It was Bill.

"It's a real barnstormer here. You know, she might actually have a chance." Ty eyed the kitchen cupboards only half-listening. "Where were you? Everything okay?"

They were checking up on him. His respect for Mattie shot up, along with his dislike. She was too clever to phone herself; instead she'd got Bill to do it. "Sure, Bill, everything's fine. Computer's all set up and ready to go." Start with the bottom cupboards. Bill rang off and Ty began a systematic search of the kitchen cupboards, his hands moving rapidly among the pots and pans, dried goods, canned goods, dishes. He could taste it, oh God!, he could taste it.

"Fuck!" He'd searched under the sink, the last cupboard, finding nothing but a garbage container, a sack of potatoes and various household cleaners.

He got to his feet and began to close cupboard doors. "Fuck, fuck, fuck!" He swiped at a canister on the counter.

The lid flew off and flour cut a swathe through the air, drifting lazily to the tile floor.

His vision cleared. He looked at the floor, at the open cupboard doors. "Jesus," he muttered. He found a broom outside the kitchen door and a dustpan in the hall closet.

Cleaning the floor took a long time. He was painstaking about it. Then he sat down at the kitchen table. He was dying for a drink. "I can't do this," he said out loud and set about making a plan. He could bundle Mason into the back seat, he'd probably never wake, and drive into town. He checked the time. Too late for the liquor store but he could buy a bottle at a hotel or bar.

He was calmer now that he had a solution. He put on his jacket, checked for his keys and climbed the stairs. He tried to take his time opening Mason's door but the thirst was upon him again and he had to get moving.

The boy was lying on his stomach, head turned toward the opposite wall, hands tucked under the pillow. Ty began to plan how to lift him, blankets and all. He reached for him.

You cannot do this, Hogan. You really cannot do this. He suddenly remembered Lydia Choi, and how he had been too drunk to hear her crying. "That was different," he muttered.

Damn right—it was far less than this.

He took a step backward. Did he seriously think he could drive into town with Mason? What if his parents came back? What if he woke during the ride? What if—even in Ty's fevered state the irony did not escape him—what if he hit a pothole?

A sigh escaped him and he took another step back. "Think about this," he muttered and backed out of the room and closed the door. There was nothing to think about. He couldn't drive into town with the boy.

He returned to the kitchen. Well, then, without him. He could be in and back in no more than forty minutes. "He'll never wake." He spoke aloud to the empty room, waiting for approval. *Let's do it.*

"He'll never wake." He was outside, with his hand on the car door. An anguished pause. "Oh Christ!" He bowed his head on the car roof, then looked up at the night sky. "Oh Christ Almighty."

A whinny drifted across the paddock from one of the colts, then silence. A breeze brought the scent of hay and horses from the barn. "Well," he said to himself at last, "think of it as a camp night. That's all it is."

He returned inside.

"Is dad an alcoholic?" He'd been about thirteen at the time, drying the dishes while his mother washed, and she had stared at the soap container for a minute. "Yes, I think he is." She rinsed a plate. "Years ago I asked my doctor the same question. He said, 'Anyone who has more than one drink a day is an alcoholic.'"

"Wow," said Ty. "Did you tell dad?"

"No." She set the plate in the rack. "I changed doctors."

This struck Ty as funny and he began to laugh. Annie put the mop down and laughed too, leaning against the fridge with her arms folded, oblivious of her wet rubber gloves. "He was a prissy man," she said. "I didn't like him for other reasons but that answer was so dogmatic I just felt he didn't really see people as individuals but as pegs to fit into holes like on a crib board."

Ty sat at the kitchen table remembering that conversation. His dad was forty-eight now. Did he ever think of quitting? Did he ever even try? Even two weeks off and one week on would probably help him. It hadn't hurt Ty. Every time he went off to camp he'd known the structure of the next fourteen days. He'd been okay with that because then he'd have a week to himself. You could quit easily if you knew there was an end to it. "Hell, I could quit for a month if I wanted, or even a year." So that made him a binge drinker, not an alcoholic.

The clarification calmed him and he sat at the table contemplating a few dry days until a thought wormed its way into his mind. *But you're getting worse.*

He attacked this proposition hard but it refused to go away. He drank more than he had at home with Barty; he didn't care any longer if he drank alone; and he no longer bothered to measure. He just filled the glass. *Shit, why bother with a glass?* In ten years' time, would it be easy to quit for two weeks? In twenty? Would he still be having this battle when he was his dad's age? When he was sixty? If I quit now, he thought suddenly, I'd be done with it.

A life without booze suddenly filled his mind's eye and it was as though he was falling off the monkeyboard all over again. Terror tightened the skin of his arms and legs and pricked the back of his neck. He heard a whimper and stood up so fast the chair fell over. He stumbled up the stairs and only just stopped himself from barging into Mason's room and hiding under his bed.

He slid down the wall outside the bedroom and hugged his knees. He could feel the thud of his heart and he bowed his head and closed his eyes. He stayed that way for a long while, thinking of home and his bedroom and hiking. When he raised his head it was with the thought, Don't look down, look up. In his mind's eye he saw again that vast limitless prairie sky. It poured into the dark corners of his mind, brightening, lifting, and he felt a strange lightness of spirit. He sat motionless, savoring it, feeling it warm him through.

* * *

Ty walked back past the manure spreader to close the gate, then returned to the tractor and continued on to the barn. Ten minutes later, the tractor and spreader parked tight against the east wall, he climbed down and smiled and stretched in the afternoon sun. He would have another session tomorrow and the day after, and the day after that. Spreading manure would be part of his keep-busy routine for the next week, disposing of the winter's accumulation of horse droppings.

He was finding the new Tyler Hogan disconcerting, a person who seemed to veer from exhilaration to uncertainty to nervousness and back again. He wished once more that he hadn't told Bill and Mattie, but the matter had been taken out of his hands last night, after they returned from their meeting.

They had admired the computer and then sat round the kitchen table comparing notes and telling Ty about their evening's work. He'd been content to listen until Bill realized the time and said he had to get to bed. "I'm off on my rounds tomorrow. Want to come?" He stood up, looking down at Ty.

"No." Short, emphatic. Involuntary.

Mattie's face fell. "Are you leaving?"

"No." That had also burst out, but with a tinge of alarm. He came to his feet trying to process a series of sharp, emotional messages that all amounted to the same thing. He did not want to go anywhere near a town and he did not want to cope with anything unexpected. Eventually, reluctantly, he'd explained.

"I've quit drinking."

Mattie's hands went, prayer-like, to her mouth, her eyes fixed on him. Bill took a step toward him and stopped.

Ty frowned down at the table, trying to think of what to say. "That's all," he said at last.

A silence.

Bill said, "That's a man-size decision."

"I mean it."

"I see that. What can we do to help?"

"Everything's . . . I just have to get my bearings."

"Understandable." Mattie got to her feet. She turned away, but not before he saw her wipe her eyes.

This morning, Bill had left in the semi after breakfast. He was off to one of the logging concessions in the hills, where he would pick up a load of logs for the mill. After that he'd be carrying hog fuel or wood chips south. He'd be away for three days and Ty would help the hired hand.

Mason had gone off to kindergarten, climbing into a van full of kids being driven by another mother. Mattie had lessons all morning, schooling horses and riders, and Ty helped to muck out the stables and water the horses. The Williamses wanted him to stay until his next job, and that suited him fine. After lunch, he and Mason went exploring for a couple of hours and that first day, the boy showed him his favorite lookout rock and a cave barely big enough for a six-year-old. Then they carried on to the perimeter of the property and walked along to the road, then down to the driveway and back alongside the paddock where the colts greeted them.

After lunch, Mason was shown the computer. He'd been dumbstruck, but only for a moment, then he watched intently as Ty started the hard drive. Once the computer had booted, he learned how to log on. He thanked Ty, but absently, and Mattie frowned. Ty gave her a small shake of his head: no offense taken. They discovered he had picked up the rudiments from his friend Janice: he knew how to use a mouse and how to pick out words on the keyboard. Ty logged him onto Khan Academy and they left him absorbed in Early Math.

Now, as Ty crossed the yard on his way to check on the colts in the paddock, Mattie came out of the house with her purse and car key. "I'm off into town. Weekly shop."

Ty nodded toward the living room. "How's he doing?"

"Completely absorbed." She glanced at her watch. "I should be back in a couple of hours, but if not, pull him off it, will you, Ty?"

"Yeah, sure."

He walked with her over to the vehicles, and leaned against the Pathfinder, watching, as she opened the door of the pickup. She looked over. "You'll be okay?"

"Absolutely."

She pulled out a lengthy shopping list. "Favorite soft drink?"

He waved it off. "Don't worry about it."

"No, really. What do you like? Bill likes Coke."

"There you go."

She laughed and made a note and he glanced away. Even a small kindness made his eyes prickle. If anyone had told him yesterday quitting would turn him into a weak emotional fool, he might have reconsidered.

Mattie was talking.

"—little stinker was playing with the lazy Susan again." She put her list away. "He likes to arrange the cans by size or color, instead of food group. Makes it harder to find out what I'm low on." She glanced at Ty then peered more closely. "What?"

"Don't blame Mason."

She gazed and gazed and gazed at him.

"You must have been annoyed not to find anything," she said at last and he thought she chose her words with care.

"I was." He shoved his hands in his back pockets and looked her in the eye. "Mason was in real danger last night, Mattie. You were right to be concerned, and—well, I'm sorry."

She looked out at the paddock and he wondered what she was thinking. "Cut yourself some slack, Ty," she said at last. "See you later."

She drove off up the narrow lane and he watched her go, then went inside and peeked at Mason. The boy was completely absorbed in the screen. Ty could see rows of things and hear, faintly, a man's voice talking.

He returned outside and walked over to the paddock and one of the colts joined him, snuffling and whuffling at his shirt-front. "Hiya, boy," Ty put his cheek against the horse's neck and breathed in the horse smell, and slapped his flank. The others joined them and he looked into their dark eyes and smoothed his hand over their sides and felt strength flow through his own body.

* * *

The truck came while he was preparing to fill the colts' water trough. He had dragged the hose over to the paddock and had walked back to the barn to turn on the tap when he heard it. The sun had just dropped below the trees and a blue Toyota Tundra came down the road and into the yard. Three men inside. Crusher Harmon got out of a back seat. He carried a baseball bat and he headed straight for Ty, slapping it in his palm.

"What the hell do you want?" Ty's stomach churned.

"I shoulda killed you before," said Crusher. "My brother's gonna lose his job because of you." He stopped, contemplating his victim, and the bat slapped against his palm.

"Don't be ridiculous. Jesus!" Ty ducked as Crusher took a step and swung the bat.

Oh Christ! How do you block a baseball bat? "It's your own stupid fault, not mine!" He ducked again and stepped back, driven by Crusher and his bat. His mind scrabbled blankly for tactics but his body, responding to months of practice, began to react automatically. His knees flexed and he forgot he was wearing work boots as he balanced on the balls of his feet, dodging, watching those deep-set, piggy eyes for clues.

He backed into the barn wall and there was a reverberating crack as the bat met the wall next to his head. Crusher tossed the bat aside and drove a fist into his face, deflecting Ty's block as he did so. Dizzy, Ty slid down the wall and Harmon reached down, dragged him upright and began to slam him against the wall with barn-shaking strength, bellowing incomprehensibly. A horse whinnied in the barn.

Ty looked into his eyes and the fleshy cheeks and kicked Crusher's knee, scraping his boot down the big man's shin. That registered, and Crusher's grip relaxed. Ty drove the heel of his left hand upward into the man's forearm. He bent his right arm and drove the elbow with all his strength into Crusher's breastbone.

It was just enough to free him, and he bolted toward the house, then saw with horror that Mason had come out onto the porch. He yelled frantically, "Get inside!"

Two men got out of the truck: Zack Harmon and Joe Feeney, the transferred RCMP officer, out of uniform.

He heard Crusher following and he turned on the hardpan, arms up, watching him. His mind cleared and he realized suddenly how easy anything could be if you only wanted it bad enough.

"I don't want any trouble," he said, backing away, a smile in his heart.

"You're dead meat, Hogan," said Crusher, coming at him with raised fists.

"Dream on, you sack of shit." Ty stepped forward, blocked one punch—a punch that, in February, had hurled him backwards over a bar table—blocked another, then palm heel up, up into Crusher's face, raking his chin, his nose, driving his head back, exposing his throat. The big man staggered back. Ty could feel the power coursing through his body and he stepped forward, whirled and launched himself. He heard a yell and drove his boot into a spot just below the collarbone. Crusher went down without a sound. Ty savored the sight of his prone, motionless form.

"I could have killed you if I'd been two inches higher," he said. He remembered Axel telling him how black belts might be charged with using a dangerous weapon if they abused their skills.

"Tyley!" It was a scream from behind and he ducked reflexively and turned. Feeney had picked up the bat and taken a swing at him. Now Ty crouched, circling, as the cop did the same. Ty sized him up. He'd had some training, probably more than Ty, but he looked somehow soft and unfit. Ty faked a move leftward, prompting a kick. He grabbed for the booted foot but missed. Zack Harmon stayed near the truck.

You moved the tongs with your back and thighs, centering the movement in your core. Ty stepped in, grabbed Feeney's right inner forearm, swung him off balance. Still holding the forearm he applied his other hand to Feeney's wrist, threw, used his knee, twisted . . . joint manipulation. Feeney screeched and fell onto his side.

"You won't be writing any tickets for a while." He sprang back.

Holding his arm, Feeney got to one knee, began to rise, half turned away. Ty kicked him hard in the kidneys and he cried out and collapsed onto his stomach. Crusher was beginning to move.

Ty felt almost euphoric. He could do this all evening if he had to. He could go on until they were broken and bleeding on the ground. They would not hurt him nor the child in his care. He focused on the only standing assailant.

"You want some of this?"

Zach shook his head. "Not my idea. Sorry." He came slowly forward, stopping next to his brother. He looked at Ty for permission.

"I'll get him into the truck, okay?"

"Why does he think I'm to blame?"

Zack grimaced. "Jodie told us last night she'd seen you with Bill Williams." He stared at Feeney, groaning on the ground. "Joe started working on Arthur, going on and on about how you were to blame. It got so I couldn't control him."

"And you didn't think of calling for help?"

Zack's eyes shifted. He'd never done that before, why start now? He shrugged and Ty shook his head.

In the end, Zack helped his brother while Ty grabbed a fistful of Feeney's collar and hauled him to his feet. He walked him, stumbling, over to the truck and shoved him in next to Crusher. Zack came round and climbed in the driver's side, and moments later, the truck was gone, back up the lane to the road.

Ty walked back to the porch where Mason stood, shivering with excitement.

"Oh Tyley," he said, his eyes shining. Ty smiled into them and it was easy to meet the boy's gaze, easy to let him see inside. He wrapped his arms around Mason and lifted him up, exulting.

"Thanks for the warning, partner."

"Oh Tyley, you were beautiful."

CHAPTER

Nineteen

THE GRASSLANDS of the Peace River were dotted with bales of hay, brown cylinders against the deep green. It was the second week in August and Ty was heading home.

He could hardly wait and, try though he might, he could not keep his foot off the accelerator. The job had been plagued with delays and had only been completed this morning. He'd come off his last night shift, said goodbye to his crewmates and set off immediately for Fort St John, five hours to the south. He'd arrived at the Chois, packed his belongings, had a quick lunch with them and taken off.

He planned to drive straight through. That would give him a day and a half with his family before leaving with Barty for Peru. He saw an elk by the roadside, grazing the thick long green grass, and slowed as he passed. The grass was shot through with yellow and red flowers. The red ones were called Indian paintbrush, according to Marilyn. The yellow looked like dandelions. Whatever. Along with the aspens and firs, they made a lush contrast to the bleak, bare terrain he'd seen in January.

His speed crept up again and he let the cruise control take over. The miles ticked by and he left the Peace and saw the meandering Fraser River in the distance. In the heat and glare of the late-afternoon sun he came to the outskirts of Prince George and was pulled over for speeding. He glanced at his watch as the prowl car pulled in behind him and waited impatiently for the cop to reach his window. "Do you know what speed you were driving, sir?" Ty said he did and apologized and handed over his license and registration and waited some more, sweltering in the August heat.

Eventually the cop returned. "Step out of the car, please, Mr. Hogan."

Ty climbed out, quelling his impatience. He walked a straight line as instructed, then stopped, facing the cop. "I can maybe save you some time," he said. "I don't drink." He looked at the cop and added, "I'm an alcoholic."

"Oh?" He was given careful scrutiny. "When did you last have a drink?"

"Two and a half months ago."

The cop studied him, nodded and said, "Get back in your car." And as Ty did so, he asked, "Quit cold turkey?"

"Yeah, I did."

The cop leaned over, one hand resting on the door. "You ever try those non-alcoholic drinks?"

Ty glanced at him. "They're a waste of money," he said. "All they do is make you feel deprived. Here's what I use." He reached over to the glove compartment and took out a chocolate bar. "Doesn't mix with booze. But everyone's different. That's just what works for me."

The cop looked from the bar to Ty. "No kidding." He nodded and stepped back. "Good luck. And watch your speed."

"I will. Thanks." He drove on with a smile.

Barty had been okay with his nondrinking status. "We're cool," he'd texted and confirmed that the Peru trip was still on. He was racing to finish his epic poem. He'd found an artist to illustrate it and they planned to self-publish in the fall.

People were helpful when they discovered he'd quit drinking. One of his first tasks was to apologize properly to the Chois, acknowledging that he'd betrayed their trust and explaining that he'd quit drinking for good. Mrs. Choi's features had relaxed and when a spare room came free, they offered it to Ty. Mr. Choi had told him an AA meeting took place regularly in the basement of the Presbyterian church. Marilyn had been glad to go with him. He had great respect for the people he met there, but found he didn't care for the philosophy. "Surrender myself to a higher power? I don't think so."

At the second meeting, he bumped into Pulaski, and thereafter he often met the Grizzly manager for coffee in the evenings of his week off.

He stopped for a hamburger, then drove on until he had trouble keeping his eyes open, pulled in at the entrance to a logging road and slept for a few hours. He was on the road again before daylight and came into Vancouver with the August rush hour traffic. He reached the terminal in time for the mid-morning ferry and stretched his legs before returning to the car for loading. He was idly watching the cars disembarking when he saw the airport bus come down the ramp, a Barty lookalike at one window. He grinned. That would be him and Barty day after tomorrow. He took out his phone and called Barty's number. No answer, no voice mail. He sat up, bothered, and called Cathy's number. There was gladness in her voice. "Gosh, it'll be good to see you, Ty."

"Listen, Cath, let me speak to Barty, okay?" An infinitesimal pause. "He's there, isn't he?" They shared an apartment.

"I'll call you back, Ty. Give me a minute." Over his protests, she added, "Just a minute."

She rang off and Ty sat up, worried. Tempted to call his mother, he held off, and a moment later Cathy called back.

"Oh Tyler, this is awful." Now he heard shame in her voice. "He's gone already. He left this morning with that—with Luke Aragio. Oh Ty. I moved back home last month because he doesn't want me around."

Barty had never mentioned that. "What flight?" Loading had started and the lane next to his was moving. "Find out what flight and what time, okay?"

By the time she called back he had been waved out of the loading line, guided through to an exit lane, onto a narrow road leading up to the highway.

* * *

He'd been standing at the international departure gate for more than hour when they arrived. He barely noticed Aragio. Barty was thinner than he remembered, almost gaunt, and very pale. He slung his backpack onto the x-ray conveyor line and glanced across it, straight into Ty's face. Ty couldn't have said which hurt him more: the look of horror on Barty's face or his violent start of fright. He turned for the x-ray screen entranceway.

"Bart! Barty!"

But Barty ignored him, stopping in the entranceway barely long enough to be wanded down. He grabbed his pack and scuttled down the corridor, his shoulders hunched. Ty could see him through the Plexiglas, followed by Aragio, blocked by other passengers, Barty, his buddy and best friend, gone. Ignoring the pain in his chest he stood motionless, one hand clenched around the glass edge that jutted out at right angles, stopping those without tickets from entering the departure area.

Sometime later he turned away. A long time later he returned through rush hour to the ferry. When he reached home, the front door opened in the dusk light and his mother was waiting there. "My poor boy," she said and put her arms around him, "my love." He embraced her and the familiar scents of mum and home greeted him. Emma came tumbling downstairs and the tears ran down her cheeks when she saw the loss in his face. "Oh Ty, Tyguy, I'm so sorry," and they stood together, the three of them embracing in the hall.

"My fault," said Ty eventually, over their objections. But he still loved Barty and couldn't bear to hear ill of him. "I wasn't being honest. I wanted that trip so badly and I was sure I could pull it off. But I didn't think about how Barty would feel, being with a guy who was always sober. I didn't want to think about that."

He could see they disagreed but he knew he was right. He'd wished that trip into his reality, but wishing didn't make it so. Pulaski had told him: "Gotta learn to be honest with yourself, kid. No bullshit."

* * *

It was later in the evening, and friend after friend phoned, then dropped by. Jason had brought Cathy, eyes red-rimmed from crying. "I thought you'd be able to talk to him," she said, as Ty hugged her.

"I wouldn't do that, Cath." And when she seemed to need more, he added, "A guy's addiction, it's a boundary you don't cross unless he gives you permission."

Alex arrived. He had dropped out, he informed Ty. He'd flunked his first year and was finally doing what he'd always wanted: becoming a plumber like his dad.

The house became crowded. Annie and Emma stayed close. Ty was their possession and while they might let others have a little piece of him, they weren't giving up their own ground, not so soon after his return.

Jason opened another beer from the six-pack he'd brought with him. "I asked your mum," he said to Ty, "You don't mind, do you?"

"No way." Ty took a brownie from a plate that materialized like magic and grinned up at his mother. Her hand caressed his cheek and she smiled down at him and was quickly surrounded by hungry students.

Jason went on, "I can't believe Barty." He swigged some beer. "What a crap friend." He glowered at Ty, hurting for him. "I never would have believed it, Ty. Never."

Ty turned away. "Leave it, Jay."

"What?"

"He was the best friend I ever had. That's all."

Another friend joined them and noting the coffee mug in Ty's hand, wanted to know if he seriously had quit. "It's just bizarre not seeing you with a beer."

"Yeah, I quit," said Ty, and added, "It's no big."

Sitting nearby, Emma heard and turned. "It's hugely big," she responded quickly and he met her glance.

"Yeah."

Someone asked what he'd been doing all these months.

"I did a lot of cleaning," said Ty with a straight face. "And got well paid for it."

Jason looked at him. "For crying out loud, Ty."

Ty laughed. "I learned how to fight. Kicking, boxing, you know. Martial arts."

Alex invited him to demonstrate so the party moved outside to the lawn. Alex was a wrestler and managed to pin his opponent two out of three times, and Ty made a note to learn some strategies for beating him.

Still later, he overheard Jason and Emma discussing her off-the-grid adventures. She and her boyfriend were going to become energy self-sufficient, she told him. "You wouldn't believe all the red tape involved. Going off-grid isn't as easy as I thought."

Ty put an arm around her shoulders. "Know what I learned, Em? Sometimes you have to bend the rules to get 'er done."

Chapter Twenty

On the Tuesday after Labour Day, Ty presented himself at the Dean's office. He sat in a chair near another male student on one side of a large waiting area. It was filled with light from a domed skylight in the center. The chairs and coffee table on Ty's side were duplicated on the opposite side, where a couple of girls sat waiting. This was the Deans' office, the Dean of Women occupying one side and the Dean of Men the other.

The student next to him was called, and Ty straightened. He had not been back here since last December. He couldn't make himself believe the Dean would deny him entry; nevertheless he was conscious of a slight tension. His eyes happened to meet those of the Dean's assistant and he smiled vaguely. She nodded briskly.

Under the skylight was a work island consisting of two desks, one for each of the two assistants, and several filing cabinets.

He gazed at a painting on the wall that faced the offices, an oil painting of a fishing trawler in rough water, crew members in yellow slickers, whitecaps on the waves, riding lights showing red in the rigging. He walked over to study it more closely and heard an assistant telling the waiting girl to step inside. He half-turned to check that no one wanted him and his gaze fell on the girl coming his way, a girl who had presumably concluded her meeting with the Dean of Women and was now leaving. She returned his look and stopped.

Ty had never seen the girl before but he knew at once he would do everything in his power to see her again. She was slender, wearing a teeshirt and capris and sandals, a loaded satchel on a broad leather strap over one shoulder. She had a beautiful figure and a neck that was just right, and her face . . .

"Hi," he said.

Her eyes moved to his face. "Hi . . . have we met?" She stopped.

"We have now. I'm Ty—Tyler Hogan." He stepped toward her, smiling, hand extended, just as the Dean's assistant spoke.

"The Dean will see you now, Mr. Hogan."

"Yes," he said vaguely in her direction. His eyes returned to the girl. She had a straight nose and dark eyebrows and eyes, and her hair was tumbled, thick, chestnut in color.

She had a cool, firm handshake. Neither of them seemed able to let go or to look away. "We've met," she said. Her mouth was wide, the lips upturned at the corners. It seemed exactly the right mouth to him.

"I'd know," said Ty.

"Kaitlin," she said and that broke the spell. She was taken aback at his reaction. "Kaitlin Grant. Why?"

Ty shook his head. "I guess I can—"

"Mr. Hogan!"

"—handle it." He turned to the assistant. "In a minute, okay?"

"You have something against Kaitlins?"

"Not against this one." He debated how much to tell her. "There's a town named after you in Alberta, did you know that?" She shook her head.

The assistant materialized at his elbow, a middle-aged woman with a large bosom under a tailored suit. "Mr. Hogan, do you really want to do this? Miss your appointment?"

"How about meeting me for coffee later?" He glanced at the assistant, "I'll be right there, promise." When he looked back, Kaitlin had a hand to her mouth.

"Oh my God."

"What?"

Her eyes had seemed like pools in which he might drown. Now they became sparkling pools, buoyant, dancing. Amusement and then something like amazement crossed her face.

"You're the one who nearly killed me. You're the one who rammed into our tree."

Ty could recall that night, nearly a year ago. But he tried in vain to remember her. He knew someone had been in his face, someone other than the constable, but for the life of him he couldn't recall her. He said so, contritely.

Kaitlin shook her head. "It doesn't matter. Listen—you know where I live, right?"

He nodded.

"I'll be home later. Come by for a drink. I've got a bottle of wine—" she stopped abruptly, then she smiled up at him and finished, deliberately, "that I've been saving for a special occasion."

"Sounds great," he was drowning in her eyes. "Oh!" He remembered.

"What?"

"Look—"

"Mr. Hogan. You have to come."

Ty wheeled around to face the assistant and bellowed, "Go away! I'm busy!"

The assistant's face flamed scarlet and she swept back to her desk. The Dean's office door opened but Ty had already turned away.

"Listen, Kaitlin." He wondered what to say, fearful of saying the wrong thing.

"What's wrong?"

Conflicting thoughts scrabbled through his mind—*just tonight have a drink—don't tell her—tell her now—tell her later—*"

"What is it, Ty?"

There was a chocolate bar in his shirt pocket. He took a breath. "Here's the deal. I don't drink any more. I'm so so sorry but I don't." One eyebrow went up, but he hurried on before she could say anything. "Not ever."

Her face seemed to alter somehow, but he could never work out exactly how until he saw the same expression after they'd made love. Her eyes became pools again. "Well, fine, we'll have coffee. Or tea. Whatever."

"But you can drink." He was anxious that she not feel deprived. "In fact, I'm perfectly okay with that. Honest."

She came close and kissed his cheek. Her lips were soft. "We'll work something out." She stepped back, smiling. "Okay?"

"Okay. Well, okay! I mean, I'll see you later." She smiled and turned toward the door. "Kaitlin?" She looked around. "Nothing—nothing." She returned his smile, then she was through the door and gone. He sighed and turned. He could have been walking on ball bearings, red-hot needles, molten fire or marshmallows, it made no difference: he couldn't feel his feet.

Across the room the Dean leaned against his doorway, arms folded, waiting. "At your convenience, Mr. Hogan."

"Sorry about that."

"Please don't apologize. The principal function of this institution, I have long contended, is as a clearing house for the assignations of the student body."

The Dean stood aside as Ty entered, and closed the door behind them both. He returned to his customary position behind his laptop, across the desk from Ty.

Ty was aware as he sat down that the Dean was speaking, and some small part of his mind urged him to pay attention, but the girl of his dreams filled his consciousness. He made a mighty effort, dragging his mind from the meeting later with Kaitlin and concentrating on the meeting now, with the Dean. He looked across the desk at the older man.

The Dean's expression altered. His annoyance disappeared. "I was going to ask what you've been up to. And I'd like to hear about it sometime, but let's cut to the chase."

Ty waited calmly. He could handle it.

The Dean stood up and held out his hand. Ty stood and they shook.

"Welcome back, Mr. Hogan."

THE END

Acknowledgments

This story was inspired by my nephew's adventures in northern Canada. Once I'd written the first draft, I drove more or less the same route as Matthew, to get a taste of the country and the people, and to interview some of those who work in the oil (and other) industries.

In the Fraser Valley of British Columbia, my starting point, Chilliwack fire chief Jim MacDonald and martial arts expert Adam Gibson were generous with their time and expertise.

In Fort St John, I'm grateful to Arnold Drschiwiski for his hair-raising reminiscences while we toured the display oil rig at the Northern Lights campus. Thanks also to Rob Smith and Doug Phillips of Scott Hydrovac for giving me some insight into their operations, their massive, complex machines and the professionals who operate them.

In Whitecourt Alberta, Bryan Passifiume, editor of the Whitecourt *Star*, was generous with his knowledge and anecdotes. My thanks also to the fire chief and sundry hospitality workers for taking time to chat with me.

In Carlyle, Saskatchewan, I had the benefit of an hour with Mark Scott and Billy Wilson of Savanna Energy; many thanks to them and to Laura Koronko for setting up the meeting. I'm grateful to the Biberdorfs, Gerald and Jeannette, for the tour of their farm near Estevan, where pump jacks dot fields of wheat and flax.

Tyson Cornfield, derrickhand with Akita Drilling, provided unstinting help throughout the later writing stages. His comments and reactions helped bring my rig to life and I can't thank him enough.

Online help came from numerous sources, including the Twitter team at Trinidad Drilling.

Editor Michael Denneny was a steadying influence, while Laurence French provided his customary sterling service in reading the manuscript and earns my gratitude, too, for suggesting the title. A big thank you to my sister for her help and comments.

As always, any errors or omissions are my own responsibility.

About the Author

Helen Yeomans was born in England and raised in Canada. She worked in book publishing in Toronto and London, then launched her own firm, providing editing and later writing services to corporate clients worldwide. She began writing fiction more than 20 years ago. *Return to Kaitlin* is her fourth novel.

Visit helenyeomans.com for more on the author or her books.

* * *

Feedback from readers is always welcome. Please consider expressing your opinion of *Return to Kaitlin* on the website of your online retailer, or on GoodReads, or by sending an email to info@helenyeomans.com.

CPSIA information can be obtained
at www.ICGtesting.com
Printed in the USA
LVHW050049080321
680835LV00008B/126

9 780969 321972